Ibarajo Road

First published in Great Britain in 2012 by
Frances Lincoln Children's Books, 4 Torriano Mews,
Torriano Avenue, London NW5 2RZ
www.franceslincoln.com

A catalogue record for this book is available from the British Library.

ISBN: 978-1-84780-320-7

Set in Palatino

Printed and bound by CPI Group (UK) Ltd, Croydon, CR0 4YY in June 2012

1 3 5 7 9 8 6 4 2

Ibarajo Road

HARRY ALLEN

F

FRANCES LINCOLN
CHILDREN'S BOOKS

For Niamh

Mo féràn rẹ nígbà yẹn, mo féràn rẹ báyí, sì féràn rẹ títí láí.

CHAPTER 1

It was Harmattan season: storms in the Sahara blew sand down over the country, staining the skies over the city of Ilaju a nicotine yellow. The sun, barely discernable as it sped into the sky, fought to give light to the city below.

We turned on to Ibarajo Road and the early morning chaos sucked us in. Hundreds of horns bellowed their drivers' anger and frustration as cars wove through the exhaust-filled humidity, swerving from lane to lane in an effort to get ahead. Pedestrians stumbled along the cracked and potholed pavements, the colours of their Yoruba dress greyed by the heat and dust, heads bowed against the aggression of the morning. Street traders jumped onto the road, open shirts clinging to their bodies, holding their wares above their heads and shouting prices into car windows.

A trader peered through at me as we crawled along,

his sunken eyes filled with hope as he held up a pair of jeans, 'Cheap, cheap. Good price. Five dollar.' I waved him away with a yawn and glanced at my watch – six thirty-five. Too early – after over a year, it still felt painfully early.

Hard to believe. A whole year since my father had announced we would be leaving our house in Hampshire. Leaving our home, McDonald's, shopping centres, TV and HMV, and coming here, to Sengharia. I had looked it up in the atlas and found it nestled in the corner of West Africa – a world away.

The car hit a pothole and my bag bounced off the seat next to me. Bending down, I picked it up, cramming my schoolbooks back inside, and saw the skin on my arm had begun to peel. I scratched at it for a moment, sorry that the tan would be lost, vowing to spend more time by the pool at the weekend.

'Turn up the air conditioning, will you, Samson?' My driver nodded and the added rumble helped mask some of the noise. I caught a whiff of monsoon drains and checked that the Mercedes' window was tight shut against the compost smell, sealing my cool, safe haven.

The sound of a siren burst through the car and Samson swerved to the left. My head hit the window and Samson swore as we jarred to a halt. A police Land Rover raced towards us, its red and blue lights punching through the dawn. A policeman stood in the open topped back, one hand gripping the roof for support, the other bringing a pistol butt crashing down on to the car roofs, daring them not to move. Samson pulled us further in towards the central reservation, but the roof shook from a blow as the Land Rover shot past.

'They are crazy,' muttered Samson.

I glanced up the road. The police had left a slipstream, and cars now poured over from the other carriageway, flowing in their wake before swerving back onto the correct side. Samson pulled away, his fist on the horn, keeping right to avoid the impatient commuters.

And in the central reservation, flanked by six lanes of screaming traffic, two boys began to run.

Even from a distance and in the poor morning light I could see them clearly. They wore crisp pressed khaki shorts and starched shirts, their knee socks gleaming white against the grey concrete of the flyover. The smaller boy ran slightly behind the other, one hand gripping his satchel, the other clasping the shirt of – his friend? His brother?

The distance to the side of the road wasn't far, just three lanes of traffic. The boys must have been waiting for a break in the constant stream of cars for some time, but the grins on their faces suggested this was a game they played every morning; something to liven up the trek to school, to talk about with their friends, to joke about their daring. Looks like a laugh, I thought. Perhaps I should dare Max to do it with me. I smiled and leaned forward to watch.

They got off to a good start, and I was wondering who would make it first when, halfway across, the smaller boy stumbled. His friend turned and shouted something as a red Peugeot tore across the central reservation towards them. The smaller boy struggled to rise, but his foot caught in his satchel strap, and he only made it halfway up before stumbling back down.

Get up, I thought. Get up. . .

I think the driver saw them at the last minute. The car swerved slightly before the smaller boy, his hand reaching for the shirt of his friend, vanished between bumper and tarmac. The first boy shot into the air, a flailing collection of arms, legs and schoolbooks. He hung there for a second, the car brakes screeching, before thundering down onto the windscreen, bouncing off the bonnet and vanishing after his friend.

Samson hit the brakes and I slammed into the back of the front seat and slid down into the foot well. I stayed there for a second, struggling with the image in my mind

'You OK?' asked Samson.

'Fine,' I managed, pulling myself up from the floor, 'Jesus, did you see. . .?' My heart pounded, the picture still floating in front of my eyes.

'Safety belt, safety belt,' ordered Samson. 'We go fast now. Bad men will come, big *wahala* for tis.'

I didn't argue and dropped back into my seat, pulling the seat belt across and locking it into place. Big *wahala*: big trouble. It was one of the sternest warnings a Sengharian could give. I'd heard Samson use it before, and, despite the air conditioning, sweat began to trickle down my face.

The Peugeot lay slightly askew across the inside and middle lanes. The shattered windscreen obscured the driver, but I could make him out still sitting there, his hands on the wheel, unable or unwilling to move. Samson put the car into gear and we inched forward, trying to find a way through the gridlock left by the accident. The car's sudden jerks threw me back and forwards.

On the other carriageways, the traffic slowed as people stared over at the scene, and gradually the flow stopped as a man in a tailored blue suit let out a yell of fury and stepped onto the road. He shouted, pointing at the Peugeot, and the noise increased as others joined him. People climbed out of their cars, fought their way through the crowd at the side of the road and began to converge on the car in a mass of anger, drawn by the man in the suit and his impassioned cries.

'Samson. . .' My voice shook.

'Don't worry, Charlie. We go now.' But there seemed to be no way through. Samson tried to edge around to the left, to squeeze through the gap between the mob around the car and the central reservation; the Mercedes lurched forward a foot before jarring to a stop. A man jumped in front of us, his arms stretched out and upwards, his open shirt flying behind him, shouting something I couldn't hear above the din of the crowd. Samson slammed his fist against the button on his door and I heard the central locking snap into place; but the man was gone, his attention turned towards the car in the road and its driver.

The man in the suit crouched by the Peugeot staring at the bodies. Then he rose to his feet, held up a fist and shouted something in Yoruba. The crowd erupted. They forced open the door and dragged the driver out, throwing him to the ground. He knelt on the road, his eyes glazed with shock and terror, as all around the crowd grew, and the noise of their cries intensified. Standing above him, one hand gripping his head, the man in the suit began to speak. His head swirled around as he addressed the mob, his free arm slicing through the air giving form to his rage, a fervent, evangelical tone in his voice that rose above all other sounds.

'What is he saying?' I asked, the words forced out of my mouth by another jerk from the car.

'*Child-killer*,' said Samson, his voice a steel whisper.

I couldn't make out who kicked the driver first; the sole of a black shoe connected with the side of his head and he let out a howl of pain. He clasped his hands together and began speaking, pleading, his words lost. Another kick, and he turned and gripped the trouser leg of his persecutor – who moved back forcing him to follow on his knees, head bowed like a street beggar. But he was pushed away and the blows rained down.

'Stop!'

The people turned. They seemed unsure of what

to make of this new command. Their attention moved away from the driver, who fell forward onto the tarmac, his clothes torn, the marks from his beating standing white against his brown skin, and their eyes searched for the one who had interrupted them.

The speaker stepped forward, his worn trousers finishing an inch above scuffed shoes. He was short, with unbrushed grey hair, but he stared up at the man in the suit with a gaze that would have cut glass. He began to speak, his voice free of the rage of the mob. He pointed to the car, indicating the boys trapped underneath. For a moment, the man in the suit seemed to waver; his followers looked around, unsure of what to do.

Another jerk from the Mercedes and the seat belt rose up, biting into my neck, forcing my eyes away from the scene. When I turned back, the leader stood towering over the old man, spittle shooting from his mouth as he screamed at him. Leave, I thought, leave, turn away and run. But the old man stood unflinching, staring up at him like a teacher observing a wayward child, and the man's tirade weakened and then stopped.

The old man turned to the driver. He crouched on one knee trying to get up, a hand outstretched, and the old man took a step towards him. The movement seemed to bring the suited man back to life and his fist hammered into the old man's chest, sending him stumbling backwards. This action was the sign the crowd had been waiting for, and two men moved forward to drag the interloper away. He made no attempt to struggle, but his eyes never left his attacker, who watched him go before returning his attention to his victim.

The driver's temporary reprieve was over. The man forced him to his knees with his hands behind his back. The thugs who had dragged away the old man returned carrying a tyre. The sight of the tyre seemed to whip the mob into a new frenzy and they punched the air and chanted something I didn't want to understand. The man in the suit snatched it and held it above his head, showing it off like a trophy.

People started to crowd closer, and the gap between the central reservation and the car widened. Samson seized his chance and our car surged forward, throwing me back into my seat, and we were through just as the man, his suit greying in the dust, slowly, almost gently, placed the tyre around the driver's neck.

I turned as we passed the abandoned Peugeot. A trail of blood seeped out from underneath the rear bumper, sliding its way towards a school satchel, encircling it as if to pull it back to its owner.

I didn't look back as we sped away. I unclipped my seatbelt, leant forward, placed a shaking hand on the seat in front of me, and took several deep breaths. 'Holy shit,' I gasped.

'Charlie? You go be sick?' asked Samson as he slowed the car.

'No. But, dat *wahala* make me weak for bodi,' I replied in pidgin. I glanced up at the rear view mirror and saw Samson's eyes widen with laughter.

'Now you go learn to speak correct! Finally my lessons are paying off,' he said, his laugh reverberating around the car. '*Na Wah* for Charlie!'

I laughed with him: a pure, cleansing laugh that drove away some of the stress and fear. I slumped back into my seat and sighed. The violence of the roadside vigilantes already seemed distant and somehow unreal as we sped across the Oyo Bridge onto Ekadan Street.

From its elevated position, I gazed out over the harbour and the quays, at the ships sailing in sitting low in the water, heavy with their cargo, and at the ones sailing out empty. The sun managed to break through the dust and played on the ocean as we neared the expat heartland of Ikoro and Mountbatten Island, and the question that had been burning in my mind now seemed safe to ask. 'Samson, was the tyre for *necklacing*?'

Samson hesitated before answering. He shifted slightly in his seat and rolled his bull-like shoulders. 'Don't you worry about necklacing, Charlie. The police dun come for sure. Dat man OK.'

I believed him. It was the easiest thing to do. The police would have arrived, I said to myself, before they doused the tyre in petrol, before they lit the match. Yet there was something hollow in Samson's reassurance, and my hands began to shake as the car cruised onto Mountbatten Island, to my friends, to school.

CHAPTER 2

The guard blinked through the side window of the car and I gave him a wave. He nodded, slouched back to his post and pressed a button somewhere under his desk. The single, black-barred gate began to open, the gold lettering reading 'Ilaju International School' sliding behind the razor-wire-topped wall, and we drove in.

Samson pulled the car up and turned to face me. 'You sure you OK?' he asked.

'I'm fine. No problem,' I said. I grabbed my school bag and opened the door. 'I'll see you at two. Thanks, Samson.'

I clambered out of the car into the early morning heat and stood and watched the gate close, the world beyond slipping away, kept at bay by steel and concrete. I turned as it finished its roll across the driveway with a clang and headed away from the entrance, moving along the flower-planted wall to the back of the gym.

I had lied to Samson. I struggled to pull my heavy, watery legs along, the saliva pooling in my mouth. I leant against the wall and tried to calm myself. I'm in school. I'm safe, I told myself. The world of the road can't reach me here; I have nothing to worry about. Yet the image of the two boys would not leave me. It had been so random, so sudden. . . And the driver? What had they done to him? What *might* they have done to him, I reasoned. Samson had said he would be all right; and besides, it was nothing to do with me.

And the thought gave me strength.

I leant against the wall of the gym for another five minutes, my familiar surroundings slowly wrapping themselves around me. The nausea passed, my mind felt clearer, and with a sigh, I gathered up my bag and headed back towards the entrance.

Several cars now lined the way, their occupants spilling out of the back seats, shouting instructions to their drivers, before scurrying up the steps to school. I watched as one girl's bag slid from her driver's hand as he passed it to her. 'Jeez, careful! My chemistry paper's in there!'

I left the man mumbling his apologies to the seventh grader and headed up the steps. The banner celebrating the school's anniversary was still up and formed a fluttering arch above the staircase.

Celebrating ten years of excellence.
1974–1984

I walked slowly, watching my feet as they fell on the marble-clad steps. One of my shoelaces was undone and I stopped at the top to tie it. I heard the Principal pass me, showing around what seemed to be prospective parents.

'The whole school was custom built to specifications by a company from America,' he said. 'To ensure quality, we imported everything from the US: the wall tiles (purple is our school colour), the desks and chairs, right down to the padlocks securing the lockers. Your son will be guaranteed the same quality you know in the States. . .'

'Jerk,' I mumbled, and headed off towards the school office. I passed the sign welcoming visitors and turned left at the octagonal courtyard past the American flag.

The talk and laughter of students filled the air, their voices never carrying to the world beyond the walls and never interrupted by any sounds from it.

Pockets of them stood scattered across the courtyard and hanging over the rails for four storeys in their uniform T-shirts, high tops, baggy shorts and mini-skirts, only their features giving a clue as to which of the thirty-two nationalities they represented.

I headed straight for the alcove, our usual morning meeting-place in the far corner of the courtyard. Max and Wael were already there: Max plugged into his Walkman, slowly nodding his bleached, spiked hair; Wael stretched out on the bench, his back to the wall, apparently studying a crack in one of the cladding tiles, his T-shirt declaring that 'Life's a Beach'.

'What's up,' I said, tossing my bag into the corner. The noise made Max look up. His head skipped a beat as he nodded his greeting. Wael swung his legs off the bench and sat up.

'Hey, dude,' he yawned, his American accent masking his Lebanese nationality. But we all spoke like that. My clipped, Home Counties English had faded away in the first month. 'Anything happen on the road today?'

I rocked slightly on my heels, and an image of a bloodstained satchel flashed in front of my eyes. I knew what they wanted. My war stories from the Ibarajo road had become popular morning entertainment:

the time we nudged a man running across and he had ended up in the monsoon drain, the naked lunatics dancing on the central reservation, any number of car accidents. But today was different. Today I didn't want to tell the story of the boys. I knew I would have to listen to gasps of 'No way!' and 'You shitting me?' and I couldn't bear that. Any thoughts of daring Max to run across with me had long vanished.

'Nothing,' I said, 'nothing today,' and I heard the crack in my voice.

Wael shrugged, looking disappointed. 'You coming dragging after school? We're going to Four Point Island.'

'Sure. If you want your ass kicked again.'

'Hey, the clutch slipped. You got lucky. . .' A groan from Max interrupted us. He pulled off his headphones and stared across the courtyard. 'Well, here he comes,' he said. I glanced over my shoulder and saw, walking towards us, The Guppy.

Max called Guppy his 'charity case' and had thought up his nickname. Short, with a side parting in his hair, The Guppy had one leg longer than the other which gave him a distinctive wobble when he walked, like a toy boat being blown across a pond. We tolerated him, allowed him to tag along, good for comic relief and copying homework, but he would never really be one of the gang.

'Hey, dudes.' He pronounced it 'dodes'; his thick Indian accent was one of Max's principal concerns.

'Dudes,' corrected Max. 'Dudes with a "u", Guppy.'

Wael looked him up and down. 'Guppy, what's up, man. Looking cool.'

'Not so cool, I think,' said Guppy, looking down at his black leather lace-ups and knee socks. 'I need the High Tops. If I have the High Tops, then I can ask Hagit to the dance.' It was the sort of comment that Max and Wael had been hoping for. They collapsed with laughter onto the bench, slapping it with their palms and occasionally managing to choke up the words 'Hagit' and 'dance'. Guppy stared at them for a moment, not knowing what was funny, and then began to laugh with them. This only encouraged them and the harder they laughed, the harder Guppy laughed. Doesn't he get it? I thought. They're laughing at you, Guppy.

But it was laughable. Hagit was a fellow senior, an Israeli, and considered the best-looking girl in the school. Guppy was only just sixteen, at least a year younger than the rest of us in grade twelve, and the thought of him taking her to the dance was absurd – for anyone.

'Guppy, you are too much, man,' said Max, dragging himself out of his fit and wiping away a tear.

'Legend,' coughed Wael. 'My mornings would not be the same without you.'

'OK, I must go,' laughed Guppy. 'I have to see Mr Lutz. I see you guys later.' He turned and then stopped. 'Oh, Charlie, tomorrow is OK, I asked my parents,' he said, and walked off.

I watched him wobble away and then turned to Max and Wael, knowing what was coming.

'You invited him tomorrow?' Max forced the question out, staring at me in amazement. I held up my hand, trying to deflect the tirade of objection from them both. My parents and sister were going away north for the weekend and had said I could have a couple of friends over to stay. Max and Wael had jumped at the chance, but I had not told them I'd asked Guppy.

'Hey, what could I do? The guy was bugging me all week!' I pleaded.

'But I thought we were going to the Crocodile Bar, dude,' said Max. 'We can't take The Guppy!'

'Look, there was nothing I could do. It could be

fun. Who knows, with a couple of beers inside him he might even walk straight.' The joke worked, and Max and Wael amused themselves with impressions of a drunk Guppy. Then Wael stopped and nudged Max. Hagit walked across the courtyard followed by her posse of girls. She turned her head slightly as she passed the alcove, flicking her hair away from her face to reveal a half-smile, her hand smoothing the side of her skirt.

'Jesus,' murmured Wael. 'She is so hot.'

'She smiled at me, dude,' said Max. 'You see that?'

'She could have been smiling at any of us,' I said.

Max laughed. 'In your dreams, Charlie. I swear to God, before I leave this shit-hole, I'm going to have her on her back.'

'Will there be girls at the Crocodile Bar?'

'No, Wael,' I said, 'there won't be *girls*. There'll be women. Lots and lots of women.'

'Do they put out?'

'You got the money, they'll do whatever you want.'

Max clapped me on the back, his smile threatening to crack his face. 'Charlie, my friend, this is going to be one great weekend!'

I left them and headed for class, pleased with their

reaction to the promises of the Crocodile Bar. I had never experienced that side of the bar's services, but they hadn't asked and I wasn't about to tell them.

The route to the classroom took me past the newly posted Honour Roll photos in the corridor. Max, Wael and I had never come close to being on it, but there at the top, his broken nose protruding from his dark, narrow face, was Guppy. Someone had circled his picture with a red marker, and above it scribbled 'Geek!'

Why the hell had I invited him?

🖻◉🖻

Fridays meant assembly, and I joined the groaning crowd in the hall. It was hot, the air conditioning struggling to cope with the additional heat of 250 bodies. We would have to listen to the principal, and I prayed he hadn't booked another guest speaker. Recess was short enough as it was.

I sat at the back and Max threw himself down next to me, immediately assuming his routine pose – his head thrown back, mouth open, pretending to be asleep. Wael was serving the last of six detentions for getting caught 'running the roofs', a race against the clock around the roof of the school. Guppy sat several rows forward, having found a seat behind Hagit.

The principal strode onto the stage and took up his position behind the lectern. He wore the same college tie he always did, wrapped around a starched, yellow collar, and he smiled around the room with teeth like a whitewashed fence.

'Good morning. We have come to the end of another *great* week, with lots to be proud of. But, I want to start by thanking everyone who participated in the track and field meet over the weekend. It was a huge success. And remember: it doesn't matter if you finished first or last. . .'

'. . .You are all winners,' I murmured, mimicking his Texan accent. This was what he always said whenever there was a competition and it irritated me to the core.

'And now,' continued the principal, 'we must move on to one of our most important concerns: fund-raising. As you know, it is extremely important to help the less fortunate and I'm delighted to say that our sponsored car wash raised over $250!'

It was his favourite topic and I had heard it all before. I reached into my bag and pulled out a car magazine as scattered applause echoed around the hall. If the principal was going to drone on for the whole assembly, I thought I might as well use the time wisely.

I was staring in awe at a picture of a Lamborghini Countach, when the applause told me he had finished. Thank God, I thought, keeping my eyes on the car, but then a wave of giggles made me look up.

The principal had stepped to one side, clapping the arrival of a speaker whose introduction I had missed, and there, standing next to him on the stage, was the old man who had tried to intervene on the road that morning. The magazine slipped from my grip as I stared at him, and I bent down to get it, the sweat forming on my palms.

The principal looked at him with a forced smile, like someone who had invited an ambassador and got his secretary. The old man gave no hint that he was aware of the principal's dissatisfaction and after shaking his hand moved to the front of the stage. He wore exactly what I had seen him in earlier that morning, his dishevelled appearance the source of all the giggles, but apart from a small, white bandage over his left eye, he showed no sign of the violence he had been involved with. He ignored the lectern with its microphone and, stepping around it, addressed us directly.

As he began to speak, the giggles subsided. He seemed to make no effort, but his voice filled the hall, pushing into every corner with an accent that I couldn't place. It seemed unreal to see him standing there, his presence splintering the routine of the day. He belonged on the road with my memory of two dead boys, in the world beyond the gates and the razor wire. I didn't want him there, in his frayed shirt, the dust from his shoes falling on the polished wood of the stage. I wondered if I should try and sneak away, but one of the teachers would be sure to see me. I would have to sit it out.

He thanked the school for its efforts, hoping they would continue to raise awareness amongst the students, and then began to speak about things I didn't understand. He spoke of 'drip-feed' charity and finding the 'root of the problem', of 'adaptation to a western-style economy'. These were things I had never heard mentioned before, but from the expressions building on the faces of the teachers, I could tell this was not what they had been expecting. I glanced over at the principal; he stood tugging at his collar and holding on to his concrete grin.

The old man continued, speaking of Africa's

natural resources that made it the richest continent on earth; of leprosy and how it was curable, but how the stigma attached to it scared people away from seeking help; of education and health care. But it was when he spoke of children being mutilated at birth and later forced to go out and beg, that the principal intervened.

He stepped forward clapping, cutting the old man off in mid-sentence and thanking him, apologising for stopping him short, but time was running out and we had classes to get back to and there wasn't much recess left.

The old man showed no surprise at the interruption and stepped back. The principal gave us a quick reminder that there was a collection box outside his office, turned to thank the speaker once more, and dismissed us.

The students rose as one, clamouring to get out.

'Jesus,' said Max. 'Assemblies have reached a new low with that guy.'

'You're not kidding,' I said. I followed him towards the rear doors, eager to push the old man back into my memory, far away from here. A tug at my shirt stopped me and I looked back to see Guppy.

'That was a fascinating talk, wasn't it, Charlie?'

'What?'

'The old man. Joseph Obohense from the Ilakaye Refuge Centre.'

'Oh, right. Yeah. Fascinating, Guppy.' I backed away, keener than ever to get to the courtyard.

'I knew you would think that. Why don't—' He stopped, a pained expression on his face. 'Damn. I have forgotten my bag. I will catch up with you.' He turned, fighting his way back through the tide of students, his thin frame buffeted from side to side. And at the edge of the stage I saw a still beaming principal usher Joseph Obohense through a side door, before I turned and forced my way out.

◪◉◪

I stared through the windscreen down the only drivable stretch of road on Four Point Island, an unfinished and abandoned stretch of tarmac by the quays. Samson stood at the end of the track with the other drivers against a backdrop of rubble and a few scattered palm trees. There was only a 150 metre stretch before the road disintegrated and my hands tightened on the steering wheel. Max and Wael flanked me, the sounds of the engines ripping through the air. Max leaned across and poked his head out of his passenger window. 'Charlie, you're my best friend, and this is going to cause me a lot of emotional pain, but I'm going to kick your ass!'

'You'll try!' I shouted back.

He punched the dashboard in delight. 'You've gotta love dragging!'

He had beaten me the last two times, and I wasn't going to let it happen again. In the distance Wael's driver held up his hand, and I wiped the sweat off my forehead. He held it for a second before swinging it sharply down. I floored it, feeling the steering wheel pull away from me as my back tried to break through the driver's seat. Out of the corner of my eyes I could see Max and Wael, both half a bonnet behind. I slammed into second, keeping my hand on the stick ready for the next gear. The end of the road rushed up, but Max had edged ahead and I found third. Wael began to drop back, slowing his speed, and I knew I should do the same. The trees seemed to grow with every heartbeat and the drivers flashed past me in a blur, I saw Max slip back and I jerked my foot off the accelerator. But I had left it too late. I punched my foot against the brakes and the wheels locked, the car sliding in a screaming cloud of dust, my knuckles threatening to burst through my skin. I shut my eyes and felt the car shudder to a halt.

I sat there for a moment trying to calm my breathing, then opened my eyes and looked out of the side window. A palm tree stood only inches away.

'That was awesome!' Max's hands slammed onto the bonnet, his face filling the windscreen. 'You're crazy!'

'Told you I'd beat you.'

I climbed out of the car and had a quick look around. There wasn't a scratch, and I patted the roof, exhaling loudly. Wael came running up and slapped me on the back.

'I'm going to get you next time,' he said. 'You got lucky. Come on, let's get back to the start.'

'Sunday,' commanded Max, 'turn the car round.'

'Yes, Master,' replied his driver.

'Time to go, Charlie.' Samson's voice had an edge to it that I knew couldn't be argued with. I made excuses to the others about having to get back to see my parents off and to cries of 'Pussy' and 'You just know you'll lose', Samson took the wheel and we headed away.

Samson waited until we were out of sight before pulling the car over and turning to face me, anger in every crease of his face. 'What's the matter with you, Charlie? I think your head is not correct!'

'I'm sorry, it was stupid.'

'You want to get killed?'

'No. Look, I'm sorry. It won't happen again. I just left it a little late.'

'I bring you here to teach you to drive. But . . . *dis thing wey mai eye see, mi mouth no fit talk am!*' He inhaled deeply. 'No more dragging. I will tell your parents.'

'Oh, come on, I said I was sorry. It won't happen again, OK? I just don't like being beaten.'

Samson stared at me for a moment and I saw his eyes begin to soften, and then he smiled. 'OK. You go be more careful next time.'

'I will.'

Samson turned back and pulled out onto the road. 'Good race, though,' he said, and I laughed, lit a cigarette and lent back in the seat.

'*Dis thing m. . .* What?' I asked.

'It means, "I am lost for words".'

'The pidgin version is better. You go agree?'

'You go *gree*,' corrected Samson. And my daily pidgin English lesson, the only one I looked forward to, began. By the time we had arrived back in Kekaro, I had added, '*traficate*', '*take light*' and

28

'money make iron float' to my vocabulary.

The guards took a black, seven-foot gate each, and hauled them open. Samson waved and we slipped up the gravel drive to the bungalow. The Dobermanns, Mitch and Rufus, came bounding across the lawn, their black coats spotted brilliant red with fallen flowers from the flame trees. I climbed out of the car and rubbed their ears; they circled me in delight before chasing each other away behind the house. Samson parked the car and walked down to the guard hut by the gates. Like the walls and the bungalow it was painted black and white, the traditional tropical colours. I waved goodbye and headed up to the door.

'Charlie!' My sister came running out to meet me, her sun-bleached hair falling around her tanned face. 'Will you come for a swim with me?'

'Not right now, Katie. I'm tired.'

'You always say that.'

'I'm always tired.'

She seemed about to protest when my mother's voice summoned her in to finish her reading. She turned and walked quickly back through the door. I followed, smiling, inwardly thanking my mother for her timing; swimming with my five-year-old sister was rarely on my agenda. I crossed the first of the living rooms to the bar, tossing my bag into a corner, and pulled a Coke from the fridge. Ruth, the maid, was setting the table at the far end of the room. She stopped when she saw my bag and hurried over, picked it up and vanished through to the bedrooms. I settled onto one of the bar stools, swigging my drink.

'Hello, Charlie,' said my mother. She stood in the doorway leading to the bedrooms, holding my bag in her hand. Ruth brushed past her, blushing, and hurried over to finish setting the table. 'This is yours, I believe?' She dropped it back into the corner. 'Please take it through when you've finished your drink.'

'Sorry.'

'Peter. . .'

The steward emerged from the kitchen, the evidence of his cooking efforts smeared over his white uniform. 'Yes, Madam?'

'There will only be three of us for dinner this evening.'

'Yes, Madam.' And he vanished back into the kitchen.

'Where's Dad?' I asked.

'He has to work late, get everything done before our trip tomorrow. But I know he's keen to discuss your school report. "Reckless" is a word that came up a lot. . .'

I muffled a sigh. I had been hoping the report would arrive after the weekend. It wasn't a conversation I wanted to have. 'I haven't done anything wrong,' I said. 'My grades are OK.'

'Yes, they are, as you say, "*OK*". But they could be better.'

Katie's voice drifted through from her bedroom, calling me to help her with her work, and for once I was grateful.

'I'd better go and help Katie,' I said.

My mother looked at me in surprise. 'All right, but this conversation isn't over. We'll discuss it more when your father gets back.'

I felt her eyes follow me as I left the room.

▣◉▣

'You're very quiet, Charlie. Is everything all right?' asked my mother. 'You didn't eat much at dinner, either.' My sister had gone to bed, and we sat on opposite sides of the living room. I lay across one of the armchairs, my legs dangling over the arm, watching the fan. I looked over at her, sitting on the sofa with her embroidery, and noticed she had coloured her hair, the flecks of grey replaced by the uniform auburn of three years ago. She wore a flower-patterned frock that hung gently over her thin frame, and she moved a needle through the fabric with precision.

She was right; my mind lingered elsewhere. The image of the boys on the road had faded a little, but it still hung there in the back of my mind. Then there was the old man with his scuffed shoes and bandage. I wondered if I should tell her about it, but didn't, unsure of exactly what to say.

'I'm fine, just tired.'

'All right then, if you're sure.'

The sound of the door made us both turn, and I saw my father stride across to the bar, put down his briefcase and walk around to his stool on the other side. My mother smiled, placed her embroidery down on the sofa and walked out to him. I had hoped he might be delayed at work long enough for me to get to bed, to avoid the discussion about my report – but no such luck. I got up with a sigh and walked out to join them.

'Evening, Dad.'

'Evening, Charlie.' He took off his tie and rolled it carefully, placing it next to the other four on the corner of the bar, his personal calendar. 'Thank God it's Friday.'

'You're very late, darling,' said my mother, taking a seat on the opposite side.

'Trouble with an import licence. My contact at the ministry has been sacked. I think I'll have to talk to Gunther. He might be able to fix it.' He took a beer from the fridge hidden below the polished top of the bar and poured it out into a glass. 'Right, Charlie. Let's have a look at this report.'

I sat next to my mother as he flicked through it, pausing occasionally to read a comment twice, scratching at his moustache and taking occasional sips of beer. I watched him, looking for some clue as to the defensive strategy I might have to take.

'Well, it's not great, is it?' he said, closing the booklet and pushing it a few inches away from him.

'That's what I told him.'

'But it's not terrible either,' he continued. I couldn't help but smile.

'I was worried about what the principal had to say,' said my mother, staring hard at me.

'Yes. He seems to think you and your friends run races around the roofs of the school. . .'

'Some people have done that, but—'

My father held up his hand, stopping the lie from forming. 'We'll discuss this in detail when we get back from Port Rose. I'm too tired now. But we will be discussing it, Charlie. There's a lot of room for improvement here.'

'Yes, Dad, ' I said, feeling the relief seep through me. There would be no talk, no sanctions. It could all wait. I was about to say I was going to bed, to get out as quickly as possible, when I suddenly remembered I had one detail of my weekend plans to sort out, a vital one – and suddenly the report was all-important again.

'I thought we might go to the Crocodile Bar tomorrow. Could Samson take us, do you think?' I said, tossing the suggestion out as casually as I could, trying to make it sound more of a statement than a question.

'Did you?' said my mother. 'Now, why would you want to go there?'

'Oh, there's just a few of the Hashers going down. It's Aussie Steve's birthday.'

My mother tutted. She did not approve of the Hash House Harriers, a running club that jogged in a sweating white hoard along a pre-marked route through the bush. I went most Saturdays. With all of my friends on Mountbatten Island, there wasn't much to do in Kekaro at the weekends. My father didn't mind, so my mother went along with it. She knew we drank there, but insisted on a strict two-drink rule, and as I was the youngest by twenty years, the others saw that it was enforced.

'No, I don't think so, Charlie,' said my mother.

'Oh, come on . . . I go down there every week.'

'Meeting the Hashers there on Saturday afternoon is one thing. Going down at night is something else entirely. I've heard what sort of a place it becomes.'

'But. . .'

'That's my final word on the matter, Charlie.'

I looked at my father, knowing it was pointless. My mother had spoken and I knew she wouldn't change her mind.

'Your mother's right, Charlie. It can get very dangerous at night. If you want to go out with your friends, you can go for a meal at the Lebanese. Just tell them to put it on my account.'

'Thanks,' I said, trying to hide my frustration and knowing further argument would be pointless. A meal at the Lebanese restaurant on Johnson Avenue wasn't exactly what I had planned; Max and Wael would not be happy.

'I think I'll turn in,' I said and turned to go.

'Charlie. . .'

'Yes.'

'Behave yourself this weekend.'

'Of course I will. Don't worry about me.'

'I mean it.'

'Relax, Mum.' I smiled, but she didn't respond, her eyes holding mine. 'Seriously.'

She nodded, and I turned and left, my mind already wrestling with how to get around my parents' ban on the Crocodile Bar.

CHAPTER 3

The noise of the lawn mower rattled me awake. I lay in bed for a moment, letting the sound drive away the last remnants of sleep, before turning over and pulling back the curtains. Through the circular security bars I saw Friday the gardener in his black rubber boots, two sizes too big, the mower dragging him along. He sped up the lawn past the swimming pool, yanked the machine right at the wall surrounding the generator shed and, his face locked in concentration, hurtled out of sight. With a smile, I let the curtain fall back. It was Saturday.

I clambered out of bed, pulled on shorts and T-shirt and walked into the living room, the marble cool against my bare feet. My mother had left a note on the bar: 'Don't forget to take the videos back. See you tomorrow, be good.'

I wandered into the kitchen. Ruth was pegging

the washing outside the back door, swaying as she hummed a hymn. Peter sat on a small wooden stool, his back against the metal termite-proof cupboards, reading the paper.

'Morning,' I said.

Peter looked up and nodded, and I wandered out of the back door for a smoke.

I sat on one of the gas bottles that fed the stove inside and lit my cigarette, relishing being able to smoke in the garden. It took three attempts, the first sign that Harmattan was ending and the rains were drawing in. I took a deep drag and watched as the smoke met the wind, struggling for a moment in a twisted swirl before being swept away.

I still had no idea how to get us all to the Crocodile Bar. My only chance was that my parents had told Samson where we *could* go, but not where we *couldn't*. If that had happened I could probably persuade him, but it was a long shot.

I finished my cigarette, flicked the butt between the covers of the monsoon drain and went back inside. Ruth had laid out some toast on the dining table and I pushed a piece into my mouth, grabbed the videos and headed off to Norman's.

My flip-flops kicked up red dust against my heels

as I walked along the laterite close that was Ali Idirs Avenue, rehearsing my conversation with Samson. But nothing sounded convincing and I kicked a stone down the road in frustration.

Norman's gate was ajar, so I walked straight through, up the driveway and into the house. The open front door led into a small hallway with a staircase at the far end. The door on the left was always shut and I assumed it led into his living room, the one on the right was always open and led into the video shop.

Norman sat on a buckling metal frame chair, his bulk matching the width of his glass-topped desk, counting money; he was very good at it. He would clamp a wad of notes between his middle and index fingers, then, using his thumb, bend the notes away from his body. With his other hand he whipped the notes backwards, one at a time, with dizzying speed, his lips twitching as he kept a silent count.

'Morning,' I said. 'I've brought the tapes back.' Norman tilted his head back an inch by way of acknowledgement, his eyes never leaving the green and red blur in his hands. I put the tapes on the desk and had a look around.

The room was hot and cramped, Norman and

his desk taking up most of the space. A small window by the door looked out over the driveway, but apart from that, the walls were piled floor to ceiling with tapes.

A horn sounded outside, and a car crunched over the gravel in the driveway. Like an illusionist's trick, the money vanished from Norman's hand, reappearing as a bulge in his trouser pocket, while he stood and looked out of the window, his chair creaking its appreciation. He peered through the grime for a second before turning to me.

'Leave the money on the desk.'

'No problem,' I said. Norman held my eyes for a moment before lumbering out. I moved to the window and watched as he approached the car. The passenger window wound down and he leaned inside, apparently greeting the driver. I turned back to the videos and immediately ducked down to the right in front of the shelves labelled 'Sex', snatched the nearest tape and backed into the corner. The red-typed label read *The Girls from Goldovin High*. I pulled a five-dollar note from my pocket and let it fall on the desktop. I had no idea how I was going to return the film. My father had long since instructed Norman as to what I could and what I couldn't rent. *The Girls from Goldolvin High* fell firmly into the 'couldn't' category. But today

I didn't care; today my father and his rules were in a hotel in Port Rose.

I left quickly, pushing the tape against my hip, the label facing down. But Norman was engrossed in his meeting, his head and shoulders pushed through the passenger window, the driver hidden from view by a tinted windscreen. I slipped through the gates and, relaxing my grip, walked back up to the house.

◫◉◫

Guppy arrived first. His father's silver Mercedes slipped up the driveway and I walked out to meet them. Despite the heat and the clinging humidity, Guppy's father was wearing a dark grey suit, the trousers pressed into creases you could have shaved with.

'Good afternoon. You must be Charles,' he said, extending his hand. I took it and felt my knuckles slip in his grip. 'So, what will you boys be doing this evening?' It sounded more like an accusation than a question. I glanced over at Guppy. He shifted his weight from foot to foot, his eyes touching everything but his father.

'Oh, not much,' I said, 'Hang out. Maybe watch a movie.'

He focused his gaze on Guppy for a moment – who appeared to be fascinated by the gravel, as if looking for confirmation.

'Good. Well, I must go. Enjoy the evening.'

'Would you like a cup of tea or something before you leave, sir?' I asked in my best English accent. He looked surprised, and a trace of a smile touched his mouth.

'Thank you, but I must be going.' He squeezed Guppy's shoulder, climbed into the back seat of his car and his driver reversed out. Guppy waited until the guards had heaved the gates closed before turning to me.

'Well done, Charlie,' he sighed. 'He was questioning me all the way here about the nature of our activities. He wouldn't shut up.'

'Relax, Guppy,' I said, slapping him on the back and knocking him forward. 'He's gone.'

'Thank God. I'm surprised he let me come. You know, he grounded me last weekend because my Maths grade was three percentage points lower. It's still an A, I told him. But he wouldn't listen.' He crossed his arms, mimicking his father, more sadness than anger in his voice, 'You must get the best grades. You will go to Harvard. You will be a lawyer. . .'

'Well, that's parents for you,' I said, surprised by his words. I had never heard him talk about anything personal before.

He looked me straight in the eye. 'Are yours like that?'

'Umm, well . . . sometimes, I suppose. Maybe not that extreme. . .' I glanced away – his question had caught me off guard.

He shrugged. 'Forget it. It doesn't matter.' Then he reached into his back pocket and pulled out a small business card. ' Before I forget, I got this for you.'

It was off-white and dog-eared, and in the middle was typed: 'Joseph Obohense' and a telephone number.

'You seemed interested, so I got this from the Principal,' he continued. 'I thought that next weekend you could stay at my house and we could go together and see what the Ilakaye Refuge Centre is like?'

'Oh, right,' I said, trying to hide my amazement. Only The Guppy would think that hanging out at some old man's refuge centre would be a fun way to spend a weekend. 'We'll talk about it next week. Maybe.' I slipped the card into my pocket and gestured that he should go in. I followed behind as he hobbled into the house, shaking my head.

Max and Wael arrived together. Wael came straight up to the house while Max told his driver what time to return for him the next day. He spoke slowly and loudly, like someone explaining something to the deaf. Wael shouted at him to hurry up, and Max banged the roof of the car twice to dismiss it.

We went straight out to the pool, idling away the afternoon with diving competitions until we had all had enough, and stretched out on the loungers.

'So, what time are we going to this bar, dude?' asked Wael, slipping on a pair of sunglasses.

'Samson's coming round about six-thirty,' I yawned, trying to sound as casual as possible. 'And it's not far from here.'

'Cool,' he said and lay back.

'This,' said Guppy 'is a perfect afternoon.' Max rolled his head over to look at him.

'Guppy, you're right. This is pretty good, but the best is yet to come. I wonder if I'll screw three or four girls tonight?'

'Yeah, right,' I said. 'I think your imagination is a little bigger than your dick, dude.' We all laughed.

'I need a smoke,' said Wael, and walked over to the table where we had heaped our shirts and shorts. He picked them up as one, sending the contents of our pockets clattering across the ground.

'Be careful with my shit, dude. Seriously,' said Max.

Wael muttered an apology, and we set about collecting the scattered wallets, coins and lighters. My cigarettes had fallen under the table, with something resting on top of them. It was a photograph: three men stood in front of a tiny single-storey house, its paint peeling to reveal pockmarked concrete. The men wore traditional Indian dress, the colours faded, their dhotis brushing the dust at their feet. In front of them stood a boy no more than eight or nine with a smile and a lop-sided stance.

'Hey Guppy!' I said. 'Is this you, dude?'

He stared at the photo in my hand, a wild look in his eyes. Was it shock? Anger? He rushed over to retrieve it, but I held it above my head and Max snatched it away.

'Is this where you live?' said Max, laughing out the words. Guppy lunged for it, but Max twisted away and passed it to Wael.

'Hey, Guppy, nice skirts,' said Wael.

Guppy finally managed to grab the photo and turned away. I watched him, waiting for his reaction. But he was laughing too.

'You think this is me? You dudes are crazy!' He shook his head, as if in sympathy with our stupidity. 'Charlie, you saw the car my father drives.'

Max and Wael turned to me, their eyes wide, probably hoping for some new bit of information to taunt him with. 'The new 500,' I said.

There was silence. Wael let out a long, low whistle. 'Sweet.'

'This. . .' Guppy waved the photo at us, still laughing, 'is from the social studies project we had to do for Mr Lutz. The one about India, remember? I was going to put it on the cover.'

'Oh.' Said Max. 'I think I might have forgotten to do that.' We laughed again, with Wael going over the excuses he planned to use for not doing his either. I watched Guppy: his shoulders dropped in relief, he turned his back on Max and Wael and gently slid the photo back into his shirt pocket. His eyes caught mine and he tried to smile but it was weak, forced.

I heard the gates open and the crunch of tyres on gravel, and I forgot Guppy's photo in an instant. Samson had arrived. I tried to ignore the sinking feeling in my stomach; if I couldn't persuade Samson to take us to the Crocodile Bar, nobody would be laughing. 'I'll be back in a minute,' I said and walked quickly away, fighting to keep my smile in place.

I found Samson standing by the kitchen door, talking to Peter. He turned as he saw me and smiled.

'Ready, Charlie?'

'Almost. How long does it take to get to the Crocodile Bar? Twenty minutes or so?'

Samson's smile faded and I struggled to hold his gaze, hoping the expression on my face was as neutral as I thought it was.

'Madam says I should take you to the Lebanese. Not the Crocodile Bar.'

'My mum said we could go wherever we wanted. I thought maybe the Lebanese, but the Crocodile Bar should be more fun…'

Samson stared, and his eyes seemed to bore through me.

'What's the matter. . .?' I said, feigning surprise. 'You take me there every week for the Hash run.'

Samson's face relaxed a little as he considered this. But I could see he wasn't totally convinced.

'OK, OK,' I said, as if I had been caught out and needed to confess something. 'We have to leave by ten-thirty.'

Samson thought for a moment and then nodded. 'OK. Get your friends. Let's go.'

The car park at the Crocodile Bar could easily have been mistaken for a wrecker's yard. A tin-roofed lean-to covered three sides, filled with cars in varying levels of decay. A set of wooden steps ran between a wheel-less Ford Cortina and a truck engine half-eaten by rust. I turned, as a clap of thunder tore through the air, and stared at a charcoal sky. A big storm was coming, but I didn't care, I didn't even feel guilt at having lied to Samson. We were here. I had pulled it off and that was all that mattered.

The wind grew stronger as we took the steps up onto the raised walkway. It wound between green, mould-covered fibreglass huts that looked like giant fungi in the fading light. Supposedly, the owner rented them out as short-term accommodation, but I had never heard of anyone staying in one.

We turned left at the first fork and walked up to the entrance. On the right was a concrete pit, surrounded by a four-foot wall, home to the crocodile that gave the bar its name.

'Holy shit, that sucker's real!' shouted Max. 'How cool is that?'

'What do they feed it?' asked Wael, leaning over

the wall, waving his hand at it.

'They are carnivores. They can only eat meat,' Guppy informed us. We stood for a couple of minutes admiring the crocodile, Max and Wael shouting to try to get it to move.

'It doesn't do much, does it.' said Max.

'No,' I said. 'Come on, let's get a beer.'

It was dark inside. Two lamps hung from the ceiling, illuminating clouds of cigarette smoke in their orange glow. A row of booths ran the length of the wall facing the three-sided bar, only the outer edges clearly visible. In the nearest booth, a group of women sat nursing drinks and glancing at the men cluttered around the room. A plastic fishing net hung above the bar, a dozen pairs of women's panties dangling from its web. The smell of stale beer and sour perfume hung thick in the air.

We pushed our way to the bar and ordered four beers. I recognised several of the customers, all Hashers, all still splattered in mud from the afternoon run. We took our beer and made our way to an empty booth, stopping several times for me to introduce my friends and have a quick chat with the drunk Hashers, moving on from one to another with the words, 'Behave yourselves.'

We slipped into the booth, into shadow, and raised our bottles to toast the evening ahead. Even Guppy grinned as we swigged beer and chatted about bands, teachers, girls and whose round it was next, sharing stories and cigarettes. The bar became louder and crowded, and the cluster of empty bottles on the table grew.

A woman approached us. She said her name was Alice and could she join us. Max moved up slightly and she squeezed in next to him.

'*How dey go dey go?*' she asked. The others looked baffled.

'We're fine, thank you,' I said. 'And you?' It seemed like the polite thing to say.

'OK, but *moni yab man*. I want to take beer.' The others turned to me for translation.

'She's fine, but she doesn't have enough money for a beer.'

Alice pulled at her sequinned dress with a red fingernail, revealing the top of a white bra.

'No problem,' said Wael, jumping up and hurrying to the bar. By the time he returned we had been joined by Faith, Alice's friend, who sidled up next to me, her hand resting on my knee.

They shared the beer Wael brought, laughing and

grinning at us. Max put his arm around Alice and she made a show of trying to stop him, before pressing in closer. Guppy had gone very quiet; he never looked at the girls and he kept checking his watch. I glanced around the bar, but no one was paying us any attention. The women had moved in en masse, and each group of men now had at least two girls with them, laughing and demanding drinks.

Faith took my hand and started to pull me out of the booth.

'We go walk,' she said.

'Great idea,' said Max, knocking over two bottles as he struggled to stand.

'Coming, Guppy?' I asked.

'Of course! I don't want to be left out.'

'Cool. It'll be fun.' But my stomach had knotted, and my smile felt as weak as Guppy's looked. I tried to force the doubt away: I had run the roofs, I went dragging every week, this is what we had come here for and I couldn't back out now. But the sense that something wasn't right still flickered in my mind.

The wind hit us as soon as we got outside. The girls laughed, holding their dresses down as we struggled along to the car park. Samson would be there and was bound to stop us. Suddenly a part of me desperately wanted him to. I wanted him to emerge from the dark and take us home, but when we got to the car park he was nowhere in sight.

'Where are we going?' I had to shout to make myself heard over the howling of the wind. Faith just pointed down the road and said something I couldn't hear. The girls headed off and we followed.

After a couple of minutes battling the wind and stumbling over the potholes, we came to a small two-storey building. It had no door, just a piece of black cloth that hung from the frame, fighting to stay in place. Above the cloth someone had painted the word 'Hotel' in red. A pile of rusted metal and wire lay stacked to one side, several long spikes pointing to the angry sky. I felt a tug on my shirt and turned to see Guppy; he stared at the building, shaking his head.

'I just need to think about it for a moment,' he said, his words barely audible.

'Don't worry,' I yelled. 'You can wait outside.' He nodded his agreement.

'I'll follow you later.' But he looked torn, unsure.

'OK.' I patted him on the shoulder and, fighting an urge to grab him by the arm and run back to the bar, I walked into the hotel as the rain began to fall.

A man stood behind a small counter talking to

the girls in Yoruba. He looked over as I came in and smiled, his teeth yellow and chipped, his eyes red-cracked from whatever was in the bottle at his elbow.

Max and Wael stood in the corner, their backs to the bare concrete wall. Wael seemed uncertain of what to do. Max was too drunk to care.

Faith walked over to me. 'Two rooms, twenty dollar.'

'You give it to him,' I said, and pushed the money into her hands.

Alice called over to Max and Wael, 'Who first one?'

'Me,' spluttered Max. He lurched over, took her hand and they vanished through a door behind the counter.

Faith gave the money to the man, who jabbed it into the pocket of his torn, white shirt, and gestured to a staircase hidden in darkness at the back.

'See you in a minute,' I said to Wael.

'I hope you last longer than that, dude.'

I managed a laugh.

Faith led me up the stairs, along a short corridor to a wooden door that hung awkwardly in its frame, as if it belonged elsewhere. We went inside and Faith shut the door, securing a small metal bolt, the kind you usually find in toilets. A cloth was draped over the solitary lamp, casting misshapen shadows onto the windowless walls. A bare mattress rested on a metal frame bed and she indicated that I should sit down. I did.

'What you go want me do?' she asked, letting her dress fall to the floor. She assumed a pose: one leg forward and bent, her hands on her hips, and pouted through her thick, crimson lipstick.

'I don't know,' I said. She laughed and knelt down, walking towards me on her knees, but her smile did not reach her eyes, and I looked away as her cold, clammy hand came to rest on mine. I gave an involuntary sniff, filling my nostrils with the smell of dank walls and sweat.

She loosened my belt, and I lifted myself slightly off the bed as she pulled down my jeans. 'This go cost you thirty dollar.'

'OK,' I choked. My voice sounded distant. 'Look, why don't—'

'FUCK OFF!' The shout burst into the room, making Faith fall backwards. It was Max's voice.

'What *dis ting*?' she said, her voice trembling as she grabbed her dress, hugging it to her body. I pulled my jeans up and rushed out of the door.

'Max?' I called. 'Wael?'

More shouts answered me, but they were fainter now and I couldn't hear the words. I sprinted down the deserted hallway and jumped down the stairs, made for the doorway and pulled back the cloth.

The storm hit me like a wave on the ocean. The rain was blinding, forced down in sheets by the screeching wind and churning the ground outside the hotel into a mud bath.

A few feet away from the door, Alice had Max by the collar. They both gesticulated wildly, shouting at each other. The man from behind the counter stood next to Alice, pointing at Max and ignoring Wael's attempts to talk to him. Guppy stood to one side, rain pouring down his face, his hands on his head.

I ran over to the man. 'What's going on?' I yelled, tugging at his arm. He spun around and pushed me in the chest, forcing me back.

'He never go pay my girl!' The stench of what he'd been drinking carried across the wind and his eyes shone wild, furious.

'Max, give her the money,' I pleaded.

'I didn't do anything!'

'Just give her the goddam money!' I heard the panic rising in my voice.

'You pay now!' bellowed the man and reached behind him, pulling a knife from his trouser belt.

The sight of the blade made Alice release her grip and she stumbled back. The man moved closer to Max, who stood rooted to the spot, staring at the knife in disbelief.

'Enough!' It was Guppy. He had stepped between Max and the man, his arm outstretched, his palm pointing at the man's chest. The man stopped and stared down at his drenched figure, before gripping him by the shoulder and hurling him to one side. Wael shouted something and took a step forward, his arm reaching down to where Guppy lay in the mud, and in the same instant the knife slashed through the wall of rain, arching up and across from the man's hip and finishing, red-streaked, above his shoulder.

I looked at the picture in front of me, a moment in time etched into the night: the raised knife, Wael's ripped, blood-soaked T-shirt, his face locked in shock and pain, the water hanging in the air. Then the ground rushed up at me.

I spat sludge from my mouth and looked up as Samson bounded over me. He grabbed the man by the arm and flung him through the air, back towards the hotel. The man slid through the mud, the knife falling from his hand as he hit the hotel wall. He struggled to get up, but Samson reached him in three strides. He lifted him by the neck and hammered his fist into his face; the man sagged and Samson let him crumble to the ground.

Wael lay face down, a red pool spreading beneath him. I struggled to get up as Samson ran and turned him over. With barely a glance at Wael's lacerated chest, he scooped him up.

'Come! Come!' he ordered. He began to run back to the bar with Wael limp in his arms, and his words dragged me to my feet. I clamped my hand around Guppy's arm and, shouting to Max, we sprinted after Samson.

CHAPTER 4

I sat perched on the edge of a small chair in the middle of the principal's office with my knees jutting up in front of me and the air conditioner blowing down the back of my neck. The principal sat behind his oak desk, his fingertips pressed together, staring out of the window. From a place of honour on the wall above his head, Uncle Sam jabbed his finger at my face, his expression an unspoken accusation. The ticking of the clock was the only sound.

The Principal coughed, clearing his throat, a gunshot in the silence that almost lifted me from my seat. He turned, and placed his elbows on his desk. 'Whose idea was it to go to the bar?'

'Mine,' I said, desperate to talk, to hide the scowl from the poster, to muffle the clock. I waited for the next question, but it didn't come. The principal stared at some papers on his desk and the silence slunk back into the room. I shifted in my seat. 'It was mine,' I repeated, trying to force a response. But the principal appeared not to have heard and his eyes didn't flinch from the papers on his desk.

I tried to force my thoughts away from the night at the bar, as I had for three days – was it three days? Three days since the frantic drive to the hospital, Wael's blood covering my arms as I pressed the towel against his chest. Three days since the phone calls to parents, the sound of Max's drunken crying and Guppy's pale silence.

The hospital had been small, little more than a clinic, but it was too far to the bigger, modern one on Johnston Avenue. A single, bare light bulb hung from the ceiling illuminating the empty reception desk and the grey, damp walls. A woman rocked a crying baby in her arms opposite a man lying in the foetal position on the floor, a leak from the roof slapping against his bare shoulder. A trolley stood abandoned to one side and, flicking off a cockroach, Samson laid the unconscious Wael down on it and then ran off calling for a doctor. Max had gone straight to the phone to try to call his father, Guppy helped me hold the soaked towel against Wael's chest.

Another cough brought me back to the office and I struggled to stay there. I tried humming tunes in my head, but they sounded like the laughter of girls or the pounding of rain. I gripped the sides of the chair and tried to picture the beach, palm trees swaying on the sand, but all I could see was a yellow-toothed grin, the flash of a knife and blood-stained hands. I remembered how the doctor had come running from the murky interior. He had ripped Wael's T-shirt open and without a word began pushing the trolley away, calling for a nurse. Guppy and I had stood and watched him go.

It was at that moment that the question first formed in my mind, one that had been burning there for three days.

'Is he dead?' The words were out before I realised I was speaking. The principal raised his head and his eyes bored into mine. 'Please,' I said, 'I need to know.'

The principal leaned back and the creak of leather interrupted the clock. 'No.'

My hands released their grip on the chair and I slumped forward.

'Wael has been very lucky. His parents have had him flown out to a hospital in Rome. He is stable and expected to make a full recovery.'

'Thank you,' I said, my voice barely a whisper.

'Ambassador Johnson is extremely concerned about this incident and his son being led astray in this manner. He is considering removing him from the school, but I have assured him that we do not condone this sort of behaviour in our students on or off campus.'

I looked at him for a moment, confused, then realised he was talking about Max's father. I remembered him arriving at the hospital about forty minutes after the doctor had taken Wael away. Guppy and I were sitting on the floor, silent, listening to the rain lashing against the building. Max's father burst through the door flanked by two US marines, holding his diplomatic identification in front of him like a shield; but there was no one to show it to. Max ran to him, and his father draped his jacket over his son's shoulders before offering him to one of the marines who led him outside. The ambassador looked at the two of us for a second and then opened his mouth to speak. Guppy beat him to it. 'Our parents are coming. I have phoned them.' The ambassador didn't hesitate any longer, and with a nod he was gone, leaving Guppy and me sitting, our backs against the wall, in a dank pool of rainwater and blood, listening to the cry of a baby and the rhythmic drip of water on the man still lying on the floor.

Then the principal spoke. 'You are to be expelled.'

The words hit me like a slap. I hadn't imagined this. I stared at him, not wanting to believe it, but his eyes confirmed what he had said. I tried to say something, anything that might make him change his mind, but all I could manage was, 'Please. . .'

He cocked his head to one side. 'Yes?'

I opened my mouth to try to speak but no words came. The principal held up his hand. 'There is one option,' he said, 'one way you can avoid expulsion.'

'Anything,' I said.

'I am giving you a choice: if you can convince me that you have found a worthwhile way to spend your time, something that will reflect well on the school, then you will only be excluded for the rest of the academic year. This will allow you to get your diploma, but it will keep you away from the other students – I do not want any more of them influenced by you. Assignments will be sent to you, or they can be collected. You will only be allowed onto the campus for examinations. You will be accompanied by a teacher at all times and will be required to leave immediately after any such exams have taken place. Do you understand?'

'Yes. Thank you.' My hands began to shake and I could feel my strength slipping away; the walls I had built were beginning to crack.

'I will expect your phone call no later than four o'clock tomorrow afternoon outlining your plans. If I consider them unsatisfactory, then your expulsion will stand. I spoke with your parents this morning. They are waiting for you outside. It is only because this is your final year at school that I have given you this choice. You may go.'

And he returned his gaze to his papers.

My parents stood up as they saw me come out, but I kept my eyes on the floor. 'Do you have everything?' asked my mother. I nodded, and she led the way out of the office.

Thomson, my father's driver, was waiting for us with the car at the foot of the steps. My father climbed into the front passenger seat and I sat with my mother in the back. The car pulled away and I turned and watched the gates close behind us, hiding the school from view. I looked up at my mother and she looked back, a heavy smile on her lips.

'Your friend's all right,' she said. I opened my mouth to reply but a sudden retch snatched the words away.

I clamped my hand to my mouth and turned away, screwing up my eyes as I fought the spasms rocking my body. 'Pull over,' my mother said, and before the car had completely stopped, I pushed open the door and emptied my stomach into the monsoon drain.

⊞◎▣

I lay on my bed and watched the ceiling fan, letting its warm breeze blow over me. My curtains were open and light from the floodlit compound cast circular shadows through the security bars. A mosquito hummed across the room, battling the flow of air from the fan before giving up and retreating to a shadowed corner. I would have to spray.

Events were much clearer in my mind now. My fear and shame had been replaced by relief, then clarity. Max's father had pulled rank to save his son. It must have been he who had called the school, and I wondered what Max had told him. Whatever it was, my answer to the principal's solitary question had confirmed it.

My thoughts moved to Guppy: his father had arrived and I saw the fear in Guppy's eyes as he approached. But he spoke softly, sending Guppy home with the driver and going to find the doctor to check on Wael. Roger, my father's friend, had come to get me. Guppy's father volunteered to stay until Wael's parents arrived. It was the last I had heard of any of them until my meeting with the principal.

I rolled over on the bed and saw my father silhouetted in the doorway. 'Your mother and I would like to speak to you,' he said, and was gone. I sat up and closed my eyes, pressing my fingers to my forehead. I knew what they were going to ask; I had no answer for them.

My father sat behind the bar, a pint of beer in front of him, cigarette smoke climbing in the air past his combed brown hair. Even sitting down, he looked tall. He had taken off his tie and placed it, tightly rolled, in front of him. My mother sat on the opposite side and I took the stool next to her. She looked at me and I saw lines of sadness pulling at her eyes.

'He'll have to go to the doctor for tests, in case he's caught anything,' she said, and I felt the blood drain from my cheeks as my father nodded his agreement, slowly scratching his moustache.

'But I didn't. . .'

'For God's sake, I wasn't born yesterday, Charlie,' snapped my father.

I had told them we had gone for a walk to sober Max up, that the man must have been a robber. They had both been kind, understanding and supportive, waiting for news of Wael and of what would happen to me. I assumed they had believed me.

They had arrived back the next day and collected me from Roger's. My father went down to the police station and returned with the news that they would not need to see me, or any of the boys; that Samson's statement would suffice. From the snippets I caught of his conversation with my mother, getting that decision had cost him a lot of money. He would have found out who the attacker was, what he did for a living, I thought, and the shame began to eat its way back.

'It's my fault,' said my mother. 'I should have seen something like this coming. The school was worried; they said so in the report. We should never have left him alone.'

'Perhaps not. But the blame lies with Charlie and his friends. Nobody else.' I tried to hold my father's eye as he spoke, but couldn't and looked away.

'What about that American man? The ambassador? The one who left them at the hospital?' My mother addressed the question to my father, who pulled hard on his cigarette, the tip flashing red and illuminating the sudden anger in his eyes.

'I don't think there is anything we can do,' he replied. 'The question is: what is Charlie going to do?'

I didn't know. I hadn't been able to think about the principal's offer, or how I might be able to save my place at school.

I stared at the bar-top, searching for an answer in the grain of the mahogany. The sound of the television drifted through from the living room, and through the glass panel of the swing door I could see my sister's feet resting on an upholstered stool, her elbow on the arm of the chair, Norman's crackling copy of *One Hundred and One Dalmatians* flickering on the screen.

My parents waited.

There must be something, I thought. Something I could do to please them, to make amends for what had happened, to make it right again.

My mother's sigh broke the silence. 'Well,' she said, 'as your mind appears to be blank on the subject, I have a few suggestions.'

It didn't surprise me; she did a lot of work in leper colonies, missions and a drug rehabilitation centre; just the sort of places the principal would approve of.

'It has to be something meaningful, something worthwhile. I was thinking you could volunteer at a place called the Ilakaye Refuge Centre. . .'

I looked up in surprise, remembering an old man and an off-white business card.

'What's the matter, Charlie?' she asked.

'I've heard of that place. A man, Joseph, he came to the school to talk about it.'

'Well, that's excellent,' said my mother. 'I have a friend there and I know they're always looking for help. So, do you think it's a good idea?'

The ring of the telephone stopped me from answering, and for a moment we all just sat there listening to it.

'Answer the phone, Charlie,' said my father.

I slid off my stool and walked through the door to the bedrooms. Just beyond the security door was a small table, the telephone ringing on top.

'Hello?'

'Charlie? Is that you?' The line hissed, but there was no mistaking Guppy.

'Yes, yes, it is. Good to hear from you.' And it was. I sat on the stool next to the table and listened to Guppy's story. It was the same as mine, except that the question the principal fired at him had been,

'Did you go willingly to the bar?' He had answered, 'Yes', and was now excluded from school too.

'My parents are very angry,' he said, 'and very ashamed. I have let them down terribly.' I wanted to tell him that he hadn't, that all he'd done was have a beer and wait outside a hotel in the rain. But his tone told me not to. 'I was wondering what you will be doing?'

I told him of my mother's idea.

'That sounds perfect.' Then he paused, as if trying to phrase a difficult question. 'Would it be OK if I came along? It would be a good way to continue to study and to regain my father's respect. He has said he no longer cares what I do.'

Having Guppy there would be better than nobody, I thought. 'It would be great, Guppy,' I said. 'It would be nice to have someone I know there.'

'It's strange. A few days ago I would have been delighted if my father said he didn't care what I did. But it's very hard to see him so upset.'

'I know what you mean.'

I returned to the living room. My parent's eyes followed me as I sat back down at the bar. 'That was Guppy, one of my friends. I told him about your idea. He wants to come along there with me.'

My father pondered for a moment. 'That's good. I would prefer you not to go alone.' He looked at my mother, who nodded her agreement. 'All right, then. If the principal and Joseph agree, then I'll arrange Samson to take you. If you're to fulfil the principal's conditions, this is something you will have to commit to. Do you understand, Charlie?'

'Absolutely.'

'Well, then, that's settled.' My parents rose and, without a backward glance, walked into the living room. I sat alone for a moment and, not knowing what else to do, went off to my room.

Later, as I was lying in bed, my mother came in. She stood for a while studying me from the doorway, before walking over and sitting down on the bed. 'I'm glad you agreed to go to Ilakaye. A good decision.' She seemed to choose her words with care. 'It will be a valuable experience.'

I stared into her eyes and wanted to tell her everything: about the boys killed on the road, about how I had felt at the bar and the hotel. But I couldn't. The events weighed too heavy to be turned into words; they were better left buried.

It was the first of the secrets I would keep from her.

'I want to go,' I said. 'It's what I want to do.' Of course, it wasn't. I wanted to stay in school, to forget everything that had happened. But this way I could make it right, take things back to the way they were.

She smiled, looking at me with an expression I couldn't quite define, before getting up. She stopped at the door and turned back. 'You have to take that video back tomorrow, the one you left on the dining table,' she said, and closed the door. I had forgotten all about *The Girls from Goldolvin High*. It was a slight rebuke in the light of everything that had gone before, but my heart was feeling sore and it cut deeper than anything else that day.

I reached over and pulled back a corner of the curtain. My father sat on the diving board, a whisky in his hand, as he did every night. He glanced up as a bat swooped down, sending ripples across the moon-washed water as it took a drink. I often watched him, wondering what he was thinking as he sat, solitary, sipping his whisky in the warm African nights. But that night I didn't want to know.

CHAPTER 5

We sat in silence in the back of the car, Guppy tying his shoelaces for the umpteenth time, never completely satisfied with the result, Samson with both hands on the wheel and his eyes on the road. We had not spoken since the hospital.

We took a familiar route along Airport Road, past the newly opened Sheraton Hotel, before turning onto Ibarajo Road. If it wasn't for Guppy sitting next to me, struggling with his shoelaces, I could have believed I was on my way to school on a typical morning, but as the national stadium loomed into view, we turned left onto Queens Road and into the suburb of Yuru Ibo.

It was immediately quieter; the roar of the Ibarajo road rushed past in an unmovable current. Samson shifted down a gear as the car slowed. We crawled along narrow, unmarked streets that slopped down at the sides towards the open drains. Planks of wood served as makeshift bridges between the road and the mud pavements, safe passage across the mosquito fields below. A man stood on one cleaning his teeth with a short stick, spitting into the drain at his feet, his movements lazy as he yawned at the dawn.

A group of children came running beside the car, shouting '*Oynibo, Oyinbo*' and slapping the door with their palms, their huge grins filling the windows. The man on the bridge shouted something and they stopped, falling behind, panting and laughing. A woman set up her roadside stall, trying to balance bottles of Fanta and Sprite on an already crowded wooden box. Another woman walked past her, an enormous metal dish filled with rice balanced perfectly on her head, a child's hand in each of hers.

The once-white houses, now stained with age and weather, formed crooked lines that stretched into the distance. A border of mud thrown by the rains crept up the walls to the warped wooden sills of the windows. Cloth hung in some of the doors, others were just holes in the wall reached by cracked concrete steps. Occasionally a face peered out, a hand rested on a door-frame, disembodied by the blackness within.

'Got it,' breathed Guppy. He stared down at his sneakers, now rendered airtight by the barrel-size knots sitting on top of them.

'What?' said Samson, his first word of the day.

'Oh, nothing,' replied Guppy. 'Just my shoes.'

I decided to grab the opportunity to talk to Samson. He hadn't even looked me in the eye when he had collected us that morning.

'What does "*Oyinbo*" mean?' I asked. Samson's eyes flicked up into the rear view mirror and met mine, before returning to the road. For a moment I thought he wasn't going to say anything. Then he breathed in and replied, 'White man. *Oyinbo* means white man.'

'Oh.' I leant forward and quickly began another question, eager to get him talking. But he cut me off halfway through. 'We nearly there.' The conversation was over. Samson didn't want to start a pidgin lesson, and it seemed I had lost another friend; he might as well not have been there, like Max and Wael. So I was stuck with The Guppy.

We turned right, leaving the laughing boys and the stall owners behind, and pulled into the side of the road in front of a pair of grey gates squeezed between two unpainted, concrete walls. A dog worried something on the ground opposite, its growls the only sound on the deserted street.

'Ilakaye,' stated Samson.

Jesus Christ, I thought, what *was* this place?

Guppy leaned over and blinked. 'Thank you,' he said, and climbed out of the car.

I sat for a moment and stared at the back of Samson's head. 'Samson. . .' I started.

'I will pick you at three.'

I hesitated for a moment, then nodded and climbed out. 'Don't be late,' I snapped, and slammed the door. I immediately regretted it, but I found his refusal to talk to me infuriating. I took a deep breath and turned to face the gates.

There was nothing to suggest what lay behind, no sign or poster. The wall ran unbroken on both sides of the gates, except for a small wooden box hung on the right. It held a bundle of grey rags, and above it was a small metal door with streaks of rust eating through the black paint.

'Do you think we should knock?' asked Guppy. I didn't have a better suggestion so I rapped once with my knuckles against the steel, sending a metallic echo across the street. The dog began to bark, startled by the sound. And the bundle of grey rags in the box began to cry.

We stared for a moment, unsure of what was happening.

'Charlie. I do believe there is a baby inside the box.'

'No shit, Guppy.' I took a step forward just as the metal door creaked open and a pair of hands emerged, picked up the baby and pulled it inside. We both stood and gaped.

'I think we should go in,' I said at last and, pushing the gate open, we both slipped inside.

I saw a woman hurrying away towards a building on brick stilts, calling something I couldn't quite make out; the baby's cries were still audible. A second woman appeared at the doorway, ushered them inside and shut the door.

'They must have an orphanage,' suggested Guppy. I nodded, and turned to take in the rest of the compound.

A clay track ran off into the distance; to the left stood a row of rectangular, whitewashed buildings with corrugated-iron roofs. I counted six – all on stilts. A separate compound stood to the right, high-walled with dull black gates. I was wondering what they were supposed to keep out, when a boy with one leg missing emerged from the nearest building. He paused just outside the door, resting on his crutches, looked at the sky, and then jumped down the three steps in one go, landing softly on the ground. He turned to us and waved, and I waved back.

'Good morning, Joshua,' said a voice from behind me, and I turned and saw Joseph standing there, waving at the boy on crutches. He looked exactly as I remembered him: a faded white shirt, ill-fitting trousers and scuffed shoes. He still wore the bandage on his head, a reminder of his scuffle with the man in the suit. The white fabric glared against his ebony skin, and a small scar ran from below his right eye to halfway down his cheek, like a stain left by a tear. He was even shorter than Guppy.

Joshua grinned, turned and swung down the track as Joseph turned his attention to us. 'You must be Charlie.'

'Yes,' I managed, embarrassed at having assumed Joshua had been waving at me.

'And. . .'

'Guppy. Everyone just calls me Guppy.'

'Guppy it is, then. And you two must call me Joseph. Are you ready to start?'

'Absolutely,' declared Guppy.

'Good. Then let me show you around.'

We followed Joseph down the path as he explained the layout of Ilakaye to us. The buildings on the left were dormitories. Turning the corner, he showed us the kitchens, bathrooms, and the dining hall, each building the same design.

'Beyond the kitchens are our workshops and gardens. But I will show you those later.'

'Is this a government institution?' enquired Guppy.

'No, no. We are privately run. All our staff are volunteers, mostly doctors and nurses, or craftsman who give us their time. A very valuable gift.'

'And how many people are here?'

'We can house up to 250 people,' Joseph told us. 'Although now we have only 123.'

'Who are they?' I asked.

'Lepers, drug addicts, the homeless, the crippled. They all come here. We are open to anyone. Although we only remain open to those who wish to learn. To better themselves.'

'Where are they all?' asked Guppy. And I realised that, apart from the two women and Joshua, we had not seen anyone.

Joseph laughed. 'Breakfast is at seven-thirty. You'll see everyone then.' Twenty minutes to go. 'In the meantime, I have a blocked monsoon drain that needs your attention.'

He led us to the side of the separate compound with

locked gates. The rains had filled the drain running along its side with a landslide of mud.

'Blocked drains mean stagnant water, which means mosquitoes and malaria. I have left two shovels for you against the wall there. It will be getting busy in a moment. Don't worry. I am in the office by the gates if you need me.'

'There was a baby,' said Guppy, 'in a box outside the gates.'

'Yes, I know. The first one we have had for some time.'

'They leave babies in a box?'

Joseph held my eye for a second before responding. 'Better than the sewer.'

'Sorry. . .' I began.

Joseph held up his hand. 'No need for apologies. Actually, abandoned babies are very rare. The whole village used to help to raise a child. But in the city there are no villages. Good luck with the drain.' And he turned and left.

We watched as he shuffled down the track, and then turned to face the drain.

'We'd better get started,' suggested Guppy. I nodded, and we each picked up a shovel and got to work.

In minutes I was drenched in sweat. I stabbed

the shovel into the piles of mud, trying to heave the thick, heavy sludge out, and often had to stop and let some slide off before I could lift it. The sun rose quickly, the air thick with humidity, and the insects darted around my head, drawn by the salt on my skin. I stopped and looked at my hands, they were starting to redden, slowly rubbed raw by the rough handle, the beginning of blisters on the top of my palms.

I wiped my face with my T-shirt and glanced over at Guppy on the other side of the mud pile. Sweat poured down his forehead and into his eyes, his clothes splattered a reddy-brown, his face locked in concentration, and he didn't look up from his work. I took a breath and dug the shovel back into the mud, and slowly the pile at the edge of the drain began to grow.

The sudden clanging of a bell made us both look up.

'Breakfast time,' I said, praying it meant a break for us as well.

The doors to the dormitories opened and Ilakaye poured out.

Children, men, women, all came clattering down the steps. Some rushed, heads down, in the direction of the kitchens; others moved slowly, hindered by crutches or old age, their clothes red, purple, green, black, yellow: brushstrokes of colour sweeping past, and their chatter filled the morning air.

They moved past, barely giving us a glance, and they were almost completely out of sight when I noticed a figure moving slower than all the rest. He wore a cloak that swept the ground at his feet, and a hood that hung low over his face. He walked with an awkward, disjointed gait and he seemed to stamp his feet into the ground as he went. As he drew level with us, he turned, and I felt keen eyes staring out from the depths of his hood. Then suddenly his arm snapped up and he cried out, taking a step towards us, his hood slipping back, the sun striking his face – it was covered in lesions, and large patches of his skin had faded to the colour of sour milk.

He raised his forearm to cover his disfigurement but continued to move towards us, his other hand outstretched, the fingers withered to stumps just above the knuckles. I let out a cry and stepped back, slipping against the edge of the drain and sitting down hard in the mud. The man kept coming and I realised he was shouting, 'Look out!'

The words were strong and clear and I instinctively looked up. A figure stood on the wall above me, silhouetted against the sky. I heard Guppy gasp and I jumped up, pushing him against the wall.

With a shriek, the figure jumped, landing just beyond the drain. He was naked and held a rock in his right hand. He faced the man in the cloak and let out a bellow that burst through my ears. The disfigured man stood his ground, speaking softly, his tone calm and soothing. Then, with another shriek, the man hit his own head with the rock, blood sliding down the side of his face, and then swung it, catching the man in the cloak on the arm. He gave no sign of having felt anything.

'Quickly,' said Guppy, 'we must help him,' and before I could stop him, he rushed at the naked man. The gates to the compound opened with a crash and a man in a white coat came flying out, a syringe in his hand.

Guppy threw himself onto the back of the naked man, who bucked around, screaming, in an effort to get him off. The doctor approached, holding the syringe in front of him, but the man swung the rock again, forcing him to back off. I gritted my teeth and ran towards them, dropping my shoulder, and brought the three of us crashing to the ground.

'Hold him!' yelled the doctor, and Guppy and

I struggled to pin his arms to the ground. His knee came up and caught me in the small of the back, pitching me forward. I turned and threw myself back on top of him.

'His legs! His legs!' shouted the doctor.

The man shrieked, an angry, incoherent babble, and I saw the man in the cloak grab his legs, struggling to control them. The doctor stabbed the needle into the man's arm and it took immediate effect. I felt his body relaxing under me, his cries grew fainter and I rolled over onto the track, gasping for breath.

I lay on my back and stared at the sky, my heart punching my ribs. I could hear other voices around us now, but I kept my eyes on the clouds. And then a woman's face came into view above my head, cracking into a toothless grin.

'Ẹ pẹ̀lẹ́, oyinbo níbo ni ẹ ti nbọ̀?'

'What?' I gasped.

'That will do, Abiyona. Go to breakfast now.' The thick Irish accent startled me and I sat up. A nun in a light grey habit stood there, looking sternly at the toothless woman who had spoken to me.

Abiyona seemed about to protest, then thought better of it and walked quickly away, muttering to herself. The scene had gathered quite a crowd, but a few quick words from the nun, and they began to move off. Then she turned to me.

'Up you get, and let me look at you,' she ordered. I obeyed, scrabbling to my feet. She lifted my chin and stared down her nose at me through half-moon spectacles, turning my head from one side to the other. 'Are you hurt?'

'No. I don't think so.'

She continued to study me for a moment, her green eyes framed by wrinkled, sun-battered skin.

'Well, thanks be to God. I don't know what Joseph was thinking, bringing children here.'

I felt a surge of anger at the word 'children'. 'I'm fine.' I said, hoping she wouldn't notice my shaking legs.

'Very well,' she said and turned away. 'Don't you go anywhere, Adebayo!' The man in the cloak, his hood pulled back up, was shuffling quietly away, but stopped at the sound of the nun's voice, like a child caught in the act. 'I want to look at that arm,' she said, and strode off towards him.

Several other volunteers had arrived. They lifted the naked man onto a stretcher, and with the doctor leading the way, carried him back through the gates.

Guppy sat, his head back, while a man held some

cotton wool to his bleeding nose. His eyes turned to look at me as I approached. 'Nits nalright. Nits not boken.'

The man helping him smiled. I couldn't help but do the same.

◫◉▣

'I am sorry this had to happen on your first day – or any day, for that matter.' Joseph poured tea into two cups as he spoke. It was cool in his office, and the chair was comfortable. I began to relax. 'But I must thank you. You were both very brave and saved that man from harming anyone – especially himself.'

'Who was he?' asked Guppy, pulling at one of the pieces of cotton wool stuffed up his nostrils.

Joseph sighed, and handed him a cup of tea. 'Occasionally we get people who are mentally disturbed, either through illness or drugs and alcohol. We cannot keep them here – we do not have the facilities or the staff to care for them properly. So we hold them in a separate compound until we can have them transferred. That man came in three days ago, unhinged by heroin and palm wine. I'm not sure how he managed to get over the wall. . .' He sighed again and sat down opposite us.

'What about the man in the cloak – Adebayo?' I asked.

Joseph took a sip of tea and before he could speak, Guppy answered the question for him. 'He suffers from leprosy.'

Joseph looked impressed. 'Yes, he does. Or from Hansen's Disease, depending which term you feel is more correct. Unfortunately he came to us very late. The disease had already caused considerable deformity.'

'But it is treatable,' continued Guppy.

'It can be stopped in its tracks. We have other leprosy patients here whose symptoms have never gone beyond a slight pigment change on their chest. But. . .' He paused and took a sip of tea, a shadow of weariness (or was it sadness?) clouding his face. 'There is still a lot of fear of leprosy, especially in the rural areas. Sufferers are banished and often do not find treatment in time.'

'That's terrible.' I said. Joseph looked at me and I remembered how I had backed away, scared and stumbling, when Adebayo had approached.

'Fear can make people do terrible things,' he said, his eyes not leaving mine. 'Only experience and education can stop that.' I broke his gaze and stared at my tea.

'Now,' he said, his voice regaining its strength.' I totally understand if you do not wish to continue here. You have had a nasty experience. . .'

I looked at Guppy. I wanted to go, away from this place of lunatics and lepers. There must be other things we could do; other places we could work, this was not what I had expected at all – but what had I expected? And I realised I hadn't given it any real thought at all. The sweat started breaking out on my palms. But Guppy looked startled at the suggestion.

'We have not finished the drain.'

I stared at him for a second: the cotton wool was making his nose twitch. And I nodded, finished my tea and after more thanks from Joseph we strode back to the drain.

It took us another hour to finish and I leant against my shovel, my arms burning. Guppy clambered out of the drain and surveyed the pile of mud.

'I wonder what will happen to that.'

'Who cares. We've earned a break.'

'Ah, grand. Well done.' I hadn't heard the nun approach, but felt a certain pride at her words. 'Now, you'll find some wheelbarrows by the workshop over there. This needs to be moved and spread over the ground at the back of the compound.' And she left as quickly as she had appeared.

Guppy set off immediately, but I stayed where I was, staring at the mud pile. My shoulders slumped and a dull throbbing pushed at the back of my head. I swept my eyes around the compound, taking in the buildings shimmering in the heat. Joshua swung past on his crutches and gave me a wave; I managed to raise my aching arm in reply.

What the hell was I doing here? I looked over at the gates and my mind filled with a dozen excuses to walk through them, to leave Ilakaye behind. I would think of something to tell my parents; even expulsion would be better than this.

I pulled up my T-shirt, wiped the sweat from my eyes and leant back against the wall. My eyes moved from the gates to the mud pile to the figure of Guppy limping away in the distance, and the softest of breezes stroked my face.

With a sigh, I jumped the drain and followed him.

CHAPTER 6

I was exhausted. My hands burned and the back of my neck itched maddeningly from the sunburn. Guppy's driver waited for him at the gates to my house and we grunted our goodbyes.

Samson still wasn't talking, but I was too tired to care. Kicking off my shoes outside the front door I went inside, wanting nothing but a cold drink and a shower.

'Well, here he is now.' I recognised the accent immediately, and there, at the bar with my parents, sat the nun from Ilakaye. 'Quite the hero he was, this morning,' she continued, then took a gulp from her pint of beer and pushed a four-inch cigar into her mouth.

'Sister Mairead has been telling us about your day,' said my mother, the concern in her voice detracting from her smile. 'Come and get a drink.'

'Thanks,' I said, 'but I need a shower first. I'm sorry I didn't know you. . . I mean that you knew. . .' I gave up trying to explain that I had no idea who Sister Mairead was or how she knew my parents. But it seemed I didn't have to.

'I didn't make the connection either.' Sister Mairead laughed, sending cigar ash tumbling down her habit. 'Sur', your mother and I have met many times at the mission in Darra.'

'Sister Mairead will be joining us for dinner tonight,' explained my mother.

I let out a sigh. Every muscle in my body ached, I stank, it was an effort to stand, and the last thing I wanted to do was make polite conversation at a dinner table. But nobody seemed to hear.

'He was clearing drains all day,' Sister Mairead continued. 'The rains make such a mess: first the one outside the secure compound and then the ones around the kitchens and bathrooms. Six in all, was it, Charlie?'

'Seven.'

'You'd better go and have your shower, Charlie,' my father said.

▣⊙◪

Dinner was less of an ordeal than I had imagined. I felt better after my shower, some of the fatigue rinsed away with the grime, and I couldn't have talked much even if I had wanted to, with my parents and Sister Mairead doing enough for twenty.

I let their voices fade into the background, my only concern getting as much food inside me as possible. A pause in the conversation made me look up, to find everyone looking at me.

'Sister Mairead asked you a question, Charlie,' said my father.

'I'm sorry. . .' I stuttered.

But Sister Mairead laughed. 'Sweet Mother of God, you'd think he hadn't eaten for a week. I was just wondering, Charlie, how things are at school.'

I looked over at my mother, who immediately reached for her wine glass. My father coughed, my sister giggled.

'I'm not at school at the moment. I was . . . I'm studying from home, that's why I'm at Ilakaye. There was an accident. . .' I trailed off and my eyes returned to my plate.

'Ah. Now I see.' Sister Mairead spoke slowly, drawing out the words, like someone contemplating the answer to a riddle that suddenly seemed obvious.

'So a bit of a penance, then? A bit tougher than twenty Hail Marys, though!'

'It's not a penance. I just wanted to do something worthwhile' – my embarrassment quickly turning to defensiveness – 'to help people.'

'And was clearing out monsoon drains a worthwhile way to spend your time today, Charlie?' The edge in her voice surprised me, and I found I had no answer, that I had not even asked myself that question. 'Well, I suppose after today you'll not be going back again.'

I rubbed my thumb over the calluses forming at the base of my fingers, and I thought of Guppy, sweat-soaked and gasping as he dug at the mud in the drains without a murmur of complaint. I stopped staring at my plate and looked directly at her, holding her gaze. 'Yes, I will.' But the words rang hollow, and I knew my heart was not behind them.

' Good.' She spoke in barely a whisper, and I thought I saw the flicker of a smile play across her eyes.

We lapsed into silence, broken only by the first spatter of rain on the roof.

'I still go to school,' said my sister, her young voice breaking the tension that had formed at the table. 'I'm five. I go to Willows. It's not the same as Charlie's.

Mummy, it's raining. Can I go for a shower?'

'I don't see why not. Ask Ruth to go with you.'

Katie sprang off her chair and rushed to the kitchen. 'Ruth, Ruth, I'm going for a shower!'

'A shower?' asked Mairead.

'She likes to stand in the monsoon drain under the porch when it's raining,' said my mother.

'How lovely. Oh, to be young. . .'

'Can't beat the clock,' said my father. 'Shall we go through to the living room?'

They all moved off, leaving me to take the plates and dishes out to the kitchen. As I went, I knocked a picture hanging on the wall behind me. I turned to straighten it and saw that it was my sister's school photo. A group of children sat on tiered benches under a flame tree, flanked by four teachers. The school building formed the backdrop, its verandas stretching beyond the frame of the photo. On the second tier, three in from the right, sat my sister, beaming into the camera. I realised for the first time that she was the only white child there.

I thought of my school; of Guppy, tortured for his accent and his ill-fitting leg, of the two anonymous boys knocked down on the road, of Wael lying in the mud with his chest slashed open; of dark hotel rooms and drunken girls; and the dripping of water on a dying man's skin.

I walked over to the porch doors and looked out. Wearing a pair of bikini bottoms, Katie stood in the monsoon drain under the corner of the roof. Water cascaded down, caught mid-flow in the beams of the floodlights, a rippled stream of silver in the night. Katie lifted her face, squealing in delight, letting the water run through her hair and into her eyes. On the porch Ruth started to sing, clapping her hands and swaying from side to side. Katie joined in, finding Ruth's rhythm, clapping and calling out in time with the song. I stood and watched, holding the image, engraving it on my mind so that she would always be there, laughing and dancing in the wind and the rain.

'Charlie?' it was my mother. I turned from the window to face her. 'It sounds like you had quite a tough day today.'

'It wasn't too bad.'

She nodded. 'You know, there are other places...' She left the thought hanging in the air, a dangling ticket waiting for me to grab. Here was my chance. All I had to do was say yes, or even nod. No excuses would be necessary.

Perhaps it was the thought of not being able to do

something Guppy could, to be beaten by him, or it was Mairead's words at the table – I don't know, I still do not know, why I looked at her and said, 'I'm fine. I'll go back tomorrow.'

⊞◉▣

I recognised the suit before I recognised the man.

It was our second week at Ilakaye. The sun hung low in the sky, the compound quiet, glowing in the sunset, and Guppy and I sat on the roof of one of the dormitories, the leak now plugged, drinking from our water bottles.

'Nice car,' he remarked.

From the rooftop we had a good view of the street outside the gates, where a stretch white Mercedes had pulled up in front of a battered church. The driver hopped out and walked briskly to the passenger door, opened it and stepped to one side, eyes front like a soldier on parade.

'Jesus. . .' I breathed, resting my water bottle against the roof as the man in the suit seeped out of the back. He straightened, slowly bringing himself to his full height, buttoned his jacket and surveyed the street around him. Without a glance at the driver he walked across to the church where several workmen were tying ropes to a signboard. He spoke briefly to someone I assumed was the foreman, who shouted a command to the others and they heaved the sign up off the ground. In gold lettering it read, 'The Church of Christ the Child'.

'I don't believe it,' I said.

'What is it? Are you familiar with this organisation?'

'Not the church – the man.' And I told Guppy about the two boys killed by the car, and how the man who had just emerged from the Mercedes had fought with Joseph before necklacing the driver.

Guppy nodded thoughtfully at this information and took off his hat – the wide straw brim was already beginning to fray – untied the handkerchief from around his neck and wiped it across his forehead. 'He doesn't sound a particularly pleasant person.'

'No, I don't think he is.' I had never seen anyone near the church before. Its windows were glassless black holes in the walls, and the grime clinging to them gave it the impression of being in permanent shadow.

The man seemed satisfied with the sign and returned to his car. The driver opened the boot, took out an old crate and they walked towards the gates of Ilakaye.

'What the hell is he doing here?' I said, as the gates pushed open and they came through. They stopped just inside and the driver placed the crate on the ground, before retreating to one side. Then, looking around as if wondering where his audience was, the man stepped onto the crate and began to speak.

From the roof it was hard to make out exactly what he was saying, but he became more animated with every sentence, his hands adding emphasis to particular phrases, the spittle firing from his mouth visible even to us.

The dormitories and workshops began to empty as people heard the shouts and shuffled towards the man on his box. Seeing the crowd, the man's sermon intensified, and he coaxed them forward with beckoning arms.

'I think we should see what this is about,' said Guppy. He pushed his hat down onto his head and swung his legs over the ladder. Gripping the sides with the soles of his canvas boots, he slid down in one fluid motion, landing softly on the ground below. I hesitated. I had seen what this man was capable of doing. Below me, Guppy was already scurrying towards him. I sighed, slid down the ladder and ran after him.

By the time we reached the gates there were at least sixty people gathered around the man. He hurled rhetoric at them like stones: They were sinners. They lived in a den of evil. They allowed themselves to be guided by a black-skinned imperialist. Their children would pay the price for their crimes against God. Only he could save them.

'Suffer the little children to come unto me!' he cried. But the crowd remained impassive, regarding him as if he were an act in a travelling show.

He seemed to sense their apathy and began to waver, but at that moment Adebayo loped out of the bathrooms, his black cloak fluttering in the evening breeze. The man seized his chance and pointed a stick-like finger.

'See the product of sin!'

The crowd turned, and Adebayo stopped in his tracks. There was a moment of silence and then a man in the crowd, a carpenter from the workshops, began to laugh.

'You hear, Adebayo? Plenty sinner.' He pretended to cover his eyes, and bent his knees, speaking in a mock whimper, '*Boju-boju*, Adebayo dun come!' The crowd roared with laughter and the man on the box looked down at his driver, unsure of what to do next. The carpenter stepped forward, his smile gone. *'Begin go, big man, you never go butta my bread.'* (Get lost, rich man. You can't answer my prayers.)"

Next to me Guppy snorted a laugh, but my attention was fixed on a woman in the front of the crowd. She had arrived at Ilakaye a few days ago, falling through the gates clutching her six-month-old baby. She held him now, the first day she had been able to do so after the agony of the drying-out process. She did not laugh with the others, her shoulders shook and tears streamed down her weathered cheeks. Then suddenly she let out a shrill cry and held out her child.

'No, no! Not tis ting for him, *abeg, abeg!*

The man seized his chance and, leaping off the box, grabbed the child and held it above his head. 'One will be saved. Who else will embrace the Lord?'

'Put him down!' Mairead's voice echoed around the compound as she pushed her way through the crowd.

The man stopped and stared at her. 'Go home, nun,' he spat. 'This child needs his own people.'

Mairead didn't flinch. 'Put him down.' Her voice carried a quiet fury and the carpenter and two other men moved forward, flanking her.

The man looked at them as if appraising the opposition. His driver fidgeted, looking to him for instructions. Then, with a laugh, he dropped the child to the ground. 'There is no hope for this one, anyway.' The carpenter lunged forward but Mairead's arm shot out, catching him on the chest and blocking his path. The carpenter stopped, but continued to stare at the man with eyes like coals. Mairead stooped down and picked up the child, its cries the only sound.

'This is private property. Please leave.' Joseph stood by the gates and he addressed the man as if he had wandered in by accident, an innocent mistake. The man's head snapped around to look at Joseph and then turned back to the crowd. He made as if to speak, but stopped, buttoned his jacket and, with a nod to his driver, they began to walk back towards their car. When he reached Joseph the man paused, lent over and whispered something into his ear. Joseph gave no indication of what the man had said, and he turned and indicated the open gate, gently pushing it shut as they left.

The crowd erupted with chatter, and the carpenter crushed the abandoned crate under his foot. However, a few sharp words from Mairead and they began to disperse. A nurse coaxed the still-sobbing woman from the ground and led her away as Mairead hurried towards the orphanage with the screaming child.

Joseph stood staring at the gates as the roar of the man's Mercedes filled the air. I glanced at Guppy and we walked over. Joseph didn't move and we hovered behind him for a moment, unsure of what to say.

Then Guppy spoke. 'Is he some denomination of priest?'

'It would appear so,' replied Joseph. His voice was distant and his eyes never left the gate. 'Although it's hard to keep up. The last time I saw him, he was a lawyer.'

'What was he doing here?' I asked.

'I expect he thought it would be easy pickings.'

'Easy pickings?'

'He seemed very interested in children,' offered Guppy.

'Yes, he would,' said Joseph. 'He sells them.' And he turned and walked towards his office as the last of the sunset dissolved into night.

CHAPTER 7

For three days, we watched the transformation of the derelict church. New glass gave life to the windows, a fresh coat of paint gleamed in the sun and a paved path now led through the gravel courtyard to wooden doors engraved with angels and scenes of the Nativity. When they had finished, the workmen chained the doors and vanished, leaving it standing empty, silently mocking the rusting roofs and crumbling walls of its neighbours.

I had not spoken to Joseph since the man in the suit had given his sermon. He spent most of the time in his office, only coming into the compound if there was a problem or a new arrival. No one spoke about the church, and when I asked Sister Mairead about it, she just shrugged her shoulders, before finding some defect in the work I was doing that needed my immediate attention. I got the hint and did not ask again.

Guppy and I kept busy repainting the outside of the workshops. Finished at last, we wandered inside in search of shade. We sat on the floor just inside the door and I took a long swig from my water bottle, pulled off my hat to use as a fan, and looked around.

The workshops were really one long building divided by activity. A group of carpenters and woodcarvers occupied the largest section, watched over by Abacha, the man who had stood up to the preacher and his driver. He moved quietly among them, each working by the sunlight streaming through shuttered holes in the roof. He paused for a moment behind a man who sat cross-legged on the floor gripping a piece of ebony between his feet as he smoothed the cheek of the woman he was creating, the flick of his knife coaxing her features from the wood. Abacha nodded approvingly and moved on to another who knelt in front of a low table, his chisel revealing a group of hunters stalking their prey.

In the middle, potters stretched and kneaded jugs and urns, while in a corner at the back Adebayo sat in front of a rectangle of wood painting a landscape from memory. I put down my bottle and, leaving the whirring of the potter's wheels and the tapping of chisels behind, walked over.

Adebayo gripped the brush between the withered remains of his hands, his movements delicate as he stroked colour into the scene. It was of an expanse of savannah, with a solitary tree off centre, under which two boys were playing. I stood to one side and stared at them. I could hear their laughter and feel the wind on their faces. I watched for perhaps a minute, and then Adebayo turned as if suddenly aware that I was there. I took a step back, feeling as if I was prying, and then Abacha's voice rang out.

'Come, Charlie.'

I turned and left, feeling Adebayo's stare from behind his hood as I walked the length of the workshops. There was something about the painting, something that seemed out of place. Then I realised: one of the boys was white. I turned and looked back, but Adebayo had resumed his work, and did not look up.

'Charlie,' repeated Abacha.

'Sorry,' I said.

Guppy had got to his feet, looking at Abacha expectantly.

'Today I go teach you to drive.'

'To drive?' exclaimed Guppy.

'We take all *distings* to the market,' he said, indicating the carvings and pottery stacked against the wall. 'I go. You drive back. Come, make I teach you correct.' And he walked briskly out of the workshops. Nothing surprised us at Ilakaye any more; we just shrugged and followed.

I could already drive, but Guppy had never been behind the wheel of a car before and was finding it difficult. I stood beside one of the dormitories and watched as the truck lurched past. Guppy's short leg meant that he had to slide forwards and sideways to step on the clutch, then, using the steering wheel, push himself sharply back as the truck jumped into gear.

The truck had once been a bare chassis and bonnet; everything else – the cabin, the flat bed, the bench that served as seats – was built out of wood, giving it the impression of an oversized toy. A hand-carved Spirit of Ecstasy stood proudly on the bonnet.

I watched as it came to a shuddering halt a few yards down the track. The door swung open and Abacha jumped down, muttering to the sky as he walked off to his workshop.

I wandered over. Guppy still sat behind the wheel, practising sliding onto the clutch, his face locked in concentration.

'How's it going?' I asked, suppressing a smile.

'I do not think Abacha is very pleased with my progress. But I'm sure I will be able to master it soon.'

Abacha returned with a block of wood and some string. Still muttering, he tied it to the clutch pedal then, with a despairing look at Guppy, said, 'Now let us try.' I stepped back as Guppy started the engine and watched as he made a run down the track, turned at the gates and came rumbling back, stopping smoothly a few feet away from me. Abacha clapped his hands and laughed. 'You see! *Nah Wah* for modern technology!'

◼◉◻

The market was only five minutes away. We followed the sloping road that led away from Ilakaye and pulled in next to a narrow alleyway. Climbing out, we each grabbed a box – Abacha crouching down and sliding his from the flat bed to his head – and in single file turned into the alley.

It was dark and humid and my elbows brushed the walls of the buildings on either side. I had to take deeper breaths and felt a trickle of sweat run down my cheek. Abacha turned left and we stepped out into the market.

Stalls stretched as far as I could see, with goods stacked high on wooden tables crammed together in jagged rows. We wove through the jostling crowd, ducking underneath the canopy of jeans, shirts and dresses, ignoring the constant hissing from stallholders desperate for our attention. Their fingers slapped against their palms, signalling us to come and look at carvings, pots, ivory tusks, jewellery and stereos, the bellow of the bartering crowds filling the air.

Abacha walked quickly and Guppy and I struggled to keep up, following the teetering box on Abacha's head as it turned left, then right, driving us through the maze of the market. We emerged into a small square, squinting against the sudden burst of sunlight. It was quieter here; the stalls were larger and their owners content to sit in the shade of their awnings and wait for customers to come to them. Guppy stumbled up beside me, exhaled loudly and put his box on the floor.

Joshua stood on the far side of the square, leaning on his crutches behind one of the stalls and smiling over at us. Abacha was already there, unloading his box and talking to someone hidden from view behind him. I glanced at Guppy and we carried our things across, heaving them on to the top of the stall.

'You look tired,' said a voice. I looked up to see that Abacha was talking to a girl. She wore a simple white shirt that finished above a pair of denim shorts. 'My name is Yejide,' she continued, and stretched out her hand. I instinctively rubbed mine against my T-shirt before accepting, suddenly acutely aware of my sweat-streaked face, straw hat and dusty boots.

'Charlie.'

'Pleased to meet you, Charlie.' Her eyes shone, and I found myself glancing away from the power of her smile.

'And this is Guppy,' I said. Guppy lifted his hat with a gentle bow.

'I have heard of both of you. Welcome to the Ilakaye shop.'

'This is very impressive,' said Guppy, 'I have been wondering where the items from the workshops are sold.'

'Not everything is sold here,' said Yejide, beginning to arrange the ebony carvings in front of her, handling them as if they were glass, purpose and thought in the positioning of every piece. 'We ship a lot to the north and abroad.'

'I've never seen you at Ilakaye,' I said, my eyes fixed on the movements of her hands.

'I usually work here. But I will be going to university soon – I hope – to begin a medical degree, so I will be spending more time at Ilakaye with the nurses from now on.'

'Oh, good.'

Joshua's chuckle told me I had spoken too quickly and too earnestly. Yejide just smiled.

'Time to go,' said Abacha. You take the truck go back.'

'It was a pleasure to meet you,' said Guppy, tipping his hat once more. And we both turned and left.

At the entrance to the maze of alleyways, I stopped and looked back. Yejide was still arranging the pieces on the table. She moved around to the front to study the display, putting her hands on her hips, accentuating a waist that curved away to smooth, slender legs. She turned, as if suddenly aware she was being watched. She tossed her braided hair out of her eyes and they immediately caught mine. I raised my hand and she flashed her smile, before I stumbled backwards into the market.

I hardly noticed the walk back to the truck. I slid into the driver's side, gunned the engine and pulled out, my mind still filled with Yejide's smile.

'She is very beautiful,' said Guppy. The truck

lurched as my foot slipped on the accelerator, and the smudges on the windscreen replaced the image of her face.

'Yeah? You like her?' I replied, a little defensively.

'My heart is reserved for Hagit. But I saw the way you looked at Yejide.'

Even after everything that had happened, Guppy hadn't forgotten the Israeli in the twelfth grade.

'So, you still think about her?' I asked, swerving to avoid one of the larger potholes.

'Of course. When we are finished here, when I have regained my father's respect, then I will return to school and ask Hagit to the dance.' He said it as if stating that the sun would rise in the morning.

We drove for a while in silence, and then, almost without thinking, I pulled up at the side of the road and yanked the handbrake on.

'What are we doing here, Guppy? I mean, you still think about school and Hagit. . .'

He turned to me with a puzzled expression. 'I do not understand.'

I pulled out a cigarette and lit it, took a long drag and exhaled, watching the smoke hit the windscreen, billowing into a cloud in front of my face.

'What do we do? We clean out drains, we fix roofs,

we paint walls. For what?' I pulled on my cigarette again as Guppy nodded, thought creasing his forehead.

'You don't believe what we do is worthwhile?'

'I don't know. It's just . . . I mean, why should we. . .?'

'Ah!' said Guppy, as if everything was suddenly clear. 'Everybody always asks that question. 'Why should this be done?' or, 'Who should be the one to do it?' Perhaps it would be better to ask, 'What needs doing?' and just do it. Joseph understands this. The people of Ilakaye understand this.'

I turned and stared at him at for a moment, unfamiliar with the assured authority in his voice.

'And you think we have to do this?' I asked.

He shrugged. 'I do. I cannot answer for you.' It felt like a rebuke and, without responding, I flicked my cigarette out of the window and pulled the truck back onto the road, feeling foolish.

The line of cars began as Ilakaye came into view. The paint gleamed in the evening sun, a jagged line of colour in the dust. Drivers leant against bonnets smoking and talking, resting their backsides on more money then they would see in a lifetime.

'What's going on here?' I said, as I slowed the truck

and came to rest behind a bright blue Range Rover. Its number plates identified it as coming from Jabarra State, several hundred miles to the north. I leaned out of the window and examined some more: they were from all over Sengharia and even from neighbouring countries.

'Some of these people have driven a very long way,' I said.

'There must be something going on in the church,' suggested Guppy. 'I cannot imagine why else such people would be parked here.'

I killed the engine and climbed out.

'Where are you going?'

'To take a look.' I wanted a break from the work of the day, and everyone's refusal to talk about the church had simply heightened my curiosity.

'Do you think that is wise, after what happened in the compound?'

'Stay in the truck if you want.' I turned and began to walk towards the church still angry at Guppy for – I wasn't sure what, but I was glad when I heard the door slam and felt him walking behind me.

The church was dark and a damp smell of cement hung in the air. It was a simple rectangle, with two pillars at each end and lines of pews stretching towards a marble altar. The pews were packed, their occupants' attention fixed firmly on the veined marble in front of them that shone from the glare of a spotlight hidden somewhere in the roof. A woman knelt in front of it, the upper part of her body caught in the light, the rest in shadow, her shoulders shuddering. It took me a moment to realise that she was crying. Her muffled sobs drifted across the lines of suits, dresses, and traditional robes, ripples in an otherwise perfect silence.

I glanced at Guppy and he shook his head, his eyes wide. A shiver ran from the base of my spine to the back of my neck. I put my hand on his arm and pulled him back into a shadowed corner as a door behind the altar opened and the man, the priest who had been a lawyer, his suit covered by a long white cassock, strode out.

He surveyed his audience for a moment and then flung his arms wide.

'Welcome,' he began, his voice a cold breeze. 'I am fortunate. I look around and I see the faces of the faithful, and I thank you for coming. Together we will see the power your faith can give you.' He walked slowly over to the woman on the floor, knelt beside her and ran a knuckle across her cheek. 'Do not worry.

Your heart is full of grief, but it will soon be emptied and filled again with joy.' He treated her gently, as a father would his child. It contradicted everything I had seen of him before, and I inched forward, drawn to his voice and his soft gestures.

He rose slowly from the crying woman and turned again to his audience, many of them now leaning forward in the pews.

'You have come here because the law can no longer help you. Because you fight bureaucracy and regulations. These things have no place in the miracle of life. No man can decide who shall and who shall not be blessed with children. Only God can decide these things. With faith, there is always a way. With our faith in the Lord we can overcome all things. Open your hearts to me and I will set them free. . .'

A man stood up suddenly and let out a snort of derision, shattering the atmosphere of the church. He stood for a moment, as if about to speak, then grabbed the woman he was with by the hand and marched out. In an instant there was a flurry of murmurings; several heads turned to watch the couple leave and all over the church people whispered in each other's ears.

A spark of anger lit the priest's eyes, but he

blinked it away. He spread out his arms again, a weary smile on his lips.

'The devil may come among us at any time to test our faith. Let yours not be as easily swayed as his.' He indicated the empty space in the pew and the crowd began to settle, their heavy silence floating back into the church. 'You who remain have proved your faith. And now that will be rewarded.' He turned to look at the woman on the ground, studying her, and I wanted him to speak again. To see the reward he promised these people.

'Like so many of you, this woman has come to me because she has been denied the right of every woman: the right to bear children. But she has put her faith in the Lord. She has come to me, and we have prayed together.'

The sobs of the woman intensified. She fell forward and began to knock her forehead against the floor, the dull rhythm punctuating the sounds of her grief.

'I know that some of you, like the man who fled consumed by the devil, may still have doubts in your hearts.' It was an accusation, his voice gaining power, and several people shifted in their seats as the priest swung his gaze across the pews before continuing. 'But today, today I will show you how faith in the Lord is rewarded. This woman's prayers have been answered!'

The woman on the floor sat bolt upright, her hands clasped to her mouth. The priest pointed his finger to the sky and turned to face the door. A figure appeared for an instant and pushed something towards him. I strained to see what it was and then the priest turned, holding a small girl by the hand. She couldn't have been more than two or three and she stared out into the church with dazed eyes.

'Behold the rewards of faith!' He turned and spoke to the woman on the floor. 'Come and claim your child, a gift from the Lord.'

The audience erupted as the woman sprang to her feet and pulled the now-crying child towards her, holding her tight to her chest, throwing her head back and shouting at the ceiling. Several women in the audience started to scream and rushed forward, prostrating themselves at the priest's feet. Many others rose to their feet, cheering and waving their hands, and as I looked closer, I saw that they were filled with money. The priest raised his hands above his head, his voice now barely audible above the din.

'All who are faithful shall be rewarded.'

I grabbed Guppy by the arm and hurried for

the door, desperate to get away from the hysteria. We ran back to the truck and threw ourselves in.

We sat for a moment trying to take in what we had seen. The priest had appeared so genuine, so caring. I shook my head, clearing it of his image, replacing it with the ones I had seen before, the ones I knew were true. I remembered asking Joseph why the man was so interested in children, and the reply came crashing back into my mind: *he sells them.*

CHAPTER 8

Joseph strained the tea into three mugs as the ceiling fan swirled the sticky air around his office, fluttering papers on his desk but offering no relief from the heat. I sat there wishing he would switch the air conditioner on, as classical music battled the hiss from a single speaker tape recorder.

'Winter,' said Joseph. 'Vivaldi. From his *Four Seasons*.' I nodded. 'Do you like Vivaldi?'

'I don't think I've heard him before.'

'Pity,' replied Joseph, handing Guppy and me mugs of tea. 'He's very good. Perhaps you would like to borrow the tape?'

'Sure, thanks,' I replied, not wanting to offend him.

'Now,' said Joseph, settling himself into an armchair, 'what is on your minds?'

It only took a few minutes for me to relate what

we had seen in the church, with Guppy chipping in every so often to add details I had missed. Joseph said nothing. When we had finished he stared out of the window, his fingers idly pushing at a protruding mound of stuffing that had burst through the arm of his chair. I was about to speak, when he took a deep breath and his gaze snapped back to us.

'So, that is how he's doing it these days.' He said it without anger, but the power in his voice made me start, slopping tea over my leg.

'Charlie has seen him before,' said Guppy.

'Really?' replied Joseph, sitting forward in his chair.

He caught me off guard. I had never mentioned that day on the road to Joseph, but it was clear from his expression that he wanted to know.

'I saw him – and you – the day you came to school to give your talk. I saw you both on the road where the boys were killed. The ones who were run over. I didn't mention it before, I. . .' I trailed off.

A shadow of sadness crept across Joseph's eyes and he nodded with the memory.

'I am sorry you saw that. I didn't know.' He watched me for a moment and I began to realise that his sadness was for me. I stared into my tea.

An incessant clicking from the tape recorder broke the humid silence. Joseph stood up and switched it off.

'Who is he?' asked Guppy.

'His name is Michael Danlami. At least it was when I knew him. He was the representative for a European children's charity.'

'I cannot believe he worked for a charity,' said Guppy.

'I am sure they would like to believe that he didn't. But he did.'

'And they gave him money?' I asked.

Joseph returned to his chair, his gaze moving back to the window, to the gates and the church beyond. 'Yes, they gave him money. He ran an orphanage in Port Rose. He would give the patrons a tour, turn his palms to the sky, and they would fill them with notes. It took them several years to realise that he was just pocketing the money, but by then he had what he needed. He bought a law degree and offered his services locating orphans for rich, childless families.'

'The charity was very foolish,' said Guppy, shaking his head. 'Why did they hand out money so indiscriminately?'

'Guilt,' replied Joseph and took a sip of his tea.

'But he seems to have found a new way to continue his work, as you saw tonight.'

'I couldn't believe those people were taken in by it,' I said. 'I mean, it's ridiculous. They really believe God tells him to give them babies? How stupid can you get?'

Joseph placed his mug of tea on the table next to him, slowly rotating it so that the handle faced the window. 'Do you think Sister Mairead is stupid?' He kept his eyes on his tea.

I felt my body tense, surprised by the question. 'Of course not. I would never think that.'

'Sister Mairead believes that a man with a staff parted the Red Sea, that the son of God came to earth and raised a man from the dead, that when she dies she will live for ever in heaven. This is her faith, and many people in that church tonight also believe this. Is it so incredible, then, that they should believe that a priest can answer their prayers and provide them with the children they so desperately want?'

'But Sister Mairead would never have been taken in by such a spectacle,' countered Guppy.

'Of course not. But Sister Mairead is not blinded by grief and fear. Those people are, and being blinded, they can upset the judgement of the most rational mind. Others who were there do not believe, but will gladly hide behind faith to get what they want. Danlami understands this.'

'Well, we need to call the police, at any rate.' There was a hint of anger in Guppy's voice, the second time that day I had been surprised by his tone. I looked over at Joseph, expecting him to agree at once, but he was shaking his head, a sudden weariness pushing at his shoulders.

'That would not be wise at the moment.'

'But. . .' Guppy started. Joseph held up his hand.

'It would be hard to prove Danlami is doing anything wrong. He would have all the necessary adoption documents, if questioned. And he is rich. That makes him powerful. I need to find out more before we consider any action.'

Guppy opened his mouth to speak but the blare of a car horn interrupted him.

'That will be Samson for you,' said Joseph, 'you'd better not keep him waiting.' Guppy and I stood up, thanked Joseph for the tea and turned to leave.

'Do not go back to the church. Stay away from Danlami.' I saw from Joseph's expression that it was not a request, and nodded, before following Guppy out of the door.

'I am surprised by Joseph,' said Guppy.

'He knows what he's doing.'

'I still think he should inform the police.'

'Well, you know, if Damlani's bought them off, there's little point.'

Guppy stared across at the church. 'It frightens me.'

I smiled, relieved at not being the only frightened one. 'Well, he's a pretty scary guy.'

'Oh, not him,' replied Guppy. 'What he is doing.'

My cheeks began to burn. 'Come on, Samson is waiting.'

We walked over to the car and clambered in. Samson mumbled a greeting, still not speaking to me, and we drove out through the gates.

The line of cars was still there and most of the drivers had retreated inside them, bitten into surrender by the mosquitoes. As we passed, floodlights burst into life, washing the walls a brilliant white, and I wondered how many others would have their prayers answered that night.

◼ ◎ ◻

I sat at the desk in my room and tried to concentrate on the history assignment that the school had sent home for me, but my mind was full of the service I had witnessed at the church. It had been so blatant, so arrogant, as if the priest had no fear. He gave sons and daughters to childless families – and for a moment the notion suddenly seemed quite innocent, almost laudable. What sort of life would they have elsewhere? The congregation had seemed well off, possibly even rich; surely the children would have a good life with them.

I pushed the chair back sharply and walked to the window, trying to shake the idea from my mind, ashamed I had even considered it. It was wrong, no matter how you looked at it. I was sure Joseph would take care of it, despite Guppy's misgivings. There was nothing to worry about there, nothing that affected Ilakye. I smiled, content with my reasoning, picked up my empty water glass from the desk and headed to the kitchen to fill it up.

The door to my sister's room stood ajar. I looked in; she lay asleep, light from the open doorway touching her face.

'Busy?' asked my mother. She stood in the corridor, he head tilted slightly to one side, scrutinising me.

'Just getting some water.'

She nodded. 'Everything all right? You look a bit worried. . .'

I glanced away for a moment before answering. 'I'm fine. Just a difficult history assignment.'

She held my eyes for a second, then smiled, and took a step closer, her gaze turning to my sister in her bed. 'I used to watch you when you were that age. So peaceful. . . There is nothing so precious – don't you think, Charlie?'

I nodded, not knowing what to say.

'I'll bring you some water,' she said, taking the glass from my hand. 'You'd better get back to your studying.' And she slipped quietly away.

I watched Katie for a moment: her body rising and falling with each breath, the fan sending ripples over her hair. I wondered what she was dreaming of. Were they the same dreams as the little girl in the church was having? I turned away, shutting my mind to the thought, and walked quickly back to my room.

◘⊙◘

In what year was the Cotton Gin invented?

I chewed at the top of my pencil and studied

the four possible answers to the first question in the World History exam. Guppy and I sat in the main office under the steady glare of the school secretary. It was cool, the air conditioner and the secretary's sinuses the only sounds, and tinted windows holding back the worst of the midday glare. The rest of the seniors had sat the test the day before, but the Principal had made it clear that we could not mix with the rest of them.

It was the first time either of us had gone back to the school for an exam. I had been nervous at first, but as Samson had driven past the gates with their familiar gold lettering, my nerves turned to excitement. I stepped out of the car and walked up the steps to the courtyard, brushing my hand against the cool brass of the railings, the smile beginning to broaden on my face.

It was class time and the courtyard was deserted. I stood and stared at the lockers, the wall tiles, the banners proclaiming sports events and the school play, everything around me twisting the world of Ilakaye into the memory of a dream. I took a deep breath, relishing the dust-free air filling my lungs, soaking up the silence and the safety.

I strolled along the covered walkway leading down one side of the courtyard to the main office, passing lines of air conditioned classrooms, listening to the buzz of the activity inside, and suddenly I desperately wanted to be among them, to open the door, fling my books on the desk and slide into my seat, back where I belonged. But I had been met by the secretary, and marched quickly into the office.

I continued to chew on the top of my pencil but my thoughts drifted far away. I thought of Max and Wael, whether they were still here, whether I would be able to see them. I imagined they would be going dragging after school, then maybe basketball at Max's place.

A burst of warm air broke my daydream as a student came into the office. She looked appraisingly at me for a moment, and then her eyes widened. She suddenly realised who I was. She gave the folder she was carrying to the secretary and hurried out. I returned my attention to the first question on the test and filled in the small oval next to 1793.

A glance at the clock told me I needed to hurry up. Next to me, Guppy was already on the second page. I began to move down the list of questions:

Which of the following men did not sign the declaration of Independence?

The war of 1812 was against which country?

In which year was the Louisiana Purchase?

What was the cause of the American civil war?

Which was the last state to become part of the United States?

I moved quickly down the page, dutifully filling in answers I had memorised from the textbook, when I felt the door open again and looking up, I saw Max standing there staring at both of us, his trademark spiked hair now a dull orange. I nodded a smile, but his face didn't move and he walked quickly over to the secretary. They spoke for a moment and then the secretary turned and disappeared into a back office.

I leaned forward and whispered, 'Where's Wael?'

Max pulled a piece of paper from the counter and began to write. He screwed it up into a ball and threw it over to me just as the secretary returned. I caught it, dropped it into my lap, and ducked my head back towards the exam paper. The door closed and I knew he was gone.

I tried to concentrate on the questions but the paper sat like a dozen books on my legs and I fought desperately against the urge to open it. Max was still here; I should still be here, not pouring sweat onto the ground in Ilakaye. Next to me, Guppy worked steadily away, I doubted if he had even noticed Max come in, and suddenly he looked as I remembered him: comic relief with a funny accent and a silly walk.

'Time's up. Please hand me your papers.' The secretary moved around and collected our answer sheets.

'How did you think. . .' started Guppy.

'Wait,' I snapped, and pushing back my chair, I unfurled Max's note like a birthday present. The secretary was speaking, but as I read the words scrawled on the paper her voice drifted away, my skin tightened and the air conditioner that had seemed so welcome now blew too cold.

'Do you understand, Charlie?'

'I'm sorry,' I said, forcing my eyes away from the words in my hand. 'What?'

The secretary sighed. 'I said, you are to leave the campus immediately.'

'Of course. I'll get my things.'

I glanced back down at Max's handwriting, my feeling of belonging chipped away with every syllable.

'Wael's in a boarding school in London. What are you doing here? Fuck off back to the ditches.'

Guppy was already on his feet, his bag slung over his shoulder. 'What are you reading?'

'It's nothing.' Guilt began to replace the pain caused by Max's words. 'I'm sorry.'

'Why?'

'I . . . It doesn't matter. Come on, let's go.' And gathering up my things, I followed him out of the office.

We got outside just as the bell rang for recess and in seconds the courtyard was packed. I walked quickly, keeping my head down, aware of the stares and the muttering. Guppy wobbled along in front of me, seemingly oblivious to the pointing fingers and the giggles; but then, school had always been like this for him. As we reached the steps, I turned back. Max was holding court in the alcove where we used to meet every morning. He looked up and saw me, a sarcastic smile spreading across his face as he brushed his hand through the air, a gesture designed to shoo me away.

I watched him strut away with his entourage before casting my eyes around the rest of the courtyard. A group of girls started to whoop with joy as one of produced a sachet of Kool-Aid from her bag. A boy walked past, chatting excitedly to a newcomer.

'. . .You can come round to my place. My dad's just got back from the States and we have M'n'Ms. Can you believe, you can't buy those here .. *So* backward. . .'

From the balcony above me, a voice was complaining that her driver was late. 'I'm gonna report him to my dad. Can you believe it? I had *cheerleading* practice. . .'

I began to laugh.

'What is so funny?' asked Guppy, 'You are acting a little strangely, if you don't mind me saying.'

'Oh, nothing,' I said, and I dropped Max's note into the bin like a used tissue. 'Well, we'd better get going.'

'Yes, I'm glad the examination was in the morning, I'm not very happy with our repairs to the dormitory door.'

'We'll have a look as soon as we get there.'

'And I need to speak to Joseph again about Michael Danlami.'

'Guppy, we've been through this. . .'

'I believe there is more we can do. It's making me a little bit angry.' With Guppy muttering about Danlami and the church, we walked over to where Samson waited and climbed into the car. We pulled out of the gates and I stared out of the rear windscreen, watching the school slip away behind us until it was lost, buried beneath its walls and razor wire, and I heard the tapping of chisels in a workshop, and saw the smile of a girl at a market stall.

CHAPTER 9

The church was always busy. The cars would arrive late in the afternoon and still be there when we left in the evening. I found I could ignore them, concentrate on my work – but Guppy could not.

'I can't believe he's doing nothing!' Guppy threw his shovel down and sat on a pile of rubble, glaring at Joseph's office and the door that always seemed closed. We were laying hardcore into the foundations for an extension to the orphanage. Four babies had arrived in the last three days and Mairead was worried that they were going to run out of room.

'You don't know he's doing nothing,' I said, sitting beside him and lighting a cigarette. It wasn't a conversation I wanted to have again, but I was glad of the excuse for a break.

'What? You want to do nothing as well? Sit there

smoking and pretend that church over there does not exist? Is that it, Charlie?'

'Hey, that's not. . .'

'Sit there and think, "Oh, never mind, he'll go away." This is just a hobby for you, isn't it? A nice break from school.'

'That's enough, Guppy.' My anger began to build. Who the hell was he to talk to me like this? 'And what about you? You told me you were here just to look good for your father. So don't go questioning why I'm here.'

'That is none of your business.'

'Fine. Then don't bring it up. What would you do about Danlami, anyway?'

'Something . . . anything . . . I wouldn't just sit around like Joseph, hiding over there in his office.'

'He's not hiding. . .'

'Oh, really? Turning a blind eye, then. Great philosophy.'

'He's not turning a blind eye! He knows what he's doing. I trust him.'

Guppy gave a snort, stood up and picked up his shovel, 'Well, I'm glad you do.'

'What's that supposed to mean?' I waited, holding his eye, trying to check the anger rising inside me, expecting another outburst. But he turned and without a word went back to work.

I sat on the rubble smoking my cigarette and listening to the scrapings of Guppy's shovel, fighting the urge to throw something at him. Joseph did know what he was doing, I was sure of that. Guppy would calm down, I told myself, but I had never seen him like this before. I turned to look at him: he worked fast, carelessly, his shovel cutting into the pile of rubble before he flung it towards the footings, leaving a trail of cracked tiles and broken concrete blocks in the dirt. I stood up and walked a few feet away, trying to avoid the shrapnel from Guppy's efforts. I wondered if I should speak to Joseph, ask him to talk to Guppy, but before I could make up my mind, a voice interrupted me.

'Could you help me with this, Charlie?' I turned and saw Yejide, a large white box in her arms, a sunrise smile on her face.

'Sure. Of course.' I dropped my cigarette to the floor and took the box.

'I didn't know you smoked...' she said. Disapproval shone in her eyes, and I looked down at the crushed fag end on the ground. 'I don't much ... really. ... Once in a while.'

She shrugged, and pushed the box in to my arms. 'We're going to the infirmary. This way.'

She turned and headed off and I dropped into step beside her. I had seen her twice since that day in the market, but had never been able to speak to her. She was always with one of the nurses or Mairead, and I was always ankle-deep in mud and rubble.

We walked across the compound together. The box wasn't heavy, Yejide could have carried three, and I knew this must be an excuse to talk to me. But with every step the silence between us seemed to grow deeper. We neared the infirmary and I still couldn't think of anything to say. I was about to open my mouth and comment on the weather, when Yejide rescued me.

'Guppy seems a bit upset. Is he all right?'

'He's upset about what we saw in the church the other day. He doesn't think Joseph is taking it seriously enough.' The words had come tumbling out, and I was instantly aware that our first conversation was not going as well as I had hoped. Yejide stopped and turned to face me; her smile had vanished.

'There's a lot Guppy doesn't understand.'

'That's what I said,' I replied. 'I guess it just annoys him that it's happening so close by.'

'Joseph knows what's he doing. And believe me, he takes it extremely seriously. However close or far away it is.'

'I'm sure . . . look, I don't doubt it.'

'I know,' she said. 'Joseph is worried. Danlami could have picked any spot for his church, but he chose here.'

'Why?'

'Easy pickings,' she said, echoing Joseph's words. 'But I think there may be something else.'

'What?'

'I'm not sure. Come on.' And she continued towards the infirmary at a pace I struggled to match.

Inside it was dim and cool, like walking into the dusk, and I squinted, trying to force my eyes to adjust to the light. A row of beds stretched out on either side of me, the uniform line of starched white sheets and black metal frames broken three beds to the right by a man lying on his side. He breathed sharply through clenched teeth, a single sheet covering his waist, sticking to his sweat-soaked skin. There was a movement behind him and I realised a woman knelt there, stroking something into his back.

'Abiyona!' shouted Yejide, and rushed over. The woman jumped up and backed against the wall, her eyes on the floor. I recognised her from the day Guppy and I had helped to subdue the man who had escaped from the secure compound.

'What are you doing?' demanded Yejide, and without waiting for an answer she dropped on to her knees and began to study the man's back. A look of disbelief slowly replaced her anger and she stretched out a hand to touch the man's back.

'Better?' she asked. The man nodded.

Yejide stood up and turned to face Abiyona. 'What did you do? What did you use?'

Abiyona slowly lifted her hand, indicating me, muttering something I couldn't hear. Yejide took a step towards her and spoke softly in Yoruba, but Abiyona just shook her head. Yejide studied her for a while and then shrugged, stepping aside to let her pass. Abiyona, head down, walked quickly down the row of beds and out of the door.

'Can you bring that over here, Charlie?' asked Yejide. I walked over and, placing the box on the floor next to her, looked at the man's back. It was covered in crimson blisters bursting from a mass of purple swelling, the skin cracked and weeping.

'Decubitus ulcers,' explained Yejide, her eyes scanning the man's ruined back. 'Bed sores.

You have to be extremely careful in these conditions; they can become infected in hours. I was bringing antibiotics but—' She stopped abruptly and, opening the box, pulled out a cotton bud. With the gentlest of touches, she stroked it across the man's skin between two of the sores, pulled it away and held it up, staring at the yellow stain on the tip. She lifted it to her nose and immediately pulled it away, exhaling sharply.

'What is it?' I asked.

'I'm not sure. It's what Abiyona was using. She wouldn't tell me what it was, but whatever it is has helped enormously.'

'They're better?' I asked incredulously

'Much better.' She walked around the bed to speak to the man. 'How many times has Abiyona come?'

'Three, I think three times,' he gasped.

'Well, we'd better send her back to you, then.'

The man nodded. 'Good medicine.'

Yejide smiled. 'Yes, it is. I'll be back in a while.' She moved around the bed and closed the box. 'We can leave that here. I'll need it later. Come on.'

I followed her to a sink at the end of the infirmary, where she began to wash her hands. 'I've tried three types of antibiotics on that man already, and Abiyona comes in with her creams and. . .' There was a hint of irritation in her voice.

'Why wouldn't she tell you what it was she used?' I asked. Yejide stopped and looked at me, before reaching for a towel.

'Because you were here.'

'What's that got to do with anything?'

Yejide dried her hands. She looked at the towel but her mind was elsewhere, as if deciding on the best way to approach a sensitive topic.

'In her words: it is not for the *oyinbo* to know.'

'I see.' But I didn't.

'Don't be offended. Some people who still practise traditional medicine are a little . . . protective of its secrets. Especially around foreigners.'

'Oh, I'm not offended,' I said, forcing my smile. 'Well, it seems to work, doesn't it?'

'Some does. But I wouldn't put my faith in it entirely.'

'Bet that guy would,' I laughed.

'Yes, he would. And he would have died of malaria a week ago,' she snapped. 'Ground-up roots aren't always enough.'

'I'm . . . sorry,' I mumbled, taken aback by her sudden burst of anger.

'No,' she said, her voice falling. 'I'm sorry, I shouldn't have shouted. It's just I get confused sometimes. Trained doctors say that traditional medicines don't work, that we should only use modern drugs. But then I see what Abiyona can do . . . and then. . .' She paused, as if unsure if she should continue, then she rolled up the right sleeve of her T-shirt, pulling the edge over her shoulder. 'Here. Look.'

Even in the poor light the scar leapt out, covering her arm from mid-bicep to shoulder.

'It's a burn. When I was seven, I broke my arm. Branding with fire is the traditional cure. That one definitely doesn't work.'

I stared at the scar, a pale mark of decay on perfect skin. 'My God, that's terrible.'

'Not really. Everyone here carries scars of one kind or another.'

'What did you do after it happened?'

Yejide pulled her sleeve back down and nodded towards the compound's entrance. 'I knocked on those gates.'

I marvelled at her courage, at what it must have taken to walk into Ilakaye at the age of seven. Yejide pulled down her sleeve and I noticed another scar on her forearm.

'Is that from the same thing?' I asked.

'That? Oh no. I fell off the roof a couple of years ago.'

'The roof?'

'It's a race. You run around the roofs of the buildings and have to jump the gaps between them. I missed one.'

I laughed. 'Sounds like fun.'

'Apart from that once, no one ever beat me.'

'Well, I was pretty fast around the roofs of my school. . .'

'Really?' She said, her eyes lighting up. 'Is that a challenge? We'll have to—'

A scream echoed around the infirmary and cut her off mid-sentence. I snapped around. 'What the. . .' But Yejide was already running.

'Come on,' she yelled, and I sprinted out of the door after her.

We sped through the compound as the doors of dormitories and workshops crashed open. Turning the corner by the secure compound, we saw a group of people forming a circle around a woman, and I recognised her immediately; she was the one who had offered her child to Danlami. Tears poured down her cheeks as she screamed hysterically, an unlabelled bottle spilling its contents into the ground at her feet. Her right fist clenched around something I couldn't see, held high above her head, and in her left she carried a knife.

As the crowd around her grew, she jabbed at them with the knife, the rusty blade sweeping the perimeter of the circle, holding everyone back. I saw Sister Mairead run over and push herself to the front of the crowd.

'Move back,' she yelled, and the crowd retreated a few steps. The woman whirled around to face Mairead, pointing the knife at her and shaking her head.

'Go back! Go back!' the woman shouted. Mairead held up her hands, a smile on her face as she took a step backwards.

'Put the knife down.' Her voice drifted across the crowd, and even the wind seemed to settle at its sound. 'It's all right, give it to me.' She took a step forward.

The woman seemed to falter. The knife lowered an inch and her shoulders shook as she took a breath.

'That's right,' said Mairead, taking another step. 'Give it to me.' She inched forward. 'It's all right.' The woman continued to lower the knife, as if it was too heavy for her to hold. Another step, and now Mairead could almost touch her. 'It's going to be all right.'

'No!' the woman yelled, and swung the knife at Mairead's face. Mairead stumbled back, tripped and fell to the ground. I instinctively rushed forward and felt several others do the same, but a voice stopped me dead in my tracks.

'Stay where you are.'

Joseph stood on the other side of the circle. His eyes swept the crowd. I looked down at Mairead; she appeared unhurt; the knife had missed.

The woman had turned to face Joseph, but seemed unable to look him in the eye.

'Níbo ni ọmọ náà wà?' asked Joseph. The woman took a step back. *'Níbo ni ọmọ náà wà?'* he repeated.

'What's he saying?' I whispered to Yejide.

Yejide looked up at me, her face a mixture of fear and anger. 'Where is the child?'

Joseph repeated the words, his eyes fixed on the woman, and under his gaze she started to weaken. The knife began to shake in her hands and fresh tears streamed down her face. She lifted her head and looked directly at Joseph, a cry slipping from her lips that tore at my heart, and she crumbled, sobbing, the knife falling as her knees hit the dust. She looked at her right hand and slowly, almost painfully, she opened her fingers. A few crumbled dollar notes fell into her lap.

'Oh God, ' I murmured.

The woman's sobs grew louder. '*Mo nfẹ́. . . Mo nfẹ́. . .*'

'What do you want?' asked Joseph as he walked slowly towards her.

'*Tèmi ni ọmọ náà.*'

'Yes, he is yours. And we will find him for you.' He bent down and, cradling her face in his hands he raised her up. 'Come with me.' Yejide and two others rushed forward to help him, and the crowd parted as they ushered the woman towards the secure compound.

I walked over to Sister Mairead, who was now brushing the dust from her habit.

'Are you all right?'

'Oh, fine, Charlie, fine, just a bruise on the backside, thank you.' And she hurried after Joseph and the others. As I watched her go, the crowd dispersed and I bent down and picked up the bottle the woman had left on the ground. I held it to my nose and coughed, feeling the burn of the coarse alcohol.

'What is it?' Guppy was eyeing the bottle with distaste.

'Something I wouldn't want to drink,' I said, as a muffled cry shot from the secure compound. 'I wonder what they'll do to her?'

'Dry her out, I suppose.' I was expecting another tirade about Joseph's lack of action, but Guppy looked shaken. He bent down and picked up the money the woman had dropped.

'How much is it?' I asked, looking at the booze-drenched notes.

'About thirty dollars.'

I stared at the black gates now hiding the woman who had handed over her child for thirty dollars and a few swigs of mind-rotting liquor. I clenched my teeth, turned and hurled the bottle in the direction of Danlami's church. It did not even reach the gates, falling in a tiny puff of dust a few metres away. I sighed, my anger subsiding in an instant; my arm felt weak, as if I had tried to hurl a shot putt.

'Come on, Guppy, we'd better—' But he had gone. I wheeled around and saw him walking towards the gates. 'Guppy?' He didn't a miss a stride, and slammed his shoulder against the gates, bursting them open. 'Guppy!' And I started to run. 'Guppy. . .!' He stopped at the side of the road to pick up a rock, and carrying it at shoulder height, he advanced on the church.

I reached him just before he threw it, ripping it out of his hands. He spun around to face me, the anger shining through the tears in his eyes.

'Guppy. . .' He brushed past me, back towards the compound. I watched him for a second, before following. I dropped the rock and walked into the compound. One by one I closed the gates, my eyes never leaving the church until it was gone, wiped away by grey steel.

CHAPTER 10

Guppy and I sat in silence on the steps of the orphanage, watching the night drag the sun down from a purple sky. No one had come out of the secure compound and its black gates were merging into the dusk. We should have left half an hour ago, but I wanted to wait, to hear any news from Joseph or Yejide. I swatted at the mosquitoes feeding on my legs and wondered what was keeping them so long.

'I don't think we can stay much longer,' said Guppy.

'Just five more minutes.'

I heard Guppy shift on the steps, and then he cleared his throat before speaking. 'I'm sorry for my . . . outburst this afternoon. I was not angry with you.'

'Forget it.'

'No. I said some things I shouldn't.'

'Me too. It's OK.'

He scratched at his crooked nose, as if lost in thought. 'Charlie.'

'Yes?'

'What do you want to do when you finish school?'

'I don't know. I haven't really thought about it much.'

'Where I am from, you do what your parents expect. My father wants me to go to Harvard and become a lawyer. Did I ever tell you that?'

'When you first arrived at my house that weekend.'

He smiled and nodded, as if remembering the scene. 'After I got in trouble, he said he no longer cared what I did. That didn't last very long, and he is getting insistent about it again. But I'm not sure if that is what I want. I love my father, I'll never forget the look on his face when I was nearly expelled from school, I don't ever want to upset him like that again. But, to be a lawyer . . . it just doesn't feel right. And then I look around here, at the people and their lives. . . I have opportunities most of them will never know, and I'm thinking of throwing them away.'

I looked at him for a moment, unsure what to say, surprised by the emotion in his voice. 'It'll work out.

Just because you don't want to be a lawyer doesn't make you a bad person, Guppy. Perhaps you just need to talk to your dad?'

He tried to smile, but it looked more like a grimace. 'Yes,' he said, 'you are probably right.

'And then there's this.' He reached into his pocket and pulled out a photograph. It was the one of the three men and the boy I had found by the pool, the day of our trip to the Crocodile Bar. 'That's me,' he said, 'with my father and his two brothers. We came from a poor family, only one step up from Ilakaye really, but together they built a very successful business. My father is here to expand into Africa. I lied to you all that day at your house, about this being for an assignment. I was ashamed. God. . . ' He stopped, his voice cracking.

I felt I should say something, that he was looking to me for support, for comfort. Guilt clawed at me: I had mocked the photograph just as much as the others.

'That's the thing that hurts the most: that I was ashamed of my family, that I lied about who they were to try and be as popular as Max and Wael and you. And now I want to throw away the opportunities my father has worked so hard to give me. What sort of a person does that make me?'

'Guppy, we all do stupid things sometimes. . .' As the words came out, I knew how trite they sounded, but I had to say something.

'You're right,' he said, the strength back in his voice, but with a shadow of sadness still clouding his eyes. He slapped me on the shoulder. 'And thank you for stopping me damaging the church. That would only have caused more trouble.'

'Don't worry about it,' I said, relieved he had changed the subject.

'Thanks. You are a good friend. ' And he extended his hand. I took it and held it firmly.

'You too, Guppy.'

A sliver of light cracked the gates to the secure compound and Joseph walked out, heading towards his office. I stood up and watched him, but he gave no sign that he had seen us. I was just starting towards him when I saw Yejide slip between the gates and close them behind her. I waved, and Guppy and I walked quickly over. Yejide met us halfway.

'How's the woman?' I asked.

'We had to sedate her. She's resting now.'

'What happened?' asked Guppy.

'It's not very clear. It was hard to get much sense

from her at times, but it seems she was approached by a man on the street. . .'

'Danlami,' whispered Guppy.

'No, it wasn't. She said she had never seen him before.'

'But she gave the child to him,' I said.

'Yes.'

'It must have been Danlami!' Guppy kicked a stone on the ground.

'It wasn't. She was clear on that.'

'Then this man must work for him,' Guppy persisted. 'It's obvious. Surely that's evidence enough.'

'It's not evidence at all. For anything.' There was a hint of irritation in Yejide's voice now. 'An alcoholic abandons her baby: it happens every day, all over the world. And what are you going to do with this evidence? Hmm?'

Guppy stood silent for a moment before slowly nodding. Yejide was right: we had nothing on Danlami.

'I just wish Joseph would let us know what he plans to do,' said Guppy.

Yejide seemed to hesitate for a moment and then began to walk off towards one of the dormitories.

'Come with me. I want to show you something.'

We followed Yejide around the side of the dormitory, to a door set to one side. All the dormitories had these annexes; they were quarters for staff who stayed overnight. Yejide opened the door and beckoned us in. She pulled at a cord to the side of the door and a light bulb flickered for a moment before pushing back the gloom.

'These are usually shared,' Yejide explained. 'But as I'm spending so much time here, I've taken over this one.' The room was small and the air close. A metal frame bed stood against the far wall, watched over by a simple wooden crucifix. 'Sit down,' she said, indicating the bed. Guppy and I sat awkwardly at opposite ends while Yejide went to a chest of drawers and pulled out a large photo album, before sitting herself down between us.

'This might help you understand how complicated this situation is,' she said.

I leaned over and studied the pages as she flipped through. Most of them seemed to be of Ilakaye, but there were pages of others that I didn't recognise, buildings and people from a different place and time. It was on one of these pages that she stopped.

'That's me,' she said. 'Ten years ago.'

The smile on the little girl's face was instantly recognisable. Dressed in a flower-patterned dress she beamed into the camera, her right hand gripped firmly by a stern-looking nun, and it took me a moment to realise it was Sister Mairead. On her left stood Joseph, his hair visibly thicker and darker, and standing slightly apart from the others, a grin creasing his face, was Michael Danlami.

'Holy shit,' I whispered. 'They know each other.'

'Joseph helped Danlami set up the orphanage in Port Rose. He introduced him to the charity. They worked together for two years.'

'But Joseph didn't know. . .' spluttered Guppy.

'Of course not.'

'What are you doing there?' I asked.

Yejide sighed, a breath of sadness in the still air. 'In those days Ilakaye was much smaller. We didn't have room for everybody. Danlami suggested that Joseph send the children up to him. He agreed. Over a dozen were sent.'

'So you were going to live at Danlami's orphanage?'

Yejide nodded. 'Joseph and Mairead decided to come up with me, to see how Danlami was getting on. It was then Joseph saw that none of the improvements he had suggested had been made; if anything, the place was falling into disrepair, and some of the children were missing. Danlami had a pretty answer for everything: there were problems getting the funds. They had been robbed. Several children had run away . . . Joseph got suspicious. He took me back with him and contacted the charity. They confirmed that there had been no problem with the funds – Danlami had simply pocketed the money.'

'And the children. . .?' asked Guppy.

Yejide shook her head, her eyes darkening to match the shadows in the room. 'Joseph never found them.'

I stared at the photo for a moment, at Yejide's face and Danlami's grin and the anger welled inside me. How was it possible? What would drive a man to do such things?

'Joseph told us that he was a charity swindler, but he never mentioned that he had worked with him,' said Guppy, amazement in his voice.

'Joseph blames himself for not having seen what Danlami was doing earlier. He never speaks about it. But he had no reason to suspect him. Danlami had done some genuinely good work in the past, helped a lot of children. Then he saw how much money he could make . . . thought he deserved it. He was still giving children homes, after all. . .' She laughed, shaking her head as she stared at the picture. 'A lot of this I didn't know at the time, but Sister Mairead told me after I recognised Danlami from this photo. Joseph thinks he helped Danlami reach the position he is today. He also knows how clever Danlami is and he won't do anything until he's sure he can get him. Danlami got away once. Joseph doesn't want that to happen again.'

Guppy nodded to himself. 'I see. Thank you for showing us this. It makes more sense of things.'

A car horn sounded in the distance. We had kept Samson waiting too long. Guppy jumped up. 'I'll go on ahead.'

Yejide watched him go and then her eyes returned to the photo for a second before she slammed the album shut. '*Omo ale!*' she spat. I didn't need a translation.

'I'm sure it will all be OK,' I offered. Her eyes met mine and I battled an almost irresistible urge to kiss her. She nodded.

'Do you want me to stick around for a while?'

'No, you'd better not keep Samson waiting any longer. Thanks.' And she stood and walked over to the chest of drawers, slipping the album back into the dark, taking my feelings of unease with it.

I stood up and walked to the door. 'You know, if you ever want to chat . . . about anything. . .'

She looked over and smiled. 'Thanks Charlie. That would be nice.'

'Perhaps we could have a drink or something. Some time.'

'Definitely. It would be nice for the three of us to get together.'

'Sure. The three of us, yes. . .' My heart sank and I locked my smile in place. 'Well, I'll see you tomorrow.' I closed the door and walked around to the side of the dormitory.

'The three of us.' It wasn't the answer I had been hoping for. But, I thought, it's a start.

◫◉◻

My father stopped the car in front of the gates to the Eko Club and touched the horn. Wiping sleep from his eyes the guard slouched from his hut, pulled open the gates and we drove in.

The Eko club was really a condominium, but the bar allowed a small, select membership of non-residents. Tuesdays had always been snooker night, but my father had not taken me since I started at Ilakaye.

His invitation that morning to take Guppy and me had been a surprise, a gesture of forgiveness that I eagerly accepted.

Guppy had not spoken about Yejide's revelations. He was quiet, withdrawn, and seemed happy to let things be.

My father parked the car and we clambered out. The hollow crack of a squash ball echoed from the nearby court as we climbed the stairs to the entrance. It was good to be back.

'It's about time I taught you how to play squash, Charlie,' said my father, and without waiting for a reply he pulled open the door and waved us inside.

Landscapes and portraits hung on the wood-panelled walls, scenes from another age encircling the room. The snooker table stood to the right, its baize top glowing like a manicured lawn at sunset. Opposite, armchairs surrounded a series of low tables, the lights soft enough to add weight to the leather, bright enough to ensure that everyone could see the occupants. Nodding and murmuring in response to the greetings, my father ushered us towards the bar at the far end of the room, our footsteps muffled by hand-woven rugs laid over black-veined marble.

'Well, look who's back from exile!' Gunter Bath

beamed at us as his voice bounced off the walls. He had one hand wrapped around a pint glass, practically hiding it from view, the other pushed against the bar for support. 'Good to see you, Charlie. And who is your friend?'

Guppy stopped trying to polish his shoe on the back of his trouser leg and gazed up at Gunter. 'Everyone calls me Guppy.'

'Then I'll call you Guppy as well,' laughed Gunter. 'Bloody stupid name, though.' Guppy returned to his polishing, his cheeks beginning to redden. 'And you,' continued Gunter, turning to my father, 'you look dreadful. You need to get out more. Emeka, four beers.' The barman dropped his head and set about pouring the drinks. I glanced at my father, but a nod assured me that that a beer would be allowed tonight.

'Why don't you and Guppy rack them up, Charlie,' suggested my father.

'Yes, yes, off you go,' said Gunter, passing us our beers. 'Your father and I need to have a quick chat, then we'll come over and give you your snooker lesson.'

Guppy seized his drink with whispered thanks and, chased by Gunter's laughter, walked quickly over to the snooker table. I suppressed a smile and followed.

'He's a very rude man,' said Guppy, rolling the

reds from the far end of the table towards me. I gathered them up and began to arrange them in the wooden triangle.

'Yes, he is,' I confirmed. 'Rude, loud and drinks too much. Everybody likes him.' Guppy snorted and began to arrange the colours, placing each ball with measured care on its assigned black spot.

'What does he do?'

'I'm not sure. I think he's some kind of consultant.' I looked over at them. Gunter's smile was gone, and as they spoke he leaned in close to my father, who nodded and occasionally held up his hand to speak, before turning his ear once again to Gunter's whispers.

There was a clack behind me and I turned to see that Guppy had taken the break. I opened my mouth to congratulate him but a familiar voice beat me to it.

'You need a little more left on the cue ball, really.' It was Brian the Expert, who was now surveying Guppy with pity. 'A little more left would have helped bring it back up behind the yellow. You left a shot open in the bottom right corner.' Brian pushed his pipe into his mouth and lifted slightly onto the balls of his feet, waiting for a response to this particular pearl. Guppy stared at him open-mouthed, at a loss for what to say.

'Good break,' I said, in an attempt to rescue him.

'Do you think so?' asked Brian, like a teacher trying to guide a student towards the right answer. I just looked at him, and after a moment he sighed, shaking his head. 'Not. Enough. Left. Spin.'

'Oh. Thanks,' said Guppy, handing me the cue. Brian nodded and waved his hand towards the table, indicating that I should take my shot, but before I could, he spoke again.

'I wanted to ask you, Charles, how you are faring at the leper colony.'

I kept my eyes on the ball, trying to concentrate on the shot, fighting the urge to throw the cue at him. 'It's not a leper colony.'

'It's a refuge,' said Guppy.

'For lepers?'

'They have people suffering from leprosy there.'

Brian nodded. 'Just as I thought. Still, I'm sure your school will have you back soon, and you can stop wasting your time.'

I drew myself up sharply from the table, but Guppy spoke first. 'It is not a waste of time.'

'Oh dear,' said Brian. 'A crusader.'

'Excuse me?'

'Allow me to demonstrate,' said Brian, picking up

a glass of water that stood abandoned on a nearby table. He inserted a finger into the water, held it for a moment and then slowly drew it out again. 'See that hole,' he said, holding the glass up to Guppy's nose. 'That's how much difference your efforts are going to make.' For a moment I thought Guppy was going to hit him.

'Brian!' bellowed Gunter. He and my father had left the bar, whatever they were discussing apparently resolved. My father looked extremely pleased. 'Now. What nonsense are you feeding these two?'

Brian stiffened. 'I beg your pardon, Gunter?'

'You're far too sensitive, Brian,' said Gunter, and patting his cheek, advanced on the Expert. 'Give me a kiss.'

Brian took a step backwards. 'I think I'll see how the bridge rubber is going.' The four men huddled over cards on the table opposite looked up in alarm. But Brian appeared not to notice. He walked quickly over and positioned himself behind the nearest player, shaking his head and tutting.

Gunter waved to the bridge players and then turned, clapping his hands together. 'That's got rid of him. So, men against boys?'

After our second thrashing, Gunter decided that

six pints of beer was all his bladder could hold and excused himself. My father led Guppy and me to a table where we nestled into the armchairs.

'Good game,' said my father, raising his glass.

'Thank you,' replied Guppy. 'You and Gunter play very well.'

'Misspent youths.'

We sat in silence for a moment. The bar was quieter. Brian had left and Sinatra crooned from a hidden stereo.

'He's an interesting man, Gunter,' remarked Guppy.

'Very,' said my father. 'When he was a boy he walked across from East to West Berlin the day before the wall went up. Only had a bar of chocolate in his pocket. Says he felt something was going to happen, but I reckon he was just running away from the orphanage.'

'What happened to him then?' I asked. I hadn't heard this story before.

'Another orphanage for a while. Then he joined the merchant navy. Jumped ship on the Ivory Coast and somehow made his way to Sengharia. Been here ever since.'

'Fascinating,' said Guppy. 'And what does he do?'

My father hesitated before answering. 'He's a consultant.'

'He offers advice?'

'Something like that,' said my father. 'I do business with him occasionally. He's married to a relation of the Oba of Irefe, a useful man to know. He can . . . fix things.'

'Who's the Oba of Irefe?' I asked. But before my father could answer, the door burst open and Gunter appeared, still struggling with his fly.

'Another frame?'

And before anyone could answer, the man who could fix things began to rack up for the next frame.

CHAPTER 11

My drink arrived on the table with a clunk and I
looked up to see the barman scowling down at me.

'Ice?'

The bottle felt slightly cooler than the air around
me, but not much. Anyway, I wasn't going to risk
amoebic dysentery from the ice.

'That's fine, thanks.' I handed him the money and
he wandered back into the tin roof lean-to, pausing at
the front to straighten the sign that read, 'The Hilten
Bar'. The bar was tucked away behind the market next
to a makeshift football pitch, and I turned my attention
to the game, sipping my Coke and trying to ignore the
nervousness eating away at my stomach. I pulled my
cigerettes from my pocket, then remembered Yejide's
face when she had seen me smoking. I looked at them
for a moment, then, with a sigh, I crumpled the packet
and tossed it in to the bin.

'Good shot,' said a voice behind me.

I automatically stood up, but my knee caught the table, sending my drink toppling over. Yejide caught it and placed it gently back in the middle of the table.

'Hardly lost a drop,' she said.

'Thanks,' I replied, trying to ignore the throbbing in my kneecap.

She picked out the least dangerous looking stool and sat down. 'Sorry I'm late. We were really busy at the stall.'

'Oh, don't worry. What would you like?'

'Coke would be nice.' I called the barman over and ordered. He lurched away without a word, leaving us sitting in silence listening to the shouts from the football pitch. I had planned a witty, open-ended conversation starter, but there was something in her obsidian eyes that wiped my memory. I became aware of a dull tapping and realised I was drumming my fingers on the table. I stopped, picked up my drink, took a sip and then scrambled to wipe away the drips that dribbled down my chin. I fought to think of something to say, but my mind had blanked and I found myself staring in to space.

The barman brought the Coke and Yejide raised

her bottle. 'Cheers,' she said. I raised mine in reply. 'Where's Guppy?'

'Oh, he told me to tell you he was busy. He sends his apologies.' I couldn't tell if she was pleased or disappointed.

We chatted about the market, Joseph, the new orphanage extension, Pink Floyd and the news that a man called Bob Geldof was trying to organise a concert to help the children of Ethiopia.

We reached a natural lull and I took a sip of Coke. It was going well, I thought to myself – just as Yejide leaned forward slightly and said, 'So, what on earth are you doing at Ilakaye?'

I realised that we had never spoken about it. That I had never actually told the whole story to anybody and had no intention of starting now. There must be some tale I could spin, I thought, something that she would believe that would leave my pride intact.

'Well, it's a bit complicated, really.'

'It's OK,' she said, 'you don't have to tell me if you don't want to.'

'No. It's all right.' I suddenly felt weak, vulnerable, and before I knew it, I was telling her everything. Every detail of the night in the Crocodile Bar came spilling out: the beer, the hookers, the knife, the hospital.

And as I spoke, I knew I was lost. That it would be the last time we would meet after this, that she would not possibly want to see me again. But I kept talking; I needed to, and as the words took shape, so did the realisation of what had happened: someone had nearly died. For the first time I truly understood what that meant, how close we had all come to disaster for the sake of a night of beer and girls.

I finished, and let my shoulders drop. I stared at the scratched, jagged wood of the table, afraid to lift my head, to look her in the eye.

'Don't worry,' she said. 'It's all right.'

I looked up at her. 'I thought. . . I thought you'd. . .'

Her laugh drifted across the table. 'You'd have to do a lot better than that to shock me. In fact, it makes you more interesting. I thought you might just be someone trying to do a bit of charity work to help us poor people. But you're here for a reason, like the rest of us.' And she smiled, her gaze touching mine. 'Welcome to Ilakaye.'

I wanted to respond, but for the second time that afternoon I couldn't think of anything to say. Except this time, it didn't matter, and we sat for moment wrapped in soft silence.

'Ilakaye?'

I looked up to see the silhouette of a young woman blocking the sun.

'Ilakaye?' she repeated. He voice was soft, barely audible, and she took a step forward, bringing herself into view. She couldn't have been more than nineteen; her robes, torn and stained, hung loose over a thin frame.

'That's right,' said Yejide.

The woman hesitated. Her reddened eyes darted around the tables, as if she was looking for someone.

'What's the matter?' said Yejide. 'Do you know someone in Ilakaye?' The woman shook her head, a trembling motion that shook tears from her eyes. Yejide stood up and reached out her hand. 'Tell me what's wrong?' The woman took a step backward and for a moment I thought she was going to run. Then she lurched forward, grabbing Yejide's hand, and began to speak, a whispered jumble of Yoruba. I looked from one to the other, straining to understand, but the expression that built on her face told me it was nothing good.

The woman seemed to break off mid-sentence and she backed away, trying to shake off Yejide's grip. 'It's all right,' said Yejide, but the woman wrenched her hand free, turned and hurried away, slipping down a narrow alleyway at the side of the bar.

'Come on,' said Yejide, and I sprinted after her.

The alleyway turned away from the market, down towards a few scattered houses and the rubbish tips. Yejide sprinted ahead and I struggled to keep up. A man emerged from the one of the houses and stumbled quickly back against the wall as I sped by. He yelled something at me and I shouted apologies over my shoulder, hurdled a chicken and sped on.

'What the hell is going on?' I shouted. But Yejide ignored me. We rounded a corner and skidded to a halt. The woman stood in a small clearing surrounded on three sides by rotting rubbish, its smell so thick, I could feel it brushing my skin. I spat a fly from my mouth and swallowed hard, battling nausea, struggling to catch my breath and trying not to breathe too deeply. Yejide stood motionless and I took a step forward. She held out her arm, her eyes never leaving the woman, indicating that I should stay where I was. We waited, listening to the flies, and then the woman stepped aside and a small boy took a stumbling step forward.

He couldn't have been much older than two, his Mickey Mouse T-shirt reaching to his knees. He gripped his mother's robes with one hand and in the other he held a small blue handkerchief patterned with red flowers. He smiled and waved, the handkerchief fluttering in the air, and the woman nudged him towards us.

'Take him,' she said.

I looked at Yejide, stunned by the words, and saw her eyes open in surprise.

'You come too.'

'*Rárá, rárá. Mi ò lè bá yin lọ.*'

'Why can't you?'

The woman shook her head. 'I must stay. They go. . .' Her voice seemed to age with every word and her body dropped, as if the pain dragged her towards the garbage at her feet.

'Who? *Tani?*'

'They go hurt us. They promise good life. They go take my boy.'

'No,' said Yejide, sudden power in her voice. 'I will not let them.' She took a step forward, her hand outstretched. 'Come with me.'

The woman looked down at her child, who smiled up at her. She stared at him, the slightest of smiles creeping across her mouth; then she nodded, picked up the boy and shuffled towards Yejide.

'What are you doing?' The words rang clear and

I wheeled around, startled.

A man stood at the entrance to the clearing, hands on hips, a smile on his face. He was short, with a well-ironed white shirt and crisp slacks, his shoes gleaming against the filth. I took a step backwards and the man laughed, throwing his head back. 'I hope my sister is not troubling you.' The woman began to shake.

Yejide eyed the man from top to toe, appraising him like someone who has stumbled across a snake. Then she tossed her hair back and smiled. 'Oh, not at all. My friend and I were a little worried about her, that's all.'

I looked at her in disbelief. The woman backed away, before coming to a stop against the rotting mass behind her.

'Thank you,' he replied. 'She is not well. . .' He touched his index finger to his head and shrugged his shoulders.

'That's what we thought. I'm very glad you've arrived. Well, we'd better get going.' She took my arm and began to lead me away.

'Wait a minute, ' I said. 'You actually believe this. . .'

The man's eyes flashed and his body tensed.

Yejide threw her head back and laughed, her fingers

digging into my bicep. '*Oyinbos*. They think they know everything.'

The man chuckled in appreciation, but it was through a brittle smile, and his eyes seemed to sink into their sockets as he slipped his right hand into his pocket.

Still smiling, Yejide led me away. 'Don't look back,' she hissed, tightening the grip on my arm. We walked quickly, and it wasn't until we had turned the corner that she released my arm.

'What the hell—' I began, but her shaking hands and the fear in eyes stopped me short.

'Run, Charlie!' she said, grabbing my hand, and we sprinted off down the alley.

▣◉◘

Despite pushing the truck to its limits, we took over half an hour to get back there with the others. We raced through the market to the Hilten, Yejide and I leading the way, no time to talk. At one point I thought we had lost the way, but then I spotted the man I had nearly collided with sitting outside his house, and we hurtled back to the clearing with its rotten rubbish.

She was gone.

'Are you sure this is the place?' asked Guppy.

'Of course,' I said. 'She was right here.'

Joseph glanced around and sighed. 'I didn't expect her to be here. We must ask around the market, see if anyone recognises her description.' Abacha nodded and set off immediately.

Guppy kicked at an old can on the floor. 'Now we know why the orphanage is so busy. Everyone is afraid of their children going missing,' he said.

'I think you might be right, Guppy,' sighed Joseph. 'But I need you to go and help Abacha.' Guppy grunted and set off, anger clouding his face.

'This is ridiculous. This should never have happened. We could have just brought her with us,' I said.

'We couldn't,' said Yejide. 'The man was—'

'The *man*. . .? He barely came up to my waist!'

'Yejide is right. There was nothing you could do,' said Joseph.

'Oh, come on. Why?'

'He was a child trafficker. I doubt that the woman would have been from Ilaju. He probably brought her in from the rural areas with the promise of money, a good job. He would not have allowed you two to get in the way. Yejide did the only thing possible in the circumstances. In fact, you were lucky he gave you the chance to leave.'

'Oh, and why's that?' I asked, hearing the insolence in my voice. I couldn't help feeling shame at myself and surprise at Yejide.

Joseph said nothing. He placed his hand on Yejide's shoulder and gave her a sad smile, before turning and walking slowly back towards the alleyway.

'That's unbelievable. This is the stupidest thing I ever heard of, we never should have left, that guy couldn't have done much—'

'Shut up! Just shut up, Charlie!' Yejide's cries were like physical blows. I stood rooted to the spot, stunned by her anger and the tears that fell from her eyes. 'You think you know everything, but you don't. He would have killed us, Charlie, without thinking twice about it. Where do you think you are. . .? You think that was easy for me. . .?' She stared at me for a second, words failing her, her eyes searching mine, and I caught a glimpse of a pain trapped deep inside, before she turned and ran back to the alleyway.

I watched her go, too shocked to follow, realising how stupid and hurtful my words had been, and how terrifying hers were, and that without Yejide I would not be there, that I was horribly out of my depth.

I turned away from the alleyway and looked out over the tips. The garbage snaked into the distance, stretching out into the countryside beyond the market, beyond the city, past the reach of walls and wire, hurrying on its way.

A breeze swirled the stink around me, pushing it into my lungs, and I turned to leave – when something caught my eye. The handkerchief with the red flowers lay squashed under a footprint. I bent down, pulled it free and shook off some of the filth and flies that covered it. I was about to throw it back to the ground, but stopped myself. I rubbed my finger over the soft fabric, feeling the smile of the boy who had carried it and the tears of the woman who had held his hand.

I folded it up and slipped it into my pocket.

CHAPTER 12

Guppy pulled the splinter from his palm with his teeth, spat it on the ground and looked up at the skeleton of the orphanage extension. 'It's coming along nicely.'

I looked at his hand. A drop of blood clung to the tip of his forefinger. 'You should get some antiseptic for that,' I suggested.

'Later.'

I shrugged. There was no arguing with Guppy these days. He worked tirelessly, almost obsessively, and I think, after what he had told me about his family, that I understood why: this is where he was from.

The rough footings that Guppy and I had dug now held the complete framework for the new wing. The walls supporting the timber-framed roof were hollow blocks filled with steel reinforcing and concrete; you couldn't dent them with a sledgehammer.

I watched Guppy as he bandaged his palm with

his handkerchief, before picking up the plane and continuing to smooth the timber for the window frames. The sun seemed to be concentrating all its efforts on Ilakaye, and I backed into the shade of the orphanage, but Guppy had not taken a break all day. His arm moved fluidly over the wood, the shavings curling up from the plane and falling in ringlets at his feet. Suddenly he jarred to a halt. The plane had hit a knot in the wood and he pushed at it, gently at first, but then harder, until he was ramming the blade against the obstacle with all his strength.

'Guppy!' It was Abacha, calling from the roof. 'Cool down. You will break the blade!' Muttering to himself, he slid down the ladder and marched towards Guppy. 'Take a rest,' he said, snatching the plane from Guppy's hand. Guppy seemed about to speak, but Abacha held up his hand. 'Take a rest.'

Guppy sat down next to me with a grunt and wiped the sweat from his eyes.

'You look tired,' I said.

'I'm all right.'

'You don't have to do it all, you know.'

'What else is there to do? We aren't allowed to go near the church or Danlami. At least, with this, I feel like I'm. . .' His voice trailed off, and he leaned back against the orphanage and shut his eyes.

I knew what he was going to say, and he was right. No one seemed to be doing anything about Danlami and his church. Our search for the girl had been fruitless. No one at the market seemed to remember her or her child; she had vanished as quickly as she had appeared. A report had been filed with the police, but nothing more had been done. Joseph was away at a medical centre in Ibe, and Sister Mairead refused to talk about anything to do with it. Yejide hadn't been around for a couple of days, and so we buried ourselves in our work, venting our frustrations on wood and concrete, building our solution to Danlami's church.

The compound was empty. Everyone had retreated inside against the onslaught of the midday sun; the silence from the extension told me that Abacha had given up, too. The trees stood silent and unnaturally still, as if painted on a backdrop; their branches drooped under the weight of the heat. A fly murmured by, and I felt my head nodding forwards, my eyes beginning to close.

Something landed in my lap and I gasped in surprise.

'Lunch,' said Yejide, tossing a similar package

to Guppy, which landed on his head. 'Thought you'd be hungry.'

She and I looked at each other in silence. We hadn't spoken since the boy had vanished. I had tried to find her but she was never around.

'Thanks,' I said. 'Look . . . Yejide . . . I . . .'

'I need to go to the bathroom,' said Guppy, handing me his package. 'I'll be back in a minute.

I stood up, inwardly thanking him for his tact. 'Yejide. I'm really sorry about what I said. You were right, I didn't understand. But I think I do now. You did the only thing. If I'd had my way, neither of us . . . well, you know.'

'Thank you, Charlie. And I'm sorry too. I was upset. I shouldn't have been so angry.'

'Don't worry about it.'

'You know, it's a shame. I was really enjoying our date.'

My heart leapt at the word 'date'. 'Shall we try it again some other time?'

'Definitely.' She took a step forward and gave me a hug. 'And I haven't forgotten about our race on the roofs, either. Come on, let's go to Joseph's office and enjoy some air con.'

We burst into Joseph's office and I felt the physical

relief of the air conditioning, like water to a parched man. Guppy arrived a few seconds later and shot me a quizzical look. I nodded, and he smiled.

We pulled up chairs around the low table next to Joseph's desk and pulled open our lunches.

'Where have you been the last couple of days?' I asked.

'I had some forms to fill in for university. Joseph thinks I should try for a scholarship.'

'You'll get it, too.'

'I hope he won't mind us using his office while he is away,' said Guppy, looking around anxiously.

'He won't,' she assured him. 'Now, let's eat.'

'What is it?' I asked.

'*Suya.* It's spiced, barbequed goat. The raw onion helps to take the edge off the chilli.'

I looked down at the slices of meat sitting on page six of that morning's *Vanguard*. We had always been told at school never to eat anything sold on the roadside, but I held my breath and slowly placed a couple of pieces in my mouth. It was the nicest thing I'd ever tasted.

We ate and talked. Yejide explained why Joseph was in Ibe; he was helping at a medical centre – mainly educational work, she said, helping people to cope with leprosy, and the rising problem of a new disease called AIDS. She said Joseph called it the new plague, and if something wasn't done soon it would be an epidemic in five years' time. Guppy spoke at length about the orphanage extension, but we all skirted around the topic of the church where children were sold to the highest bidder, and of the woman and the boy who had vanished.

Then I remembered the question I had wanted to ask Yejide for days: 'Who's the Oba of Irefe?'

Yejide looked at me with surprise, and I explained about Gunter and his wife.

'If he's married to a relative of the Oba, then he really is well-connected,' she said, her eyebrows raised.

'But who is he?' pushed Guppy.

'He's a traditional ruler.'

'So he's part of the government.'

'No,' she said. 'Well not part of the official government. They're tribal rulers, a bit like kings and queens in Europe, except here, people still listen to them and they have a lot of power.'

'So the Oba of Irefe is a king?' asked Guppy.

'Sort of, I suppose,' said Yejide. She put down her lunch and walked to a map of Sengharia pinned on the wall. 'This is Irefe,' she said, pointing to a spot in the south-east, 'although it's not the capital of the old Yoruba kingdom – that's outside the new borders of Sengharia. It was once an important town, and the Oba – the ruler – an important man. So you could say your friend is married to royalty. Very powerful royalty, too.'

'Fascinating,' said Guppy.

My father's description of Gunter as a man who 'could fix things' suddenly became very clear. He had the ear of an Oba, an ancient ruler, and I understood why he was such a useful man to know.

A blast of hot air pushed through the room, and looking over, I saw Joseph standing in the doorway. Guppy jumped out of his seat like a criminal caught in the act and started stammering apologies. But Joseph held up his hand, a smile on his face. 'It is all right, Guppy. Looking at the progress you have made on the orphanage, I would say you deserve an air conditioned break.' Guppy's face shone. 'And what's this?' he continued, indicating Yejide standing by the map. 'A Geography lesson?'

'When did you get back?' asked Yejide.

'About five minutes ago.'

'Yejide was telling us about the old rulers,' I explained.

'Ah. Not Geography then. History. Can I smell *suya*?'

'All gone, I'm afraid, Joseph,' said Yejide.

'Pity. I'm hungry.'

'Yejide was saying that the old rulers still have quite a lot of influence. It was fascinating,' said Guppy.

Joseph coughed out a laugh. 'Some, I suppose. But they have little relevance in modern Sengharia. Quaint history.'

'Interesting, though,' I said, surprised by his dismissal.

'Perhaps. But now they are nothing more than a hindrance to democratic progress, hanging on to positions that no longer have any meaning. Sengharia must look forward, not backwards.'

'But isn't that denying the country its history?' asked Guppy.

'No more than suggesting that Britain should return to a monarchical dictatorship. Now, I'm afraid I need my office back. I have a lot of work to do.'

I threw the newspaper that had held my lunch into the bin, and, murmuring our thanks, we wandered back to the heat of the compound.

A shout made me turn, and I saw a man in a grey suit standing by the main gates,. Sweat flecked his face and he held a large brown envelope in his hands. Two policemen flanked him; wooden-stocked Uzi submachine guns hung casually over their shoulders.

'Joseph Obohense!' The man with the envelope looked around nervously as he repeated his shout. The policemen looked bored.

The door to the office opened and Joseph came out. He surveyed the men for a moment before walking over, a smile on his face. 'Welcome to Ilakaye,' he said. What can I do for you?' Without a word the man raised the envelope and brought it down sharply in front of Joseph. 'For me?' The man simply nodded.

Joseph took it with thanks, tore it open, pulled out a single sheaf of white paper and began to read. The man wiped a handkerchief across his forehead, a quick side-step bringing him closer to one of the policeman, his eyes flickering over Joseph's face searching for some indication of a response. But Joseph remained impassive. He read the document with care, and then looked up at the man.

'Is there anything else?'

The man visibly relaxed, shook his head and with a curt word to the policemen, walked out.

'What's all that about?' asked Guppy, his eyes following the three men.

'No idea.' I watched Joseph as he walked back to his office, the paper held loosely at his side. As he reached the door he seemed to stumble a little, leaning against the wall for support, before vanishing inside.

'I don't like this. . .' said Yejide. And, as if to confirm her thoughts, Mairead came out of the orphanage and hurried after Joseph.

◫ ◉ ◻

Guppy and I sat in silence as Yejide paced the ground in front of us. We had exhausted all possible theories about the man with the envelope, and were lost in our own thoughts. It had been three hours, but the door to the office remained shut. I was beginning to think it was nothing to worry about, that it was just some routine matter.

'At last. . .' said Yejide, running across to Mairead, who barely had time to shut the office door before Yejide was upon her.

Guppy and I stood watching. Mairead led her away from the office and leant close, speaking quickly, her hand on Yejide's shoulder. After a moment she stopped and gently lifted Yejide's chin with her hand, before offering some parting words and moving away towards the orphanage.

Yejide stood still for a moment as if unsure of what to do. I took a step forward, but Guppy held my arm. 'Wait,' he whispered. She looked first at the office and then turned and walked towards us, and I saw a tear slide down her cheek.

Pushing Guppy's hand away, I rushed over. 'What is it? What's happened?'

'There's a problem,' she said, her voice a cracked sigh. 'The authorities are revoking Joseph's lease. They are demanding that Ilakaye be handed over.'

'Who to?' I said, knowing the answer, but dreading it.

'Michael Danlami.'

CHAPTER 13

Guppy watched me, waiting for a reaction. I tried to catch Yejide's eye, looking for some sign of what she thought, but she stared into the distance, one finger stroking her cheek, her face unreadable.

It had taken some effort to stop Guppy and Yejide from barging straight into Joseph's office. Guppy clearly needed some time alone, some time to think things through. And so I left him to himself. Later, we walked down to the Hilten Bar and sat on wooden stools by the monsoon drain, swigging warm Coke straight from the bottle. The football pitch was deserted and we hardly noticed the early evening bustle of the market, all our attention concentrated on the Danlami news.

Then Guppy told us his plan.

'Well?' he asked. I stared at the ground, my foot

carving a semi-circle through the dust to the clay below.

'I don't really think it would work, Guppy,' I said, avoiding his eyes. 'I barely know Gunter. . .'

'You could ask your father to talk to him about it,' persisted Guppy, 'I am sure it could work.'

'Guppy, this really is a police matter. Something for the authorities to work out. My dad's friend's wife's . . . whatever he is, isn't going to be able to do anything, even if he wanted to.'

'A police matter!' scoffed Guppy. 'Danlami has bought them ten times over.'

'Listen. . .' I began, and I trailed off, looking to Yejide for support. But she shook her head.

'Guppy is right. The police will not be able to help. But the Oba might. I'm not sure, but he might. It's worth a try.'

Guppy breathed in deeply, his chest swelling out and a smile growing on his face.

'Thank you, Yejide. So, you'll talk to your father, Charlie?'

I held up my hands in submission. 'Sure. I know what he'll say, but sure. Why not?'

'Good. I must get back.' Guppy downed the last of his Coke and headed off down the alleyway.

I watched him go for a moment, wobbling into the distance, before turning to Yejide. 'You really think that the Oba will listen to us?'

'I don't know,' she sighed. 'But it's worth a try. Anything's worth a try.'

We sat in silence for a moment watching the sellers at their stalls, the late afternoon sun gleaming on the ebony and ivory. 'Would you like another Coke?' I asked.

'No, thank you. Come with me. I want to show you something, it should have started by now.'

She walked off quickly into the labyrinthine alleys of the market and I followed behind, my thoughts still locked into how I was going to approach my father about the Oba, interrupted occasionally by a jostling customer or a shout from one of the traders. Yejide stopped suddenly, forcing me onto tiptoe to prevent a collision.

'I thought you should see Joseph's school,' she said.

I moved around her and saw that the alley opened onto a large courtyard flanked by the backs of stalls. The eight rows of wooden stools were as straight as rulers, and on each stool sat a child of ten or eleven. They wore an assortment of T-shirts, shorts and dresses, the only uniform their bare feet. Each held a small exercise book and a pencil and stared intently at a man writing on an easel-held blackboard at the front.

There was silence; even the racket of the market seemed to be kept at bay here.

The teacher finished writing and stepped to one side, revealing a long division sum. 'You may begin,' he said, and instant scribbling rustled the silent air. After no more than a minute a child in the far corner stood up, her book held in front of her; others began to follow until the whole class was on its feet. Except one: a boy in the front row, smaller and younger-looking than the rest, kept his seat, his head bowed.

'The answer, please,' said the teacher.

All the children sang out as one: '7.4, *Olùkó.*'

'Correct. You may sit down.'

The teacher waited until the class had settled before approaching the boy at the front. He held out his hand and the boy handed him his book. The teacher studied it for a second before returning his gaze to the bowed head in front of him. I braced myself, expecting a tirade, but it never came. The teacher bent down beside him and began to go through the problem. He spoke softly, guiding the student through the process, never rushing. Eventually the boy nodded that he understood and the teacher moved back to the board, quickly writing out another sum.

'Why don't you try this one?' he suggested.

The class waited in silence while the boy wrestled with the numbers. He then rose uncertainly to his feet.

'6.5, Olùkó?'

'Correct. Well done.'

The class applauded.

'What's a school doing here?' I whispered.

'It's another of Joseph's projects,' she replied. 'He buys the materials with some of the proceeds from the Ilakaye shop. The teacher, the Olùko, is a professor at the university. He volunteers here three evenings a week. The children are all from the market. They work with their parents during the day and then come here. Most are illiterate when they start, but . . . well, you can see. There's a lot more at stake then just Ilakaye. This place, the work in Ibe, it will all go.'

We stood and watched the class for a while. The teacher finished with Maths and began to hand out copies of a book. The small boy at the front read aloud from *Danny, the Champion of the World* and I listened entranced. I barely noticed when Yejide slipped her hand into mine. I turned and she smiled at me. 'We'd better get back.'

I didn't know what to say as I felt her fingers tighten on mine, I just nodded and, hand in hand, we walked back through the market and up to Ilakaye. We went in silence, hands entwined, and stopped at the gates. There was no one in sight. I looked into her eyes, and she smiled.

'You're a good man, Charlie. I know you are. I feel like you really believe in what we do here. You want to help.'

I said nothing, trying to bury my feelings of doubt at the plan to catch Danlami.

She moved towards me and we stood in the twilight and kissed, as the world around me melted gently away.

◫◉◨

'You're very quiet, Charlie.' said my mother. 'What's on your mind?'

'Are you in trouble again?' asked my sister.

I nearly dropped my fork. 'No, Katie. I am not in trouble.' She shrugged, and returned to her fish and chips.

'Of course Charlie's not in trouble again,' smiled my mother.

'A boy at school got into trouble today,' continued Katie. 'He shot a spit ball at Dorothy but it missed and hit Miss Mathews. He went *really quiet.*'

My father snorted into his wine and my mother shot him a silencing look. 'Well, Katie,' she said, 'he probably knew that what he did was very wrong and was thinking that he mustn't do it again.' Katie nodded in agreement.

'Well, Charlie, been shooting spit balls at anyone?' asked my father laughter flickering across his eyes.

I managed a grin. My heart had been full of Yejide's kiss since coming home, banishing all other thoughts. Then I remembered what she and Guppy had asked of me, the conversation I needed to have, and I had sunk into a nervous silence. It was asking a lot. Joseph did not want us interfering with Danlami, he had made that very clear, and I found it impossible to shake the man from the rubbish tips from my mind. But, I had said yes, and I couldn't back down now.

I had been battling with how to approach my father about Gunter, and decided that the direct way was probably the only way. I took a deep breath and said, 'I need to speak to you about something.'

'Is everything all right?' said my mother, sitting bolt upright, her eyes scanning my face.

'It's about Ilakaye. I need to ask Dad's advice about something.'

My mother relaxed. 'That's good,' she said. 'I'm glad you feel you can talk to us about any trouble you're having.'

'What's on your mind?' asked my father.

I put down my knife and fork, slowly pushing them together, feeling my parents' eyes on me as I listened to the quiet scrape of metal on ceramic. 'I was wondering if you would talk to Gunter for me. I think I . . . *we* might need his help.' I saw my mother cast a look of concern at my father, but he kept his eyes on me, studying me, as if trying to glean something from the creases in my face.

'Gunter?' he said, and took a sip of wine, placing the glass slowly back on the table. 'Now, why would you need Gunter's help?'

I didn't tell them everything. The first mention of someone selling children across the road would have had me banned from ever returning to Ilakaye, and once more the secrets piled up inside me like old unwanted books. But I told them about Danlami and his move to take over, of his history with Joseph and how we were sure he had bribed the authorities to get the decision. I told them about the school I had seen that day and how everything would be gone if we didn't do something. I finished in a rush, explaining how Gunter might be able to help because of his connections with the Oba. Then I took a deep breath and waited for their reaction.

No one said anything for a moment. They both just looked at me.

'Well,' said my mother, 'it seems your involvement at Ilakaye has moved beyond clearing the drains. This is terrible news. What does Joseph think about your idea?'

Her voice was soft and respectful, and it took me by surprise. My father continued to study me, his face expressionless.

'Well. . .' I began, buoyed by their reaction. 'We thought it would be better to wait and see what Gunter says, and then we would have something solid to offer Joseph.'

'We?' asked my father.

'Guppy and I. And Yejide. She works there too. You haven't met her.'

'Can I get down now I've finished?' said my sister.

'Yes,' replied my mother. 'Come on, let's say

thank you to Ruth and Peter, then we can watch a video.'

'Come over to the bar, Charlie,' said my father. 'Bring your wine.'

I followed him over, and he took his customary place behind it. I sat down across from him, my newfound confidence evaporating as I saw the seriousness in his eyes.

He topped up his glass and lit a cigarette. 'This isn't the sort of thing Gunter gets involved with. We do some business together: he knows the right people when you have trouble with an import licence or an invented regulation, but he gets well paid for it. He's not really in the charity business.'

'I thought it might be worth talking to him.' I tried to keep my back straight and hold my glass in the casual fashion of the men at the Eko club. 'He might be interested,' I said, taking a sip of wine and spilling some down my shirt.

My father stared into the distance for a while before speaking. 'Why does this man Danlami want Ilakaye?'

'I'm not sure.' I avoided his eye. 'He's swindled one charity. Perhaps he thinks he can get money this way.'

'Does Joseph accept donations in cash?'

'No. No, I don't think he does.'

'I'm sure Danlami knows this. It doesn't make sense. No. I'm sure the authorities will be able to sort this one out, Charlie. There's no need to bother Gunter about it.'

I almost agreed. I wanted to. I had done what Guppy and Yejide had asked me to, and there was no need to push the point, but I found that I couldn't just let it go.

'We think Danlami's bribed the authorities.'

'Bribed the authorities . . . yes, you mentioned that. I still don't understand why this man is going to such trouble over this. . .'

'Perhaps it's just the land he wants.'

'Does Joseph own the land?'

'No, it's leased from the government.'

'That's what I thought. And it's hardly what we'd call a prime location, is it?'

'No.' I felt my shoulders drop. I was losing and I knew it.

'Well, as I said, this seems to be a matter for the auth—'

'Look, does it matter *why* he wants it? He's a thief and a liar. He destroyed the orphanage that Joseph helped to build in Port Rose and now all the work at Ilakaye could be gone. All the work Joseph has done. All the work Guppy and I have put into that place. Who cares why he wants it. He's sick! He *does* want it and that's all that matters to me!' My voice echoed in my ears, and I realised I was up on my feet. My father stared at me, and I quickly sat down again. I couldn't remember ever having raised my voice to him before.

'Well. . .' he began.

'I'm sorry, I didn't mean to get so. . .'

'It's all right. You feel strongly about it. That's not a bad thing. Not a bad thing at all. Does Guppy feel the same way?'

I nodded.

'And . . . sorry, what was her name?'

I felt my cheeks redden. 'Yejide. She's just a friend.'

'Of course.' He took a long drag on his cigarette. 'Well, I think I must see what I can do.'

'So, you might speak to him. To Gunter, I mean.'

'Yes.' My father stubbed out his cigarette as if sealing his decision. 'This is a good thing you're doing.'

'Thank you.'

'Wait here for a moment.' And he stood and

walked through to the living room. I watched him talking to my mother for a few moments before heading for the telephone.

I couldn't make out much of his conversation with Gunter, but caught phrases like 'a good cause' and 'owe me a favour'. After a few minutes he returned.

'Gunter will see you tomorrow at eight.' He gave my shoulder a squeeze and leaned in closer. 'I hope you know what you're doing.' And he walked through to join my mother, leaving me alone at the bar staring at my glass of wine and the growing realisation that I didn't know what I was doing – that I was afraid.

CHAPTER 14

Gunter's bungalow squatted in the centre of the compound, the floodlights wrapping it in a patchwork of shadow and orange glow. Our feet scrunched over the thick gravel, and I looked back to see the night guards staring at us from the gates, as if unhappy that our shoes were breaking the silence of the night. It had rained earlier, the humidity wrapping itself around us like an invisible fog; my shirt began to cling to my back.

Guppy and I stopped at a door at the side of the house. A spotlight hung just above the frame, and we stood for a moment fixed in its glare.

'Shall I knock?' asked Guppy.

'That would be a good idea.' I was still unconvinced about Guppy's plan and had told him before we left Ilakaye that he would do all the talking.

He rapped twice with his knuckles, took a step back and we waited, the heat from the spotlight burning on my face. There was the sound of footsteps and the door swung open revealing Gunter's silhouetted frame.

Guppy put his hand up to shield his eyes. 'Mr Bath?'

'Mr Guppy,' laughed Gunter. 'And Mr Charlie. Come in, come in.' He stepped aside and I followed Guppy into the hallway.

The air conditioning washed over me as Gunter led us through the sitting room to a small bar nestled in the far corner.

'First, beer. Then business,' stated Gunter, pulling three bottles from a fridge hidden under the bar. 'Sit down, sit down.'

Guppy and I slid onto the stools, and Gunter ripped the tops off the bottles with an opener, sending them spinning and clattering over the bar-top. I glanced around the room: an array of tribal masks and pictures hid the walls, gentle scenes of village life and African savannah crammed between the hostile stares of the wood-carved faces. On the side-tables, statues of ivory jostled for space with ebony heads, and the perfume of stained wood scented the air.

Gunter pushed a glass towards me and raised his own. 'Welcome,' he said, and we lifted our beers in reply, whispering thanks.

'That tusk is quite magnificent,' Guppy remarked, indicating the wall just above Gunter's head. I glanced up and was amazed I had missed it. It must have been four feet long, mounted on wooden supports. A carved hunting scene adorned the top edge, the natural curve of the tusk giving the figures and animals movement, as if running over a hill of white stone. Every detail was there: the claws of the lions, the smiles of the men, the leaves on the trees and the grasses on the ground, all carved in miniature perfection. It was breathtaking.

'My pride and joy,' said Gunter. I found it in a market fifteen years ago. However, I'm lucky to still have it. Your mother, Charlie, lent my wife a video she had rented from Norman's: *Bloody Ivory*.'

'Oh, that's right,' I said. 'My mother's hidden all our ivory in a cupboard now. She won't buy it any more.'

'My wife wanted to do the same. But I managed to persuade her not to. Why hide something so beautiful,

I said to her. You'd just be compounding the sin.' And he laughed his raucous laugh. 'But now. . . How can I help you two?' And he settled himself on to his stool, his eyes moving between the two of us.

It seemed that Guppy had not forgotten our arrangement and, clearing his throat, he began to tell the story of Danlami and the church.

Gunter listened in silence, taking in everything Guppy was saying, occasionally nodding encouragement. When Guppy had finished, Gunter looked at him thoughtfully for a while before speaking.

'Thank you for telling me all this. I am glad you felt you could come to me. This man sounds very unpleasant. However, I am a business consultant. This is beyond the reach of my usual activities. I'm sorry, I don't think I can help you.'

I felt my shoulders drop, but not in disappointment – in relief. The authorities would deal with Danlami; I would go back to work at Ilakaye, clearing the drains, helping with the orphanage. I would finish the year and return to school. I lifted my glass and took a long swig, my thoughts already on my next date with Yejide.

Then Guppy spoke again.

'I understand that this is not the sort of activity you would normally become involved in, but we thought that as it directly affects the people in this area, that perhaps your wife might inform the Oba. . .'

Guppy left his sentence hanging in the air under Gunter's gaze, a gaze that had become steel. His face hardened as he stared at Guppy, who held his eye without flinching. 'That is an . . . interesting request,' said Gunter and snapped his head round to look at me. My eyes dropped to my beer.

'What makes you think she can help you?' The air conditioning buffeted my sweat-streaked shirt, sending a chill down my spine.

'We knew that she would be concerned about this,' said Guppy, but I caught the flicker of uncertainty in his eyes, a slight slouching as Gunter's eyes bored into him.

Gunter was silent for a moment and I was about to offer my apologies, when he slammed his glass onto the bar top. My body jerked in shock and I braced myself for his anger; but he was laughing. 'Wait here,' he said, and he walked around the bar and vanished through a door at the other end of the room.

'I think it is going quite well,' remarked Guppy.

'I'm glad you think so,' I said.

'There is a little more to Gunter than laughter and beer, I think.'

'Yeah,' I said, 'I think so too,' and took another long gulp from my glass.

We sat in silence for about five minutes, listening to the hum of an overhead fan, before the door opened and Gunter's wife followed him into the room. She wore traditional Yoruba robes of blue and silver, the shimmering material wrapped around a slim waist, the blouse hanging gently on sculpted shoulders. She glided towards us and extended her hand.

'Good evening. I am Mrs Bath,' she said, her accent carrying the hallmark of a British public school. 'Gunter has already told me a little about your problem. Perhaps we would be more comfortable around the coffee table.' And indicating that we should follow, she walked to the centre of the room and settled on the edge of an armchair, her knees together, her hands in her lap. Guppy and I perched ourselves on the sofa. Gunter stayed at the bar, sipping his beer and watching. 'Now. Why don't you tell me about this Michael Danlami.'

She listened attentively, a woman of power holding court. When Guppy had finished she leaned forward slightly and asked, 'How do you think my uncle can help you?' And it took me a moment before I realised she had directed the question at me.

'Ummm. . .' I glanced at Guppy. This was the question I had been dreading. What did we think he was going to do?

'Well,' I said, my mind racing, 'a friend of ours at Ilakaye told us that he still had some influence, that people still . . . look up to him, and that maybe he might be able to raise public awareness of the problem.' I watched her face and held my breath. A slight smile curled in the corner of her mouth.

'Yes,' she said, 'that is something he might be able to do.' And I realised that the question had been a test, one it seemed I had passed. 'Sometimes the authorities can be slow to act on some matters. But these are strong accusations. I will need proof. Bring me some proof and I will see what I can do.'

And before I had time to take in what she had said, she rose, shook our hands and slipped back through the door, leaving us standing by the sofa, engulfed by Gunter's bellowing laughter.

⊞◉⊡

The truck hit a pothole, jerking me off the box and onto the flatbed. I slammed my fist into the back of the cabin and heard Guppy's 'Sorry!' fly past my ear on the wind. He still hadn't quite mastered the truck.

We pulled up alongside the entrance to the market. I hopped over the side and unloaded the two boxes of carvings for the Ilakaye shop, listening to Guppy's mumblings as he tried to get the handbrake to stay on. Eventually, he stumbled out of the cab and I pushed a box into his arms.

'Come on,' I said, and we headed into the market.

'Yejide thinks this would be a good time to tell Joseph the news.' Guppy's words came out in a rush, and I could hear him trotting along behind me, his breathing quick, like a child on his way to a party.

'I know she does, but he might have left.'

'Oh, I think he'll still be there.'

Yes, he probably will be, I thought. I would have to tell him that a man he regarded as having no place in a modern Sengharia wanted to help. I knew what his reaction would be.

'And he can be the proof,' continued Guppy. 'The proof Mrs Bath wants. He'd be able to give evidence about Danlami's activities in Port Rose.'

'I suppose so,' I said. The fear I had felt about taking the problem to the Oba had faded. I had done my bit; it was up to Joseph now.

We turned the corner to the Ilakaye stall and Joshua greeted us with a wave. Joseph stood next to him.

'Ah, well done,' said Joseph as we heaved our boxes onto the stall. 'These should go down well with the afternoon trade.'

We helped Joseph and Joshua to unpack the paintings and carvings, arranging them across the rough wooden planks. Guppy was trying to catch my eye, but I kept my concentration on the work until a kick in the ankle told me I could no longer avoid it.

'Joseph.'

'Yes, Charlie?'

'There's something I'd like to discuss with you – well, that Guppy and I would like to discuss with you.'

'Yes. . .?'

'It's about Danlami. We've heard that he's trying to take the land, to have Ilakaye closed down.'

'Yes,' said Joseph, as if I had made some comment on the weather.

I blurted out the story of the Oba. Trying to emphasise how he could help, Guppy chipping in occasionally to reinforce a point or clarify a detail. When I finished Joseph nodded thoughtfully, a soft smile on his face.

'I see you know some interesting people, Charlie, and I have no doubt that you are acting with the best intentions. But I must ask you – no, I insist – that you do not pursue this matter any further.' I could feel Guppy's sigh. 'And I will tell you why,' he continued. 'I have battled, all my adult life to bring the rule of law to all I see and do, to all aspects of my life and my work. The Oba operates outside that law. It clings to a sense of power that was lost to his title decades ago. You are fighting corruption with illegality. . .'

'But. . .' Guppy started.

Joseph held up his hand. 'Thank you for your concern. But you will not go any further if you wish to continue your work with me.' And he returned to the box he was unpacking, his face turned away from Guppy's shattered expression.

We walked back towards the truck without speaking. I led the way, not wanting to have to look at Guppy, to see his expression. My foot hit a stone and I lost my balance, stumbling forward and landing on my face in the middle of the track. The traffic in the alleyway didn't flinch; the people rushed past me on either side, one man stepping over me to get to the stall he wanted. I pushed myself up onto my knees and almost immediately felt hands grip me underneath my arms, pulling me too my feet.

'Are you all right?' asked Guppy, brushing dust from the front of my shirt.

'Fine. Thanks.'

He nodded and walked on. I followed behind him, realising that I had never had a friend like him, that it was only since coming to Ilakaye that I had seen him clearly, as if the Guppy at school had been nothing more than a blurred image, a reflection in the mirror of my own ignorance.

Perhaps it was the stoop in his shoulders, the way his shoes scuffed through the dust as he limped through the crowd. Perhaps it was the image of Yejide's face outside the gates of Ilakaye and what she had said to me: *You are a good man. I know you are.* But I had not supported her as much as I could have done – not in my heart, at least, which was, perhaps, the greater betrayal. I stopped a few feet away from the truck and, calling to Guppy, said things I would never have said even an hour before.

'Danlami's going to get what he wants – he has so much influence.'

Guppy nodded.

'We need to get that evidence for the Oba.'

'I do not see how.'

'I think I do.'

'Tell me.'

CHAPTER 15

Norman sat in the chair behind his desk, a wad of dollars running through his fingers and beads of sweat oozing from between the wrinkles in his forehead, squeezed out by his concentration.

'I'd like to borrow the video camera,' I said.

He didn't move.

I coughed, and raised my voice a little. 'I'd like to borrow the video camera.'

He flicked his wrist towards me as if shooing a fly, his head twitching a little to the right. 'Only tapes. You borrow a tape.'

I stood and stared at him, watching the constant movement of his lips as he counted his money.

'Four hundred and fifty eight. . .' I sang.

His fingers jerked, then stumbled, like the legs of a tripped sprinter. 'What you want!' he shouted, slamming the stack of notes down on his desk.

'I want to borrow. . .'

'Only tapes! You no borrow camera. Very expensive, brand new, only one in Ilaju. You don't want a tape? Go home.'

'OK,' I said, shrugging my shoulders and trying to sound as casual as possible. 'I'll go and tell Mrs Bath you didn't want to help.' His face sagged. 'Oh, didn't I mention, she popped round yesterday to visit my mother. She's got a big party on and everyone's heard that you've got one of these new cameras. She thought it would be fun to film the party. I volunteered to come down and ask you. She was *so sure* you wouldn't mind. . .' And I couldn't help but smile as he heaved himself out of his chair and waddled into the back room.

⊟◉▢

'I can get through there,' whispered Guppy.

I swatted a mosquito on my cheek, feeling it smear across my skin, and peered up through the gloom of the night at the window above the vestry door. It was ajar, but only just. 'Are you sure? It's only about a foot square,' I hissed. 'If you get stuck, we're screwed.'

'I can get through there.'

I peered round the side of the church to the road beyond. It was deserted, the spill from the lights of Ilakaye washing it a dull orange. There was a shout and a reply but they seemed far off, perhaps from the market.

'OK,' I said. 'Let's go.' I backed up to the wall and, making a cradle with my hands, nodded at Guppy. He planted his foot and I grunted as he kicked himself up, my arms taking his full weight. Then the pressure slackened and his feet moved to my shoulders.

'All right?'

'Just a minute. I need to try and get in backwards.' The sole of his shoe twisted painfully on my shoulder and then was gone. I moved quickly away from the church wall and watched as he squirmed his way through. I heard a thud that seemed to echo through the night and I glanced around the wall again, scanning the road; but there was no one. Then the door opened and I stepped into Danlami's church.

'Told you I could get through,' beamed Guppy.

We moved silently through the vestry, my nostrils full of the ancient smell that seems to be reserved for old churches and forgotten cellars. The air was like a blanket and I felt the sweat beginning to creep down my face, the tension clawing its way across my skin.

I pushed aside the curtains that led to the church proper and peered around, searching, letting my eyes become accustomed to the light. Suddenly Guppy cried out, and I wheeled around as he backed into me.

'What is it?' I gasped, grabbing his arm and preparing to run.

'Nothing. I just. . .' and he pointed across the vestry. Danlami's robes hung against the far wall, the sleeves jutting out, a spectral figure against the dark plaster.

'For Christ's sake. . .'

'Sorry, Charlie.'

We continued past the curtains and out through the rows of pews, our footsteps like taps on a stone coffin. There must be somewhere. . . I thought.

Guppy spotted it. An alcove set above the main entrance, almost invisible in the semi-dark. It was Guppy's turn to be the ladder and I scurried up quickly, heaving myself over the wall and onto the unfinished floor. It was small, but big enough, about eight feet deep and six feet wide, the outline of a bricked-up door still visible on the right-hand wall; the stairs that must have fed it had vanished. I wondered what it had been for. I turned and faced the church: there was a clear view of the pews and the altar beyond, the wall at the front of the alcove providing cover.

I waved down at Guppy. 'It's perfect.'

◫◉◿

I tilted my hat further back on my head to catch the burn of the sun and took a swig of water. Cupping my hand, I poured a little in and rubbed it like an ointment over the back of my neck. 'Come on, you bastard,' I muttered.

'He will be here,' said Guppy. 'I am sure of it. I have been keeping a very close eye on that place. It's this time every week.'

I shifted my position a little on the workshop roof, trying to ease the growing numbness in my backside.

'There!' exclaimed Guppy. And, coming quickly down the road, gliding on a sea of dust, was Danlami's Mercedes.

'The driver always comes the day before,' explained Guppy. 'He goes into the church for a while and then goes off again. I suppose he checks to make sure everything is ready.'

The Mercedes came to a halt outside the church and Danlami's driver lumbered out. But he didn't make for the door. He stood by the car, his feet shuffling on the road and his head turning left and right. He pulled out a handkerchief and mopped his brow with a trembling hand.

'What's he doing?' I asked.

He backed slowly towards the rear door and, continuing to scan the empty road, opened it, paused for a moment and then ducked inside, emerging with a white cloth bundle in his hands. He walked quickly towards Ilakaye and vanished from view behind the wall in front of the drop-box. Even before he re-emerged, I realised what he was doing.

'Go! Go!' yelled Guppy, and we slid down the ladder and started sprinting towards the gates, with Guppy shouting for Joseph. Out of the corner of my eye I saw Mairead emerge from the orphanage and I jabbed my finger towards the wall, already too breathless to speak. Guppy stopped at the drop box but I hit the gates at a run, ignoring the pain that shot up my arms as I punched them open with my palms and flew out onto the street.

But the car was gone; a fading copper cloud at the bottom of the road.

▣◉▢

We buried the child that evening in a small plot behind the orphanage. He had been dead for perhaps a day, the doctor said: dehydration.

All of Ilakaye was there, crowded around the hole in the ground, watching as the men lowered the tiny coffin, shadows staining the wood as black as the earth. The child's mother stood opposite me, the one who had sold him for a handful of dollars and a bottle of gin, two attendants from the secure compound supporting her slumped frame. She looked up occasionally, her dead eyes blinking at the crowd as if unsure why she was there.

Two men stood on either side of the grave, the ropes between their hands as they rhythmically lowered the coffin, pausing with each movement to chant a few lines before continuing. I tried to listen but the words held no meaning for me, drifting past like the tears of the wind. With each drop of the little wooden box, I felt a stab at my soul. How could we have thought we could beat this man? The plan with the video camera seemed so trite now, our efforts futile, the hole left in a glass of water.

Closing my eyes, I saw two boys in school uniform, their bodies tossed into the air on the Ibarajo Road; I saw Joseph's face as the mob dragged him away,

Danlami with a tyre in his hand; my sister laughing in the rain. And I wanted to run; to hide behind guarded steel gates and razor wire, to go back to where I had started.

Yejide's hand slipped into mine, and my eyes flickered open. The crowd was dispersing and I could hear the thick thuds from the clods of earth as they knocked on the top of the coffin.

'Come on,' she whispered, and began to lead me away. Guppy stood staring at the grave, but I did not know what to say to him. We walked in silence to her room, and I slumped onto the bed. She closed the door and took a seat next to me, her hand resting on my thigh.

'Joseph has filed a police report,' she said, her voice barely above a whisper. 'They said they would come tomorrow.'

'That's good.'

'You'll probably have to talk to them.'

'Of course.' My voice trailed away and we sat in a dark silence. A gust of wind pushed through the window and the bare bulb hanging from the ceiling began to sway. I reached into my pocket and pulled out the flowered handkerchief, crumpled and dirty.

'I found this in the tip. It belonged to the boy.

I don't know why I kept it.' Her hand tightened on my leg. 'I wonder where he is now. Far from home, in a stranger's house asking for his mother? Or maybe there's a grave for him too. . .'

'We'll stop it. I know we will. I know we left him, and it was the only thing to do, I'm sure of that. But I won't leave another one. Not ever again.'

I watched the bulb for a moment, back and forth, like a pendulum brushing away the time, and then turned and looked her in the eye. 'Before I came here I thought I could anything. I used to do all those stupid things – you know, racing cars, running around on rooftops, thinking I was brave. But I'm not. I'm afraid, Yejide. I'm always afraid. Since I came to Ilakaye, I can't remember a time that I wasn't.' I stopped and turned my head away, not wanting her to see the tears in my eyes. 'But Guppy isn't. And you're not. It makes me. . .'

'It's all right to be afraid. And you're wrong: I'm afraid too. It nearly happened to me, Charlie – Danlami nearly took me. And now he's back. Sometimes I feel like he's come back for me. I can't sleep.'

I put my arm around her, knowing there was nothing I could say, and we lay down on the bed, holding each other, listening to the sounds of the night.

The police didn't come the next morning, and by lunchtime there was still no sign of them. Guppy was pestering Mairead every hour and always got the same answer: Joseph has been in touch with them, I'm sure they'll be here soon. At four o'clock Guppy emerged from the orphanage and sat down next to me on the steps, shaking his head.

'She said the same thing,' he sighed.

'I thought she would,' I said. 'You know, there's one thing I don't understand: why did he bring the child back here? Why didn't he just dump it somewhere?' My mind was clearer now, Yejide's comfort had beaten back the despair and my resolve was beginning to strengthen. I wasn't going to let this bastard beat me.

'I have been thinking the same thing,' nodded Guppy. 'He looked afraid to me. Perhaps he thought we could help. Perhaps he was hoping the child was not dead.'

'Too bad,' I said.

The door to Joseph's office opened and he came out. Guppy and I sprang up and ran to intercept him.

'Is there any news from the police?' asked Guppy.

Joseph looked at us for a moment and I could see

the bags under his eyes, the weight in his shoulders. 'I am afraid not. They are very busy and assure me that they will send someone down at the earliest opportunity.'

'Danlami bribes the police,' I said.

'I am aware of that. But we must use the system. It is the only way. He cannot bribe all of them. Our news will get to the right ears eventually.'

'He doesn't need to bribe all of them,' exclaimed Guppy, 'just the right one.'

A flash of anger streaked across Joseph's face and he straightened himself up. 'I am doing all I can. I am in contact with an Inspector Adan, and I have no doubt of his honesty. He is also helping me with Danlami's claim on Ilakaye. Now, was there anything else?'

'No.'

'Then you will excuse me.' And he strode away towards the workshops.

I watched him go for a moment, knowing what I was going to do, and it felt like a betrayal of everything he believed in, everything he was trying to achieve at Ilakaye. Danlami has left us no choice, it has to be done, I told myself. Joseph's way will not work, there isn't time.

I turned to Guppy, 'Do you still think Danlami will come this evening?'

'Oh, yes. I don't think he will let a dead child get in the way. He'll be here.'

'Are you ready?'

'Yes.' And we walked off to find Yejide.

▣◎▫

Guppy scurried through the window and opened the door for us. We had brought a short ladder from the workshops to help us get into the alcove and we wasted no time in moving through the church.

I hurried up the ladder as fast as I could with the camera on my back and pulled it up behind me, praying it couldn't be seen from below. Guppy assembled the tripod and secured the camera in place, checking the viewfinder to ensure that it took in the whole of the altar area.

We saw the problem. The camera took up far too much space; there would not be room for all of us.

'I'll wait downstairs,' said Yejide.

'Forget it,' I replied. 'There's nowhere to hide down there.'

'There's a broken pew in the back corner pushed

up against the wall. I can hide there; no one will see me. Besides, someone might need to get out quickly and call for help if. . .' She didn't need to finish. I knew what Danlami was capable of, what his men were capable of, and the thought of leaving Yejide down below was nauseating, but at least she would have a chance to run. We had no way out of the alcove.

She kissed me. Guppy turned his reddening face away and climbed down the ladder. I watched as she slipped between the broken pew and the wall, turned and waved, then vanished from sight.

'She'll be OK,' said Guppy. 'Don't worry. We should try and get comfortable.'

Even with Yejide gone, there was only just enough room for us to sit with the camera in the middle and Guppy and me on either side. Almost as soon as we had settled, I heard the sound of a car pulling up outside. A door opened and closed and there were footsteps on the gravel.

I took a deep breath and looked over at Guppy, my friend. He smiled at me, and I managed a broken grin back, my mind distracted by the thought of Yejide below. It will be OK, I told myself. She'll be OK. And with a shaking hand I reached up and pressed *Record*.

CHAPTER 16

One of the men was shouting. They must have stopped just inside the front door, their voices muffled below the alcove. I shot a questioning look at Guppy, but he shrugged his shoulders and pointed at his ear.

'You fool!' The words ricocheted off the walls of the church and shot into the alcove. I jerked backwards and my head cracked against the wall; there was no mistaking Danlami's voice. The men had moved out from under the alcove, their footsteps echoing through the church, and I guessed that they had stopped at the altar. I braced myself, trying to make no sound, but my heart sounded like raps on a wooden door and my breath the sighs of a congregation.

'Your mess is costing me a fortune!' continued Danlami. 'Adan is charging even more now that Ilakaye wants an investigation into that child.'

Guppy's eyes flashed with anger at the police

inspector's name and he glanced up at the camera. The red light was glowing; it should be getting everything.

'*Mo tọrọ àforíjì*. I thought it would be better this way.' The other man's voice sounded like a boy at confession, and I guessed it must be the driver.

'You're sorry. . .?' spat Danlami. And with a shriek I heard the stinging echo of skin striking skin, followed by a hollow grunt. 'The other child had better be here on time or big *wahala* for you.'

'He will come, *oga*, he will come,' pleaded the second man. And their steps faded into the vestry.

My body relaxed and I saw that Guppy was smiling. As slowly as I could I reached up and switched off the video. We would need plenty of battery for the main event. We shifted ourselves around as best we could, trying to get comfortable, and settled down to wait.

The heat grew and I longed to stretch. The urge to look over the wall of the alcove to check on Yejide clawed through me. But I knew I couldn't. They could come back at any moment. The dust and fallen plaster congealed with the sweat and stuck to my legs and arms like putty. The hum of the mosquitoes crisscrossed past my ears, and the wall was a constant pressure on my back.

I tried shifting my back against the wall, but whichever position I tried was painful.

'Where is he!?' It was Danlami again.

'He will be here, *oga*,' came the reply.

'We are running out of time, I need the child for the service tomorrow.'

It took a second for what Danlami had said to sink in – tomorrow. We had the wrong day. My body tensed with anger, Guppy stared into space in disbelief, his face tight with frustration.

'Come,' commanded Danlami, 'let's go.'

All at once the creak of the door filled the church, followed by the whimpering of a baby.

'You are late!' roared Danlami. The reply was lost in the baby's cries. I pressed the Record button on the camera and strained to hear what they were saying, but the baby's distress filled the air masking all other sounds, a desperate hymn in a forsaken church. Then the men's voices grew louder. They seemed to be arguing about money; whoever had brought the child was obviously not satisfied with what he had got. Someone said three thousand, and it was Danlami who laughed; then another figure was proposed and the haggling started.

Occasional words and phrases rose above the din:

'very healthy' . . . 'beautiful daughter' . . . 'boys more valuable' . . . 'agreed price' . . . 'trouble to find'. . . and suddenly I recognised the other voice: it was the man from the rubbish tip. My breath caught in my throat. Yejide lay only a few feet away. My hands began to shake and fresh beads of sweat trickled down my face. I pulled out my handkerchief and wiped it across my forehead, staining the printed flowers with the sweat, then gripped it tight, murmuring to myself, 'She'll be OK, she'll be OK.'

Eventually the voices stopped and I heard the door open, but the child still screamed somewhere below. Relief poured over me. They were gone, and we wouldn't have to come back. If the camera had caught the sale, we didn't need to film a service. We had him. I looked over at Guppy, and the smile on my face vanished in an instant. He was crouching with one hand on the camera, peering over the wall.

'Get down!' I hissed, and made a grab for him, my hand knocking against the tripod of the camera. It wobbled and began to tilt forward, I tried to reach for it but I was off balance. It hit my head and I waited for the crash below.

It never came.

I looked up and saw Guppy standing over me,

the camera securely in his hands.

'Are you all right?' Yejide's whisper drifted into the alcove and with an effort I scrambled to my feet;. One of my legs had gone numb and for a moment I thought I might topple over the edge. I steadied myself against the wall and looked down. Yejide stood below us, one side of her body caked in dust.

'What are you doing. . .!'

'Relax, Charlie. They've gone,' said Yejide.

'But the baby. . .?'

'Take a look.'

The baby lay on the altar, a screaming parcel of rags. There was no sign of Danlami or the others.

'I'm getting the child,' stated Yejide.

'Wait! They'll be back any minute,' I pleaded. 'They're not just going to leave it there for the night.'

She turned and looked up at me. But there was no arguing with the look that met my words. 'Just wait a moment for us. Guppy, pack up the camera.'

I shinned down the ladder as fast as I could, but my leg still protested, and I half-slid, half-fell, down the final rungs. I looked up at Guppy. He had the camera in the bag, but struggled with the tripod. One of the legs seemed to have jammed. My eyes swept the church, my ears catching the slightest sound.

'I'm going for the child now,' said Yejide.

'Wait!' Guppy finally managed to cram the tripod into the bag, slung it over his shoulder and began to climb down. Come on, come on, the words pounded through my head. He reached the ground and dropped the bag by the archway, then went back for the ladder.

'Leave it!' I said, not bothering to whisper any more. 'Get the bag.' Guppy obeyed. 'OK, let's go.' Yejide tore down the aisle and scooped up the baby from the altar, with Guppy and me limping along behind.

'Go through the vestry,' I called, sure that they must be out at the front. Yejide nodded, but no sooner had she turned, than Danlami strode out from between the curtains, followed by his driver.

Everybody froze, and a moment of complete stillness cut into the church as Danlami realised what he was seeing.

'Run!' I yelled, and Yejide turned and sprinted back down the aisle. She had only made a few steps when her body flew backwards, and she slid, clutching the baby to her chest, across the floor to the altar. She let out a cry of pain and Danlami let her go, turning to face me. I didn't think, I didn't hesitate, I reacted on pure impulse. With a cry, I drew back my fist and leapt forward: four months of manual labour and twelve stone hit Danlami square in the face. He staggered backwards, tripped over Yejide and his head struck the altar with a crack. He slumped to the floor and lay still.

My eyes moved immediately to Yejide, and by the time I realised that the driver had moved towards me, it was too late. His punch caught me in the chest like a sledgehammer and I felt my feet leave the floor before my back hit the ground. For a moment I lay there clutching my chest and gasping for breath. Guppy cried out, and I looked up to see the driver pinning him against one of the pillars, holding him there as if he were made of paper, his fist raised. I looked around for a weapon, but my chest was in agony and I had trouble focusing.

Then Yejide spoke:

'Help us.' It was a request, and her voice eased through the violence in the air. 'You brought the baby back, you brought the other one back to Ilakaye. Help this one.'

I heaved myself up off the floor and the driver's head snapped round, sensing a threat. I held up my hands and took half a step backwards.

'Help us. . .' Yejide continued.

'*You dey craze!*' shouted the driver. 'I never bring a child there!'

'Yes, you did. You tried to help him.'

The driver stared at her, but didn't move. I looked at Guppy, his face twisted in pain, but knew I could do nothing. The baby's cries began to weaken as Yejide rocked it in her arms.

'The baby,' said the driver, 'the first one . . . did he live?'

Yejide shook her head. He continued to stare at her before turning his attention to Danlami, who was beginning to stir at the foot of the altar. A bead of sweat clung to the driver's chin and broke on the floor below. Then his shoulders slumped, he dropped his fist, released Guppy and took a step backwards.

'Go,' he murmured. We wasted no time.

▣◎▢

'Oh, don't be such a baby,' said Mairead, as I flinched and inhaled sharply. 'They're not broken.' I looked down at my blackened knuckles, and despite Mairead's pinching and prodding, I couldn't help allowing myself a proud grin.

The baby lay on a table at the other side of

the orphanage, next to the sheet of polythene that separated it from the unfinished extension. Yejide and one of the nurses were examining it, nodding and smiling. Guppy stood next to them, a collar of bruises around his throat, unable to tear his eyes from the baby girl's face. She reached out a tiny hand and gripped his little finger. Guppy turned to me, his eyes a tangle of emotions; he looked fit to burst.

'Any other injuries I should know about?' Mairead demanded.

'My chest hurts a bit.'

'Let's have a look, then.'

It was a struggle, but eventually I managed to get the sweat-soaked T-shirt over my head.

'Mother of God. . .' she said, in an exasperated sigh. A deep purple bruise, like a stain, spread across my lower chest. Mairead's fingers were already jabbing at it, checking for broken ribs.

'How's the baby?' I called over.

'She seems in good health. I'd say, about . . . eight months old?' replied Yejide, directing her question at the nurse, who nodded agreement.

'She needs a name,' said Guppy. 'We must give her a name.'

'Any idea—S?' My second word hit soprano pitch

233

as Mairead made a particularly searching prod.

'Kambiri,' offered Yejide. 'I think that would suit her nicely.'

'What does it mean?' asked Guppy.

'May I join this family?'

'Yes,' said Guppy, his face alight. 'Yes on both counts. May I pick her up?'

Yejide and the nurse exchanged looks. 'Of course, Guppy. If you want to.'

Guppy bent down and scooped her up, drawing her to his chest as if she was made of crystal. 'Hello, Kambiri my name's...' He hesitated, and for a moment I thought he was going to tell her his real name, but he smiled and said, 'Guppy. Everybody calls me Guppy. I can't wait to show you around.'

Kambiri giggled, and pushed a finger up his nose.

I couldn't help but laugh. My head spun, the adrenalin still pumping. We had done it. We had the evidence we needed for the Oba. Danlami would be finished. Joseph, however, was not going to be happy. The thought cleared my head. Would he hold to his threat and stop us from working here? But then, he didn't yet know about Adan's betrayal.

'There,' announced Mairead. 'There doesn't seem to be anything seriously wrong. You'll be sore for a while, though. Ah! Here comes Joseph.'

I looked out of the window and saw him walking purposefully towards the orphanage. Mairead sighed. 'I think you three will have some explaining to do.' And she headed out to meet him.

Yejide looked at me and shrugged, seemingly unperturbed. Guppy was so caught up with Kambiri, I don't think he even heard what Mairead had said. But I worried. If I couldn't come back here, where would I go?

'Well, it looks like—' I never finished my sentence. A crash splintered the calm of the orphanage, and looking out, I saw Danlami erupt through the gates. I got up as quickly as my ribs would allow and headed for the door. Yejide beat me to it and was halfway towards Joseph before I had got down the steps.

'You!' bellowed Danlami, his index finger inches from Joseph's nose. 'You have robbed me!'

'You are quite mistaken—' began Joseph.

'Liar!' And turning, he saw Yejide and me heading towards him. 'Here they are, the ones you sent to attack and rob me!' As I grew closer, I saw with some satisfaction that his upper lip was badly swollen, he had cotton wool up one nostril and a makeshift bandage on the back of his head. I looked around for the driver. He stood by the gates, his eyes fixed firmly on the ground.

'Rob you?' asked Joseph. 'Of what?'

Danlami made no reply, his face twisted with rage.

'I can assure you that these two have been in the compound with me all day.' Both Mairead and Yejide shot glances at Joseph. Even Danlami seemed surprised by this blatant lie. He leaned in towards Joseph, his voice lowered.

'We will see. Tomorrow I will return with the police. I will take your land. I will expel all the beggars and lepers, and put it to good use. I have Inspector Adan's word that there will not be a problem with the handover.'

Joseph seemed to rock slightly on his heels at the mention of the policeman's name – a name he had put all his faith in.

Danlami smiled, seeming to sense Joseph's reaction. 'Oh, yes. He is very much in favour of what I'm doing. I will see you all tomorrow, when I take back what is mine.' And he turned on his heel and left.

Nobody spoke for a while. Joseph stared after Danlami, a winter expression weathering his face.

'We have evidence,' said Yejide eventually. 'We can stop him before tomorrow.'

'Adan. . .' whispered Joseph. 'I cannot believe it. Of all the people. . .'

'It's true,' I offered. 'We heard Danlami talking about him in the church. But Yejide's right. We have the evidence we need.'

'No,' said Joseph, shaking his head.

'But—'

'It is not . . . the way . . . I WANTED!' His fury shocked me, engulfing the air, and Yejide stumbled back half a step.

Mairead put her hand on his shoulder. 'It's too late now,' she murmured. Joseph looked up at her, then turned his gaze around the compound. Joshua was heading towards us and Abacha and Adebayo emerged from the workshops, drawn by Danlami's appearance. The nurse appeared at the door of the orphanage, holding Kambiri, and in the distance the dinner bell sounded.

I looked at Joseph. His whole body seemed to droop, as if being slowly pulled into the clay under his feet.

'Joseph. . .' whispered Yejide, a tear running down her cheek.

He turned to her and raised his hand, his fingertips touching her cheek, brushing away the tear, and he smiled. But it was a smile filled with sorrow. 'Do it,' he said, his voice barely audible. And he shuffled off towards his office, pausing at the steps to steady himself on the handrail, before vanishing inside.

CHAPTER 17

Guppy drummed his fingers against the glass top of Gunter's patio table and stared out across the floodlit lawn. Gunter's Dobermann patrolled the perimeter, his sleek body dissolving into shadow, only his eyes visible, glowing like reflections of the moon.

'I wonder why he asked us to wait outside.' Guppy's face was sweat-streaked and there was a tear in his grime-laden T-shirt.

'I think it's because we stink, Guppy.'

'Ah.'

His eyes moved to the patio doors. They revealed nothing but the dim outline of furniture patterned by our reflections.

'Do you think she's watching it?'

'I hope so.' I picked a bug out of my Coke, drawing it slowly up the side of the glass before flicking it away in a spray of froth.

'She's watching it. She would not ask us to wait so long if she wasn't.' He studied his face in the doors for a moment before returning his attention to the lawn.

We sat in silence, alone with our thoughts. I battled an irrational sense of guilt. Joseph's shout of fury still echoed and I wanted to talk to him, let him understand why we had done what we had done, apologise.

'It had to be done – even Joseph agreed in the end,' said Guppy, his eyes studying me closely. I nodded.

'More drinks.' The bottles clinked down on the table. Gunter had approached without a sound. 'I hope you don't mind sitting outside, but I thought as it was such a lovely night. . .'

'That's just what Charlie was saying.'

'Excellent.' Gunter pushed the bottles towards us and I poured mine immediately.

'I have been watching your film,' continued Gunter, and Guppy sat bolt upright. 'It makes interesting viewing. Although you could have found a better camera angle.' He attempted a laugh, but it sounded more like a cough. He shifted in his seat and I noticed there were beads of sweat on his forehead and upper lip, but he had just come out from the air conditioning.

'And your wife?' pushed Guppy. 'Your wife has watched it?'

Gunter ran the back of his thumb across his forehead. 'She is watching it again as we speak. I must confess I didn't expect you two to take such . . . *strong* measures to get what you wanted. You have opened a big can of worms here.'

'But will she show it to the Oba?' asked Guppy.

'From what you said earlier there is no time for that. Be patient. She will let you know what she can do.'

We lapsed into silence again and I took another long swig from my glass.

'Why did you decide to stay in Africa, Gunter?'

Gunter beamed, apparently glad to have something else to talk about.

'Ah! That's an easy one, but not to put into words.' And we watched as he stripped off one sock and shoe, strode out onto the lawn and then turned, his arms wide, and faced his audience.

'I knew where I should be when I did this,' and he rubbed his bare foot into the ground. 'Then you know. You can feel it. It's in the earth waiting for you.'

I looked at him as if he was cracked, but Guppy sat fascinated, and Gunter smiled at him.

'You understand,' he said to him. 'I can see it in your eyes.'

But in an instant Gunter's smile was gone, and I followed his eyes to the doors behind me. 'I think you have the news you've been waiting for.' And he strode quickly towards the doors, opened them a crack and slipped inside.

We watched as Gunter and his wife talked.

'What are they saying?' whispered Guppy. He couldn't take his eyes off them.

I finished my Coke and watched the Dobermann. He had spotted a lizard, and stood, motionless, studying it. And then he sprang, snatching it up in his jaws, before trotting over to some bushes and spitting it out.

'Here he comes,' said Guppy, and I turned to see Gunter stride out onto the patio. Guppy jumped to his feet. Gunter stepped to one side to allow Mrs Bath to enter the night.

'Please sit down, Guppy,' she said, and he lowered himself back into his seat.

'You have done a good thing to bring this to my attention, a very good thing. What Danlami has been doing is terrible.'

Guppy moved as if to speak.

'You risked a great deal to catch this man, and

he needed to be caught. Although,' she added, 'I would prefer it if you did not use my name to acquire video cameras.' A light remark, but there was a sting in her words. She went on, 'When people bring this sort of behaviour to our attention, it is only right that something must be done.'

Gunter tried to muffle a cough, turning his head away.

'You have been strong enough to find the evidence. I hope that you will be strong enough to bear its consequences. When the Oba acts, it is with the justice of the people. Not everyone understands this. I want you to understand it. Do you?'

Guppy didn't move. 'I think so,' I said. But I didn't.

'You will. I have spoken to my uncle. Danlami will not be able to take over Ilakaye.'

The words seemed to settle over me, touching but not quite penetrating.

'We have also received a request regarding this man. An unusual one, and we have agreed.'

'From whom?' asked Guppy. 'What was it?'

'I do not think it matters. I only hope that tomorrow you find it is indeed what you wanted. What you expected.' A smile touched her lips, but it was distant, fogged, like a harmattan moon. 'Good luck to you both. Remember tonight.' And she turned, her silk robe drifting around her, and walked back into the house.

I looked at Guppy: his head dropped, and I felt the same sudden, overpowering tiredness. We had done it. I should be shouting, cheering, but suddenly my chest ached and the pain in my knuckles seemed to grow. Guppy picked up his glass, but put it down again without taking a sip. I wanted to say something, but it was an effort to hold my head up.

'It is getting late,' said Gunter. 'You should be off. Good luck tomorrow.' And he followed his wife back into the house, shutting the doors firmly behind him.

I'm not sure how long we sat there. Eventually Guppy reached out and put his hand on my shoulder. Our eyes met and we both began to smile, some of the fatigue lifting as the news began to sink in.

'Well done.'

'You too.'

'Come on.' And we dragged ourselves up from our chairs, skirted the patio and headed down the drive. At the gates, I stopped and looked back. Mrs Bath stood, silhouetted in the window, watching us. Then she turned and merged with the shadows of the house.

Joseph had not left his office all morning. None of us could work. News of Danlami's announcement about taking over Ilakaye had spread rapidly and pockets of people stood scattered around the compound, their chatter clouding the air. Only Adebayo seemed unperturbed: he sat in the workshop, his paintbrush caressing a new canvas. I sat behind him and watched. It was cool and quiet and I was glad to be away from the crowds outside. Guppy's inability to settle had driven everyone to exasperation, until he had finally gone off to play with with Kambiri.

Yejide appeared in the doorway and I smiled. She walked over and sat down next to me, her hand finding mine, her head resting on my shoulder. There was no need to talk.

We both watched as the face of a child, a *pikin*, began to flow from Adebayo's brush. It was a girl, and her eyes glistened with laughter. My hand tightened around Yejide's and I felt the pressure returned. Turning my head I kissed her lightly, and for one perfect moment the world stood still.

There were three bangs on the gate, and Yejide rose immediately.

'*Wahala dun come,*' said Adebayo, his eyes never leaving his work. I stood up and followed Yejide out into the piercing heat of the sun.

Mairead walked towards the gate and held her chin an inch higher than normal. She reached the gates and pulled one wide open, stepping aside and sweeping her hand out towards the compound.

A police officer walked through, the compound captured in his mirror glasses, and the sun glistened off a belt buckle that strained to contain his paunch. He nodded to Mairead, pinching the rim of his hat and smiling, but there was no warmth in it, only danger.

Adan, I thought.

Guppy appeared at the orphanage door and walked slowly down the steps, stopping at the bottom and running his hand over his face.

Adan stepped to one side and three more policemen walked through, automatic rifles slung over their shoulders and military-style berets stuck to their heads.

'Where is Joseph?' enquired Adan. 'I need to speak with him.'

The door of Joseph's office opened and he walked out. He had put on a tie, the knot half-hidden under his right collar. 'Good morning, Inspector Adan,' he said.

Adan extended his hand; Joseph crossed his behind his back. They stared at each other for a moment and Adan looked about to speak, when the second gate flew open and Danlami marched in, followed by his driver. Adan welcomed him with a nod.

Guppy took a step forward before turning to Yejide and me, his mouth wide with shock. My mind reeled. What was he doing here? I looked at Yejide, but she just shook her head, tears welling in the corner of her eyes.

Guppy walked towards us. 'I don't believe this. I. . .' But he couldn't find the words. And we stood, beaten, watching Danlami's sniper eyes sweep across the compound.

'I understand you already know Michael Danlami, Joseph,' said Adan.

'Yes.'

Danlami's eyes came to rest on the orphanage.

'And you are aware,' continued Adan, 'that he has questioned the legality of your lease on this land.'

'Yes.'

What had gone wrong? Where was the Oba?

Adan pulled a document from his breast pocket. He unfolded it with care, and studied the words written there. Then he looked up again at Joseph, his expression hidden behind his sunglasses.

'Just read it, you bastard,' mumbled Guppy.

'I have here the official report disputing any and all claims by Michael Danlami to this property. We can find no fault with your lease or with your activities here.'

Adan's words hung in the air, and I stared at him, not daring to believe what he had just said. The eruption of cheers from around the compound was deafening. Guppy jumped up and down, slapping me on the back. Yejide threw her arms around me, crying openly, and I picked her up, whirling her around, caught in the tide of relief and euphoria, cheering as loudly as anyone. I had never felt such excitement and I marvelled at the totality of the Oba's power. It seemed good, it seemed right; this was how things should be.

'WHAT?' Danlami's roar sliced through the joy of the crowd, and Adan turned to face him.

'I think my words were quite clear.'

'No. You have made a mistake. You . . . you work for me!' And Danlami took a step towards him. In one snap, the nearest policeman swung his rifle up, one leg slightly back, his right eye staring down the sights into Danlami's face. The silence was instant.

Danlami stopped in his tracks before stumbling

back a pace, his hands raised to chest height. 'I don't understand. . .'

'I think you should leave,' said Adan, each word the flick of a blade.

Danlami seemed lost, his attention jerking between Adan and Joseph. 'You have not heard the last of this,' he said. 'We had an agreement.' But his voice cracked, the rage now replaced by fear. He turned to his driver. 'Start the car.'

The driver looked at him for a moment before walking towards the policemen, where he stopped and turned to face Danlami, his arms crossed. Danlami stared at him in disbelief, but the policeman's gun was still drawn on him, and he didn't make any move towards the driver.

'Give me the keys, then.'

'I think you should walk,' said Adan.

Danlami looked at Joseph, his eyes filled with loathing, before turning and walking towards the gates.

'Wait.' Joseph's voice was soft, but there was a hint of urgency to his tone, almost a question, and Danlami stopped, hesitated, and then turned to face him. I let my hand drop from Yejide's and took a step forward. For a moment nobody spoke, and then Joseph turned to Adan: 'Thank you, Inspector, I think your work here is finished.'

Adan looked at him, the crease of a smile on his face. 'I know. If you want to delay, that is your business.' Then he pinched the rim of his hat and began to walk towards the gates.

'Stop, stop... What are you doing?' shouted Guppy, moving towards the spot where Joseph stood, his eyes locked on Danlami. 'You can't leave him here, you have to arrest him, you—'

'Quiet!' Joseph's shout stopped Guppy in his tracks. The policemen paid no attention, walked over to their car, climbed in and pulled quietly away, followed by Danlami's Mercedes and its new owner.

Guppy turned to me, bewilderment on his face. I had no idea what was going on; it made no sense to leave Danlami standing there. I glanced around the compound: everywhere people stood, still and staring, the happiness eclipsed by a grey uncertainty.

'What do you want?' asked Danlami, his eyes stained with contempt, but in the dark silence of the compound I could hear the tremor in his voice.

'To help you,' replied Joseph.

Danlami threw his head back and spat out a laugh. 'Help me, Joseph? I don't need your help.

I don't want your help.'

'Stay here.'

I couldn't believe what I was hearing. The man belonged in jail, not at Ilakaye, or anywhere near it, but the crowd in the compound showed no surprise at this offer.

Danlami just laughed and took a step towards Joseph. A murmur rippled across the crowd and I saw Abacha tense, but Danlami stopped and spread his arms wide. 'To stay with my old friend. Of course, how nice, thank you,' and he bowed his head, then snapped it back up and spat at Joseph's feet. 'I am not one of your paupers!'

'I could have had you arrested,' said Joseph.

'No. This is a minor setback. He was never going to arrest me and you know it.'

'Then you know what is waiting for you.' It was barely a whisper, but the words hit Danlami like rocks. His head jerked to the side, straining to see beyond the gates, but unwilling to take his eyes off Joseph. I looked out towards the church and saw a man in a faded red shirt leaning against the wall, his hands in his pockets, his eyes fixed on Danlami. And suddenly Yejide's hand gripped mine. 'Oh God,' she whispered, 'What have we done. . .?'

Tension poured through her hand into mine, fear in her eyes; it spread around the compound like a stench; something was terribly wrong.

'Joseph, I never would have thought . . . not you,' said Danlami.

'It is out of my hands now. Stay here, it is the only way.'

'Oh, Joseph,' said Danlami, with mocking disappointment, 'you are wrong.'

'Really? About what?'

'There's always more than one way.' A smile formed at the corner of his mouth, and then, with startling speed, he sprinted towards the orphanage.

The compound exploded with shouts and cries. Abacha's voice rang out as he sprinted after Danlami. Guppy ran after him, his fist raised, followed by Yejide; but I found I could not move. Beyond the gates, the man in the red shirt barked orders at a crowd that came flooding from behind the church. They carried sticks and rocks, a few carried knives, but one, bigger than the rest, held a tyre. And with a sudden, terrible clarity, I understood.

Someone crashed into me from behind, tearing my eyes from the road. In front of me I could see Danlami streaking across the courtyard. But he didn't stop at the orphanage; he raced past it and threw himself at the outer wall. His fingers found the top and he swung his legs over just before Abacha's hands found their grip, and vanished into the shadows beyond.

Outside I could hear the shouts of the mob and the ringing thump of wood on metal. Beyond the wall was a deserted and gated patch of land owned by the government. Danlami had chosen his spot well. A sudden crash told me that they had broken through the gates, followed by more shouts and cries, but angrier now, like an argument. Some voices remained, moving past me on the other side of the wall, while others became distant, heading down the road towards the market.

'Quickly,' shouted Abacha, 'They never find him. He jump the back wall. He will be in the streets now. We can catch him with the truck.'

'No!' it was Joseph. He stood staring at the wall Danlami had escaped over, 'No one is to leave the compound.' He spun his head around to ensure that everyone had heard. At his words, the noise began to die away, and Mairead barked instructions. Any sense of joy had dissolved in the cries of the mob, and people began to drift back to their work. Abacha looked at Joseph for a second, nodded and headed back towards the workshops.

Guppy leaned against the wall, his chest heaving. Yejide stood next to him, looking around at the dispersing crowd as if unsure of what to do.

'Charlie,' said Joseph, stopping me before I could say or do anything. 'Close the gates, please.' I nodded, and headed across the compound, feeling the weight in my legs and the sweat on my face, my mind numb.

When I reached the entrance, the man in the red shirt still stood by the church wall watching me. He waved his hand, and I instinctively jumped back as a truck skidded to a halt in front of him. He eased himself away from the wall, vaulted into the flatbed and thumped the roof. The tyres spun in the dust before catching, and I stood by the gates watching him go, held in his gaze until he faded from sight.

◻◉◻

We sat on the steps leading to Yejide's room. Overhead the sky darkened. Most people were at dinner. I couldn't remember Ilakaye being so quiet.

'He's gone,' said Guppy. 'That's the main thing.'

'That's true,' I said, as much to myself as to Guppy,

but I found no comfort in the words. I never imagined what they had planned for Danlami; Mrs Bath had tried to tell me, but I had not listened.

Guppy passed me the bottle of beer we were sharing and I took a swig, before handing it to Yejide. She lifted the bottle to her lips, and I saw her hand tremble slightly. We had spoken little of what had happened. I hadn't tried to talk to Joseph, none of us had; he had retreated to his office. I didn't understand why the mob had not just come into the compound and taken him. Perhaps they had been told not to, not to risk harming anyone else. Someone knew – Mrs Bath? The Oba? Perhaps even Joseph. But I couldn't ask him, I couldn't look into his eye and see the sadness above the scar.

'It wasn't our fault,' I said. 'We didn't know . . . something had to be done. . . He was selling children, for God's sake.' But the words evaporated into the air.

'Do you think they've caught him yet?' asked Guppy. It was a question that had haunted me for hours, and I looked at Yejide, but she turned her head away and brought the bottle up quickly to her lips.

The car horn cut through the dusk and I jumped at the sound. Guppy heaved himself off the steps and began to walk towards the gates where Samson sat waiting in the car. I moved to Yejide and touched her cheek, unsure of what to say. She managed a smile in return and I headed after Guppy.

I stopped at the point where Danlami had escaped and stared at the wall. The night had begun to thicken, the dark slipping down from the sky, staining the trees beyond. Somewhere, I knew, Danlami was hurrying through the gloom. And suddenly, desperately, I wanted him to run, to escape the howling mob and the petrol-soaked tyre – to give me peace.

CHAPTER 18

Guppy and I stopped outside the gates and looked over at the church. The signboard proclaiming it 'The Church of Christ the Child' lay splintered over the gravel. Someone had boarded up the windows; the planks of wood stretched across the glass like dirty bandages. It looked as if it had been abandoned for years.

'I wonder what will happen to it?' asked Guppy.

'I don't know. Maybe Mairead knows someone who can take it over.'

'That would be nice.' We stood and stared. 'Come on, let's go in now.'

Guppy headed straight for the orphanage roof where Abacha waited with the last few roofing sheets stacked beside him; Joshua swung out from the dormitory, and, jumping the steps in one, headed for the workshops; Adebayo shuffled towards the kitchens in search of breakfast; Mairead helped a man across the compound, a plastic kettle in her hand, a reed mat under her arm; through the window of his office I could see Joseph behind his desk, a document held close to his eyes. The sounds of the busy were everywhere.

I had expected a change, a scar in the air, something to mark the events of the last two days. But Kambiri's giggles as the nurse tickled her on the orphanage steps were the only sound that held any memory of what had happened. Ilakaye was as it had always been, and I found comfort in that. Danlami was gone and we could carry on.

I looked around, wondering where I should start. Guppy and Abacha would probably need help with the roof. There could be a collection of carvings waiting in the workshops for the market. It would be busy in the kitchens at this time. But then, I hadn't checked the drains around the secure compound for weeks.

'Charlie!' Yejide was walking towards me from the hospital. I'd forgotten how beautiful she was. She leaned up and kissed me on the cheek. 'Sleep well?'

'Not bad. You?'

'No, not really. Not at all, in fact.'

'Let's go off somewhere,' I suggested. 'You look

like you need to talk.'

'It'll have to wait. I'm going to get Guppy. Joseph wants to see us.' And she hurried over to the orphanage.

He wants to see if we are OK, I thought. But I wasn't sure what to say to him.

'I am extremely busy!' exclaimed Guppy.

'This is important, Guppy,' persisted Yejide. 'Joseph wants to see us.'

'Ah. . .'

He shinned down the ladder and I met them at the door to Joseph's office.

'Do you know what this is about?' I asked Yejide.

'No. I suppose it must be about yesterday.'

I nodded in agreement, and knocked on the door.

'Come in.'

Joseph sat in the ancient armchair by the window studying some papers, his cassette player struggling with whatever classical tape it was chewing.

'Ah! Sit down, sit down. Thank you for coming.' We all tumbled in and I felt the temperature go up immediately. Joseph placed whatever he had been reading on the coffee table and sat back, his hands together. He looked at us and smiled, but it failed to hide the stress in his eyes.

What's he looking so worried about? I thought. He should be happy.

'I was thinking that in the light of recent events, it might be an idea for you three to get out of the city for a while,' he said.

'You want us to leave Ilakaye?' stammered Guppy.

Joseph held up his hand. 'Not at all, Guppy. I don't know what we'd do without you. However, the fact. . .' He stopped, as if unsure of what he wanted to say, or if he should say it. '. . .the fact that Danlami is still at large is worrying, and I think a change of scenery would be good for you. I thought you might like to spend a few days at our project in the north.'

'But the orphanage. . .' said Guppy. 'It's almost finished.'

'Abacha has promised to halt work for the week that you are away. Don't worry, you will be here to see it completed.'

Guppy visibly relaxed.

'Well, what do you think?'

'I think that would be fine,' I replied, relieved that Joseph hadn't kicked us out, but a growing sense of unease clawed its way through my stomach. 'Do you think we are in danger from Danlami?'

'It is just a precaution, Charlie. And I do think

it will be good for you to see our other work.'
He smiled, but it felt weak, forced.

I looked at the others: Guppy nodded in agreement,
but Yejide didn't take her eyes off Joseph.

'Excellent. Then that's settled. I spoke to your
parents this morning. They all agreed that it would
be a rewarding experience – although I saw no reason
to mention Danlami. Samson is to drive you, stay and
bring you back. You leave tomorrow.'

I turned to go, but Guppy hesitated. 'Joseph. . .'
he said.

'Yes?'

'About Danlami. I have been worried about him.'

Joseph smiled. 'And I have been worried about you,
Guppy. Is there anything you want to talk about?'

Guppy shifted his weight on to his shorter leg, his
body tilting two inches to the left. 'No, I don't think so.
I didn't expect what happened. I thought the police. . .'

With a sigh, Joseph got up. 'Never forget that I said
you could take the tape to the Oba. It was something
that I did not want to do, but Danlami left me with
no choice.'

'When they catch him. . .' began Guppy.

'I hope they will not. Put it out of your mind. He
knows that this is the only place where he will be safe.

I hope he will not do anything stupid, and that he will find his way back here.'

'You want him here?' I asked, unable to hide the amazement in my voice.

'Ilakaye is open to everyone, Charlie. I told you that. There will be consequences for Danlami, of course, but they will not come from the Oba and that mob. It is said that the Oba acts with the will of the people. What you saw is not the will of the people. It is one man wielding total power over a few that will do his bidding. That is a dangerous combination. I will continue to fight for the rule of law in my country. It is my rock of Sisyphus.' He managed a cold laugh and turned his head to look out over the compound. 'And I will see it. One day I will see it. . .'

He seemed lost for a moment, and then suddenly remembered we were there. 'Now, you'd better get off. Try to put Danlami out of your minds. His operation is over and that is a good thing in itself. But now I must concentrate on making sure that justice, not vengeance, is done.'

He turned back to his papers with a sigh, and we walked out of his office. Guppy closed the door behind us, and for a moment none of us spoke.

'Well, it looks like we're in for a good trip,' I said

to break the silence. 'Sounds great, right?'

'Possibly,' said Yejide. 'But I think Joseph is playing the whole thing down, trying not to scare us.'

'What do you mean?' asked Guppy.

'He's worried. More worried than he would say. I could see it in his eyes.'

'Worried about Danlami?' I said. 'I don't think we need to worry about him any more. It's just a precaution.' And I forced a laugh.

Yejide turned and looked over at the wall that Danlami had escaped over, 'I'm not so sure,' she said. 'Danlami's clever. He won't give in that easily. Joseph wants him to come back, and I think he probably will, but not to stay. To. . .'

I looked at her, waiting for her to finish. 'To what, Yejide?'

'Think about it, Charlie. He's lost everything. No one will help him now he's wanted by the Oba. Desperate men are very dangerous.'

'You mean. . .' began Guppy.

'I mean,' said Yejide, choosing her words with care, 'that he blames us as much as Joseph.'

We stood in silence with Yejide's words ringing in my mind as the wind quickened and the clouds fought the sun.

CHAPTER 19

The first hint of dawn streaked the horizon, forcing the clouds out of hiding as I heaved my bag into the boot. It would not be long before daylight stretched into the sky, dispelling the lukewarm damp of a tropical morning.

Yejide's words still hung over me, and I had not slept well. The thought that there might be a man hunting us was hard to digest. But if she was right and we were in real danger, then the sooner we left, the better.

'Charlie.' Samson emerged from the guard hut. This was one aspect of the trip I had not been looking forward to. Our friendship had never recovered from the night at the Crocodile Bar. He stopped by the boot and surveyed the sky. 'Good. No rain today, I think. I hope it is the same further north. Rain would be a problem.'

I mumbled agreement and turned to go back to the house.

'You have done very good things at Ilakaye.'

I stopped. 'Thank you.'

'I'm looking forward to this trip. We can talk in the car. Like going to school.'

'That would be nice.' I made to speak again, unsure of what I was going to say: an apology perhaps? A thank you for saving Wael's life? But he shook his head before I could say a word.

'We're OK now. *Sabi?*'

'*I sabi am.*' And as the knowledge broke through me I realised how much he meant to me. He offered his hand and I slapped mine against it, holding the grip for a moment before breaking with a click of our fingers.

'Charlie!' My mother stood at the door, Katie by her side, and with a smile to Samson I walked over.

'Be careful,' she said.

'I will.' I looked into her eyes and was suddenly overwhelmed with a desire to stay, to hold on to her, as I had when I was younger and afraid.

'Are you all right, Charlie?' she asked.

'Oh fine, a bit nervous, that's all.'

'You'll be fine. It will be a great experience.

Listen to Samson, he's in charge.'

'And bring me back a present,' said my sister.

'What would you like?'

'Something nice.'

'Of course, Katie.' And I gave her a hug.

My father walked over to the door and we shook hands. Then, with final goodbyes and good lucks, I climbed into the car and we pulled away. My sister chased the car down the drive, waving all the way, the dawn sun on her face. I waved back, until we turned out of the gates and she was gone.

⊞◉▣

Samson's voice woke me. I was not sure how long I had been asleep, but the view outside the window told me we weren't in Ilaju. We had stopped at a checkpoint, a line of razor wire blocking the road. Samson stood outside talking to a policeman; another policeman leaned against an oil drum, watching the exchange without interest.

'Where are we?' I asked.

'About five hours outside Ilaju,' said Yejide. 'You've been asleep.'

'And you were snoring,' added Guppy.

Outside, Samson's conversation became more animated, but his voice remained calm and he kept a smile fixed on his face.

'What language are they speaking?' I asked.

'Hausa,' replied Yejide. We are out of Yoruba land now. Here they are mostly Hausa and Fulani.'

'What do the police want with us?'

'Whatever they can get.'

The policeman shot a comment at his companion while running the palm of his hand over the roof of the car. The officer by the oil drum laughed. Samson shrugged his shoulders, then, holding up his finger as if an idea had just occurred to him, walked around to the boot, opened it, and held up two calendars showing bikini-clad girls stretched over forklift trucks, with an engineering company's logo printed at the top.

The officer pushed himself away from his oil drum and mooched over. He walked unsteadily and as he drew closer, I saw the red lines in his eyes. He was drunk.

The two of them pored over the pictures, grins on their faces, and then, laughing, they took the calendars, pulled back the razor wire and waved Samson away.

I watched the policemen through the rear windscreen as they shrank into the distance:

they leaned against the oil drum, still studying the calendars.

'That is wrong,' said Guppy. 'They should not be extorting things from people like that.'

'They probably never get their pay. They need the money,' replied Samson. 'What did we lose? A few minutes and two calendars.'

'How did they get out here?' I asked.

'They would have been dropped this morning, and if they are lucky, someone will go and pick them up this evening.'

'Well, at least now they have something else to look at,' said Yejide with a tut, and my involuntary grin earned me a slap on the shoulder.

◫◉◱

We travelled for another hour before Samson turned off the main road and followed a dust track through the bush before emerging into a clearing.

'Are we here?' asked Guppy.

'No,' replied Samson. 'But I thought you might enjoy the view.'

I turned in the direction of his finger and saw steps climbing up between a series of rocks that stretched into the sky, like giant pebbles tossed from the heavens.

'From up here you can see the whole city. But it is quite a climb. Come on.'

The steps varied in height from a few inches to a foot and even in the cooler air, we were drenched in sweat within minutes. Guppy found it the hardest with his mismatched legs, but he climbed without making a sound.

It took us forty minutes to reach the top. Guppy and I fell to the ground, as much with relief as fatigue. We sat for a moment to recover, and then I lifted myself slowly to my feet and turned to look at my reward.

Africa stretched before me. The glow of the savannah filled my eyes, beautiful and ancient, and I felt the stirrings of forgotten knowledge: of wonder, of discovery, of the essence of dreams.

'We will stay just a few miles north of the outskirts, at the game reserve,' said Samson, and my eyes moved to the town east of the rocks.

A blanket of tin roofs covered the landscape, glowing copper and orange in the light, a rusting sunset fallen to the ground. In the centre, separated from the rest of the town by a large tree-lined square, rose a tower of white ceramic, steel and glass. A monument from another place and time bolted into the ground.

'What's that?' I asked.

'The headquarters of the National Oil Board,' muttered Samson. 'It cost millions.'

'So is there a lot of wealth here?' asked Guppy. 'But the rest of the town. . .'

'There is wealth here for the Army, for the Obas, for the dictators and for the men of the National Oil Board,' said Yejide, 'but not for anyone else.'

'A tanker for me, a tanker for my brother,' laughed Samson. 'But nothing for you.'

We stood in silence. The wind played on my face and I saw clearly for the first time the tear in the land. I remembered Joseph's voice in a school hall so long ago telling me of the troubles of adaptation and change, and, as I slid my hand around Yejide's waist, I started to listen and to understand.

CHAPTER 20

I slept badly, images of Danlami invading my dreams, and I woke disorientated, the mosquito net blurring the walls around me. Then my mind cleared and I lay still for a moment as the reason behind this trip drew beads of sweat. I scrambled out of bed, pulled on my shorts and took a swig from the bottle of water next to my bed.

Opening the door of the chalet, I stepped out onto the wooden walkway that joined it to the three adjacent chalets, relishing the cool, dry breeze. The car stood alone a few feet away in the expanse of clear ground that served as a car park. The sign welcoming visitors to the Akari Game Reserve leaned into the morning breeze; its picture – a Land Rover driving past a herd of elephants – barely discernible on the warped wood. It was quiet, peaceful, and the fears of the night began to ebb away.

A baboon jumped onto the roof of the car, a yawn exposing its spear-like teeth. I stepped back, but it paid no attention to me and looked around as if deciding how to spend its day.

The door to the chalet next to me opened and a yawning Guppy stepped out.

'Morning, Charlie,' he said, scratching his arms. 'I think there was a hole in my mosquito net. Did you—' The sight of the baboon cut him short and he raced back into his chalet, emerging a few seconds later with a camera.

'This is fantastic,' he whispered, clicking off three shots before the baboon, obviously feeling it was too early for this sort of attention, jumped off the roof and galloped away.

'I can't wait to see more of the wildlife,' he said, staring at the back of the camera as if it might give him some clue as where to find it.

'We're here to work, Guppy.'

'Here to hide, more like. Ridiculous.'

'Joseph thinks it's for the best. . .'

'We'll have some time off, I'm sure,' he said, ignoring my comment about Joseph. 'Shall we go for breakfast?'

If the days here were going to be anything

like Ilakaye, any time off was going to be spent recovering – but I just smiled and we headed off in search of food.

The main building was a short walk from our chalets along an overgrown path lined with rusted light fittings, their casings cracked, the bulbs long gone.

'These must have been to light the way at night,' remarked Guppy. But several of them still had wires protruding from the base, the ends wrapped in rotting tape. They had never worked.

Two statues of men in traditional dress guarded the entrance to the lobby, their wooden bodies bleached by the sun. One of their spears had snapped halfway down the shaft, leaving the warrior brandishing a short stick. We walked past the deserted reception area to the restaurant beyond. Samson and Yejide were already there, lost among a sea of empty tables. Samson waved and we walked over.

'What's on the menu?' I asked, pulling out a chair.

'Plenty things,' smiled Samson.

I picked up the faded sheet of paper and began to read: *croissants, sausages, bacon, scrambled eggs, smoked salmon. . .* It was a list of the unobtainable, things I hadn't tasted in months.

'This is incredible!' I said, and quickly waved the solitary waiter over, firing off a series of requests. He looked at me for a second before shaking his head.

'Beans and yam.'

'I'm sorry?'

'Beans and yam. I go bring for you.' And he walked off.

Yejide looked at me and laughed. 'There are lots of things on the menu. They just don't have any of them.'

'Great.'

'I like beans and yam,' said Guppy.

'Good,' said Samson. 'Chop quickly. We need to go.'

◨◉◩

It was a twenty-minute drive to Joseph's centre. We turned out of the reserve and headed down a laterite road, the city following us in the rear windscreen, before we turned off onto a track leading into the bush. A few scattered huts dotted the landscape like giant shrubs, with naked children playing outside the doors, their laughter mingling with the bird song. The houses quickly became denser, until Samson stopped the car in front of a collection of larger buildings and we climbed out.

'Here we are,' he announced.

There was no wall, no gates, not a concrete block or metal roofing sheet in sight. Most of the buildings followed the same simple design: a four-foot clay wall and a thatched roof supported by wooden pillars. Others had full walls and screened windows, and I took these to be sleeping quarters or infirmaries.

'Good morning!'

I turned to see a man striding towards us, waving. The sheen on his black shoes seemed dust-repellent and he had carved a parting along the right side of his head. He greeted Yejide by name and they embraced briefly, before she introduced us in turn.

'And you must call me Simon. Come on. Let me take you for a tour.'

Simon talked for over half an hour as he led us around. He explained how all the buildings followed traditional designs, using only materials that were indigenous to the area.

'I have lived in Ibe all my life,' he explained, 'well, excluding three years at Durham University. I read architecture and designed the buildings myself.'

'This is how Joseph imagined Ilakaye,' said Yejide.

'Simon drew up the plans, but they wouldn't give him planning permission for it. Said it was unsafe and ugly. What they meant was, it looked backward. Too African.'

As I wandered through the compound, I couldn't believe that anyone could justify that decision. There was a sense of harmony and balance, like taking a long walk alone through the woods.

Simon led us into one of the workshops. Its design allowed the breeze to flow through it, channelling the hotter air out through a vent in the roof, making the interior wonderfully cool – the world's first air conditioning.

'What sort of work do you do here?' asked Guppy.

'Very similar to Ilakaye,' replied Simon. 'Although we don't have as many drug addicts. That, for now, seems to be a disease of the bigger cities. Our main job is educating the local children and adults. We teach all the major subjects as well as training carpenters and wood carvers. We also cast bronze using the Lost Wax Method. Our aim is to give the people an alternative to digging for the Devil's Shit.'

I glanced at Yejide, taken aback by Simon's words, and she mouthed, 'Oil'.

'Where is everybody?' asked Guppy.

Simon looked at him. 'It's Saturday. Nobody works on Saturday and with the villages so near, very few people live here. Only the sick.'

'Is leprosy a problem?' I asked.

'Of course. But we are dealing with a far worse threat now. AIDS. A lot of people suffer from it.'

'Can you treat them here?'

'Only the symptoms. The virus that causes it, HIV, was only identified last year, in France, and there are no approved drugs yet. People have been dying, but it has been blamed on tuberculosis or other diseases, and we still do not have official recognition of the problem here. But we know what it is. The symptoms are identical to cases in the United States. We can only wait, and that is difficult to do. We see more and more people every month. But I am confident that we can keep it under control. Once people are aware of the problem, once the United States and Europe realise what is happening, it will stop escalating. We will not see a repeat of the prejudice and ignorance we saw with leprosy. I have no doubt of that. Meantime, our main aim is education.'

He led us out of the workshop and over to the largest of the buildings. He leaned his hand against the clay wall and looked across rows of stools to the blackboard standing at the far end. 'Education is the key. The young are the key.' He fell silent for a moment and then shook his head, aware that he had allowed his mind to wander. 'Well, I think that is everything.'

'Thank you,' I said. 'Where would you like us to start?'

'I'm sorry?'

'The work,' I said. 'What work do you want us to do?'

'Work? Oh no, we just thought you would be interested in seeing the place. Joseph has given me strict instructions, what with everything that has happened in – well . . . it doesn't matter. We both thought you might as well try and enjoy yourselves.'

'Sounds good to me,' I said.

He smiled and turned to head back to the gates, but stopped. 'Just one thing,' he said, his gaze hardening, 'it's better if you do not leave the game reserve. Not without Samson. Just. . .'

'. . .a precaution?' said Guppy, a hint of irritability in his voice.

'Exactly. And you would do well to heed it.'

◧ ◉ ◨

Yejide led us through the track in the bush. The news that we had five days with nothing to do was some of the most welcome I'd ever received. Only Guppy looked disappointed.

'Where are we going?' he asked, pushing a branch away from his face. 'And why do we need our swimming trunks?'

'It's a surprise,' said Yejide. 'Not far now.'

We trekked along the path for another fifteen minutes, pausing occasionally to negotiate the growth that had spilled over and blocked our way.

'Are there snakes, Yejide?' enquired Guppy.

'Oh, don't worry. They'll be much more frightened of you than you are of them.'

'It's not that. I've forgotten my camera.'

I caught a flash of white through the trees, and pushing away the branches we walked out into a sandy clearing.

'The Akari spring,' announced Yejide.

A stream of silver cut its way through the undergrowth, the steady current emerging from a rock face to the right and snaking out of sight into the greens and browns of the surrounding bush. A narrow bridge linked the two shores, and as I watched, a bird, brilliant yellow, floated onto the handrail.

'Why did I forget my camera. . .?' whispered Guppy.

I don't know how long we spent lying in the water; we talked about so many things, but there were times when we said nothing and sat back in the stream, listening to the life around us.

We swam up to the mouth of the spring and laid our hands on the rock, feeling deep into the earth, touching the source of its secrets. Yejide lay on her back and allowed the current to drift her downstream. She stopped at the bridge and stood looking up into the sky, sunlight captured in the water that dripped from her hair

I floated down towards her, and from the corner of my eye I saw Guppy clamber out of the stream and grab his towel.

'Where are you going, Guppy?' called Yejide.

'Oh . . . I thought I'd just go for a bit of a walk or something. . . I'll see you in a minute.' And he picked up his things and limped off down the track.

I knew he must be feeling a bit embarrassed, but I didn't care, and, reaching for Yejide, pulled her back into the spring.

'Careful,' she laughed.

'Are you OK?' I asked. 'We never did have our talk

about. . .' I didn't finish the sentence, not wanting to mention Danlami's name.

Yejide thought for a moment, before replying, 'Yes. Yes, I am, I think. I was afraid of what might have happened, but it didn't.'

Yes, I thought, it didn't. 'Do you think he's still out there?'

She thought for a moment. 'Yes. But I don't think he'll be able to find us here.'

I smiled, relishing the reassurance, pulled her close and we held each other as the water eddied gently around us, carrying away the last of my guilt and fear. We sat listening to the songs of the birds, and I realised I wanted nothing else, needed nothing else, that I was completely happy.

Guppy had decided it was time to go. He emerged from the bush, slapping at mosquitoes on his legs, and stood awkwardly to one side as we pulled our clothes on over our swimming things. I didn't want to go anywhere, but the light was fading and we had to get back. We pushed through the trees and I felt the branches close behind me, like the seal on a secret, as we headed back silently towards the chalets.

We hurried into the main building, hungry and thirsty, to find Samson shouting into the telephone.

He wheeled around as he heard us approach and sighed with relief.

'It's OK she dun come,' he yelled. Holding the receiver to his chest he called Yejide over. 'For you. It is Joseph.'

I froze.

'What is it?' asked Yejide.

'He never tell me. But you must try and speak loud, the line is very bad.'

Yejide looked at me, before taking the phone and slowly pressing it to her ear. 'Yes, I can hear you. . . No . . . of course I don't mind . . . no, go ahead. . .'

The rest of us stood, waiting, Samson's eyes sweeping the doors and windows. I watched Yejide, trying to guess what the news might be.

'Thank you. . . That's . . . I know, I know. I'll speak to you when we get back. . . I will. Bye.'

She turned and faced the counter, placing the receiver carefully back on its hook as if it were made of glass.

'Yejide?' I asked.

She turned, and I saw she had tears in her eyes. I rushed over and put my hand on her shoulder. 'What is it? What's happened?'

'It's all right, it's good news. It's just a surprise.

A bit of a shock.' I stood and waited as she dried her eyes.

'Tell us!' exploded Samson, unable to contain himself any longer.

'I've been awarded a scholarship to Cambridge, to study medicine.'

Samson cheered, clapping his hands in the air. '*Nah wah* for Yejide!' he sang and, rushing over, enveloped her in a bear hug. He let her down again and caught my eye. His smile dropped. 'Come on, Guppy. I need a beer.' And they hurried into the restaurant.

I had known she would leave; she had told me the very first day we met. But it did nothing to soften the suddenness of the reality.

'Congratulations. It's wonderful news.'

She nodded. 'Thank you.'

I stood awkwardly for a moment and then gathered her up in a hug. 'You deserve it.'

She gently pushed me away and stared into my eyes. 'They want me to complete a foundation course before I go. It's research skills mainly, but in their letter they say it's mandatory.'

'You'll have no problem with that.'

'I have to leave for the UK next Friday.' Tears began to well up in her eyes again. 'I'm sorry, Charlie.'

I stood rooted for a second, feeling the second blow sink in, before pulling her close. 'No, no. Don't be sorry.' I held her tightly. 'Don't be sorry.' But I longed to tell her not to go, to stay at Ilakaye with me, that she should be sorry for leaving me – and the thought sent a splinter through my heart.

'Come on!' shouted Samson from the door of the restaurant. 'I have sent the waiter out for *suya*! We must celebrate!' And he vanished back inside.

Mustering all the courage I could find, I smiled. 'Yes, come on. This is something to celebrate.'

'Charlie. . .'

I pressed my finger against her lips. 'Not now. Let's go and have something to eat.'

◧◉◨

I managed to banish my own selfish thoughts during dinner, and we laughed, ate and drank until the waiter fell asleep on the opposite table. Guppy and Samson said their goodnights on the chalet walkway and Yejide and I sat and looked at the stars.

'It's what I've always dreamed of. To be able to go and study, to bring what I learn back here, back to Ilakaye, like Joseph and Simon have done. To carry on what they have started.' I took her hand and squeezed it. 'But I hadn't counted on meeting you.'

I had no idea what to say. And when she pulled me up by the hand and led me into her chalet, I went without a word.

She closed the door behind me, gently pushing against the wood until I heard the catch click into place. Then she walked slowly towards me, put her hand on my cheek, pulling my face towards hers, and looked into my eyes. 'I love you,' she whispered.

The image of a girl in a decrepit hotel room flashed before my eyes, and I felt a sudden stab of guilt. 'Yejide. . .' I started.

She smiled, and let her shirt fall to the floor. I slipped my arm around her waist, my fingers stroking her face, utterly myself for the first time, joyous and vulnerable.

'I love you too. I loved you the first time I saw you at the market. I've loved you ever since.'

'Stay with me tonight.' And she led me across to her bed, where the shadows waited, soft and welcoming, and the night air breathed its song.

CHAPTER 21

I had not really spoken to Guppy for three days. Yejide and I spent our mornings walking in the bush and the afternoons lying in the spring. We all saw each other in the evenings, but I never lingered, longing for the dark comfort of the chalet and the feel of Yejide's skin on mine. Guppy had spent every day at Simon's compound.

'You look a bit pale, Guppy,' said Yejide. 'Are you feeling all right?' We had finished a hurried dinner, Samson had already turned in and Simon had just dropped Guppy back.

'Fine, thank you.' He called the waiter over and ordered a beer, his movements slow, laboured.

'Are you sure you're all right, Guppy?'

'I'm fine, Yejide.' The waiter brought his beer and Guppy poured it, his hand shaking.

I had never seen him drink more than one beer, but he drank three before he began to talk. Simon had taken him out beyond the compound to a temporary shelter for those who would not come to the main compound. 'I've never seen anything like it,' Guppy said. 'It was awful. There was a tent – well, a tarpaulin really, and everyone just slept under that. There was a pit for the sewage; I've never seen so many flies . . . the smell. . . And the children. . .' He stopped, and took a long swig of beer.

'I don't understand,' I said. 'Why won't they go to the compound?'

'Simon says they are afraid.'

'Afraid of what?'

'It's true,' said Yejide. 'Sometimes they prefer to only see the traditional doctors, other are just ashamed of their condition. Or, of course, they have been banished.'

'Leprosy?' I asked.

'And AIDS,' said Guppy. He took a long swig of beer. 'I'm going back tomorrow, but. . .' He downed the rest of his beer, bringing the glass down with a thud that shook the plates.

'Take a day off, Guppy,' I suggested.

'Maybe. I'll see how I feel. It's hard, just hiding

up here doing nothing.'

'You could relax, for a change.'

'Charlie's right, you should take a break,' said Yejide.

Guppy just smiled. 'One for the road?'

'Definitely.'

'I have to go to the bathroom first,' said Yejide, and slid out from behind the table. I looked at Guppy, tired and thin. He had washed his face but some of the dirt still clung around the edges, staining it two-tone brown, and I thought of him alone at Simon's compound surrounded by disease and the dying.

'I'll come with you in the morning,' I said. And I meant it. His face lit up, and his shoulders straightened, his hand coming to rest on my arm.

'I knew you would. Thank you. I am very lucky to have friend like you, Charlie. But you have a girl to be with. There's plenty more time to dig ditches with me.'

I smiled, loving him for his generosity. 'Guppy. . .'

'Yes?'

'I owe you an apology.'

'Don't be silly. For what?'

'At school I never really. . . Well, I didn't treat you very well.'

'Don't worry about it. And that's not entirely true: you invited me for the weekend, after all.'

'I'm really glad I did.' I raised my glass and he clinked his against it, before taking a sip and placing my glass slowly back on the table.

'You did it all, you know,' I said.

'What do you mean?'

'If it wasn't for you, we never would have stopped Danlami.'

'That's not true,' he said, frowning at me over his beer glass. 'You and Yejide did just as much to—'

'Guppy, please,' I said, cutting him short. 'I want to tell you something: I would have given up if you hadn't been so persistent. You have such ... such drive in you. You've taught me so much.'

He stared at me in amazement, and I turned away, embarrassed. I hadn't planned to say anything, but I knew it was true, knew I had to say it.

'Thank you, Charlie. That means a lot.'

I nodded and smiled, and we touched glasses again. I wondered if I should ask him about his father and his plans for Harvard and a law firm. He hadn't mentioned it for some time. I doubt he wants to speak about that, any more than I want to talk about Yejide, I thought, and pushed the idea from my mind.

'One thing I don't understand, though, ' I said.

'What?'

At Ilakaye, you do everything. You won't let anyone, or anything get in the way. But at school, when everyone laughed at you, you never did a thing about it.'

'Yes I did. I laughed right back at them. Seemed like the best thing to do.'

⊞◎◻

Our fifth and final day in Ibe came around with that unnatural speed reserved for things unwelcome. We had heard nothing from Joseph, so could only assume that everything was OK and it was safe to go back. But we had one last thing to look forward to. Samson had found us a safari guide, and we rose early for a drive into the reserve.

Tanko had originally been hired by the hotel to take tourists out, but they, of course, had never come, and like everyone else he now laboured for the National Oil Board. He had warned us in advance not to be too disappointed. There was very little wildlife left. A handful of men struggled on to keep the reserve intact, but the poachers were everywhere and ivory and skins sold well.

We left while it was still dark; Tanko said he knew a spot where we might be able to see some lions. The car jerked and bounced along as we headed into the bush. Tanko refused to use the headlights and how he saw where he was going, I will never know. We came to a stop at the foot of a hill and Tanko climbed out.

'Wait,' he said. We watched as he climbed onto the bonnet and stood, hands on hips, staring at the hill. A minute passed and he had not moved. Guppy shifted his weight, the slightest sound, and immediately Tanko's hand came up, ordering silence. He stood for another ten minutes, before jumping silently to the ground and signalling for us to get out of the car.

The sun followed us in silence up the hill. Tanko led the way, stopping us occasionally, and we stood like trees in the airless morning until he motioned us on again. We reached the summit as the dawn broke and for the second time, the splendour of the land overwhelmed me. It welcomed me as if I was the first wanderer ever to set foot there. And below us, a pride of lions sought out the cover of a nearby tree. Guppy reeled off shot after shot, while Tanko looked down, nodding, a paternal smile on his face. I moved away from the others, taking a seat on a rock, and watched the lions under the dawn-painted trees and listened to the grasses whisper their secrets.

No one was happier than Tanko at our success, and the sight of an elephant half-hidden among the trees was the crowning glory. After Guppy had taken enough shots to fill an album, we headed back. Tanko punched the steering wheel in delight. 'You see! There go be life here! There go still be life!'

◻◉◻

We sat in the middle of the deserted dining table, Guppy standing on one of the chairs singing 'My Way', while I tapped out the accompaniment with the beer bottles that covered the table. It was our last night and Samson had let us order freely. Guppy's performance had drawn the staff out of the kitchens, and they stood in the corner whispering to each other and looking puzzled. He finished with a flourish and we banged our approval on the table.

'Photograph!' Samson demanded, picking up the camera and pointing it at Guppy.

'No, there's only one shot left,' Guppy said, jumping

off the chair. 'Take the three of us.' We huddled together, Guppy in the middle, and grinned into the flash of light.

'That will be a good one,' said Samson. 'But I am sleepy. And I must drive tomorrow.' He put down the camera and walked unsteadily away.

I felt the atmosphere drop immediately. Guppy suggested another singing contest, but we all knew the party was over. My heart was heavy. Tomorrow we would drive back to Ilaju, within a week Yejide would leave, and I would be lost once more.

'Well. . .' began Guppy, raising his glass. Yejide and I raised ours in return, but Guppy never finished the toast. There was no need. We downed our beer in silence and then, with a pat on the back for me and a peck on the cheek for Yejide, he limped off.

Yejide and I walked the grounds. There were so many things I wanted to say, but I couldn't seem to order the words in my head and I knew that every breath I took brought the morning closer. She seemed to sense my unease and encircled my arm with hers, resting her head on my shoulder. 'It's all right,' she whispered. 'I love you. That will never change.'

'I'm not sure what I'm going to do without you.'

'You'll be fine. I'm not going for ever.'

'Three years is a long time. . .'

'We'll see each other before that.'

'I hope so. Besides, we never had that race around the roofs,' I said, trying to bring some lightness to the situation.

'I don't really feel like it any more,' she said.

'Neither do I.'

We stopped, and sat on a bench by the two weary warriors at the entrance looking up at the sky. It was a perfect night, but I longed for the clouds of the monsoon or the dust of harmattan to blow down and block the racing sun, to trick the dawn, to leave us sitting quietly in the night.

I packed slowly, folding my clothes as carefully as I could. I placed the small, bronze bangle I had bought for Katie into the suitcase, took a final look around my chalet and stepped outside, ready to head for the car and the journey back to Ilaju.

Samson had phoned Joseph and told us he felt it was safe to go back. But he had said nothing about whether Danlami had been caught or not.

I turned to lock the door, but the sight of Guppy stopped me. He sat on a stump at the other end of the car park, lost in thought. He didn't notice me as I watched him pull off one shoe and slowly rub his foot into the ground. As his toes buried themselves in the dust, a smile spread across his face.

It is an image of him I will always remember.

CHAPTER 22

'Welcome back!' Joseph clambered down the steps from his office and came over to meet us. 'Did you enjoy yourselves?'

'It was wonderful,' I said.

'You didn't think I'd send you up there and make you work?'

'It was very interesting,' said Guppy. 'I can't wait to get my films developed.'

'I can't wait to see them. Tomorrow afternoon, I hope, at the party.'

'Party?'

'For Yejide. Who, I might add, I need to speak to. And you should be getting home. It's late.'

'Joseph. . .?' I said.

'Yes.'

'Is everything all right now? Has Danlami been caught?'

Joseph scrutinised me for a moment. 'No. But he has not been seen. I think he has gone – where, I do not know. But I think we can all relax now.' He took Yejide's arm and ushered her away. She turned and mouthed, 'See you later,' and I raised my hand.

I had already been home to drop off my bags and speak to my parents. We had chatted about the trip, and I had told them about the Akari spring and Simon's work. But I hadn't mentioned my relationship with Yejide; I didn't know what to say. Something deep inside me had changed for ever.

'Are you all right?' asked Guppy.

'I suppose so.'

'She'll come back for the long holidays. And besides, she's not going for ever.'

And, of course, she wasn't. But I had no idea where I would be when she got back.

'Give me ten minutes, will you, Charlie? I want to check on Kambiri.' And he jogged over to the orphanage, leaving me standing alone in the courtyard. I walked over to the infirmary. Sister Mairead stood by a bed near the door peering at a thermometer. She gave a satisfied grunt, before dropping it in to a cup and taking it over to the sink. The smell of antiseptic burned my nostrils.

'Need any help?' I asked

'Judas Iscariot. . . ! What are you doing in here?'

'I just got back from Ibe,' I said, startled by her tone. 'I was wondering if you needed any help.'

She took me by the arm and led me towards the door. 'The infirmary is restricted for the time being, Charlie. It's nice to see you, and thank you for the offer, but you can't be in here at the moment.'

'What is it? What's the matter?' I looked past her into the dim interior of the infirmary. Beds had been squeezed together to make room for more, while others jutted out at odd angles; two patients lay on mattresses against the far wall, all but hidden in the shadows.

'We think it's this new disease, AIDS, but we can't be sure yet. We'll be moving them to the secure compound soon, but for now, this is out of bounds.'

The patient she had been treating let out a noise that sounded half-groan, half-sigh, and she hurried over. She pulled back the blanket, revealing dark discoloured growths on the man's neck and shoulders and a livid rash running up to his face. He opened his mouth to groan again, his tongue covered in a thick white coating.

'Why are you still here, Charlie?' said Mairead,

her eyes never leaving her patient.

I hurried out and walked over to the workshops, sitting down heavily on the steps. We had only been away a few days, but the disease that Guppy had seen in the north had now found a foothold here too.

One of the cooks passed, complaining to Abacha about food going missing from the kitchens. Every day for nearly a week, it seemed. Abacha caught my eyes and raised his to the sky. The cooks had a reputation for being paranoid about their stores. I turned away suppressing a grin, glad for the distraction, and looked over to where Samson waited. He had left the gates open, and there, by the church, stood the man in the red shirt, the one who had been in charge of the mob the day Danlami escaped. He stood hands in pockets, his eyes fixed on Ilakaye – watching, waiting.

■◉□

The preparations for Yejide's party had been going on most of the morning. Every spare table in Ilakaye had been carried to the courtyard and covered with whatever could be found, forming a rickety patchwork line across the courtyard. The kitchens had made two enormous cauldrons of rice and pepper beef, and we all sat in the afternoon glow, eating and chatting. Only Adebayo stayed apart. He collected his plate of food and shuffled over to the dormitory steps, where he sat and pushed the food into his hood.

Yejide sat at the head of the table between Joseph and Mairead. She wore traditional Yoruba robes of purple and gold, the sunlight glinting off the metallic thread. I sat halfway down sandwiched between Guppy and Abacha, their jokes and laughter flying past me, my attention held by the girl at the head of the table.

With a rap on the table, Joseph called for silence. He stood up and cleared his throat. 'We are here to bid farewell to one of our residents. She arrived here a scarred and scared little girl and is leaving an accomplished, confident woman to study at one of the great universities of the world. I am proud to have known her, to watch her grow. She knows that she will be leaving with a piece of her left deep in all our hearts.' His eyes caught mine for a second and I turned away, unsure of whether to smile or cry.

Joseph finished to loud applause and Mairead got to her feet. She spoke of similar things and the more I listened, the more I swung between sadness and joy – joy to have known Yejide, to have been with her, to have been a small part of her life so far. And yet the pain of her leaving would not go.

I reached for my drink to join the toast, touching the cup to my lips before placing it quickly back on the table. With the speeches over the chatter continued, and I got up from my seat and wandered away. Tired of making polite conversation, I just wanted to be on my own.

I walked past the dormitories towards the kitchens, feeling physical relief as the noise of the party receded. I slipped into the gap behind the kitchens and the outer wall, relishing the cool of the shade. The sun never seemed to reach that part of the compound.

Leaning against the kitchen wall, I brought my foot up behind me and heard the crack of breaking wood. I swore at the dust and turned to look. Like all the buildings at Ilakaye, the kitchen stood on stilts, but to stop rats from moving in underneath Abacha had attached planks of wood that covered the gap between the ground and the kitchen floor. He wouldn't be pleased to learn I had just broken one.

I knelt down and looked at the damage: the plank wasn't broken, it had just come loose. I searched the ground for the screws, but couldn't see them.

Putting the plank on the ground, I pulled at the one above it and it came away in my hands. So did the one below. Abacha wouldn't have been this careless.

A shadow flickered in the corner of my eye and I turned, staring down the length of the wall, squinting into the gloom. Was something moving? But I could see nothing.

I shrugged it off and turned my attention back to the hole. I leaned in closer – and quickly pulled away. A sour stench of rot and excrement filled my lungs. What the hell was under there? I held my breath and peered through the gap. In the dim light I could make out a small tin bowl and the remains of what might have been yam hidden beneath a crust of flies. I pushed in further and saw a tattered reed mat lying flat on the ground, an empty water bottle lying next to it, and something that looked like cloth. Turning my face away, I reached in and pulled it out, scrabbling quickly to my feet, away from the smell and the flies. It was a suit jacket covered in dust and grime, the colour only just discernible – blue.

I stared at the jacket, unwilling to believe what it meant. He was here. All this time he had been here. I thought of Yejide, Guppy and Joseph sitting, laughing at the table, unaware, unprotected. I dropped the jacket and began to run, willing my feet forwards. But I had not taken more than three strides when a scream cut through the air.

I rounded the dormitories at a sprint to see the orphanage nurse stumbling towards the tables, her left hand gripping her right arm, blood seeping between her fingers. And behind her, by the orphanage door, stood Michael Danlami holding Kambiri under his arm.

His shirt was filthy and torn, the left side hanging in tatters around the top of his mud-encrusted trousers, his face streaked with dirt and the marks of fresh scratches. In his right hand, he held a long, narrow shard of glass, the hilt wrapped in a rag. He pointed it at the table, sweeping the jagged point along the rows of people, scanning them with dead eyes. Fear gripped my stomach. Around me I could hear shouts as people rose quickly to their feet, thuds as chairs hit the ground and plates clattered to the floor. Guppy jumped to his feet and shouted something I couldn't make out. Mairead hurried forward and grabbed the bleeding nurse, helping her away. Then Joseph got up – and at once the noise began to subside.

He moved slowly away from his seat and stood between Danlami and the table with Abacha following a step behind. Keeping my eyes on Danlami, I moved down the table to Yejide, listening to Kambiri's little cries. Guppy stood, his fists clenched, his body trembling with rage. Don't move, Guppy, I thought. Don't do anything.

'Put her down,' said Joseph.

'Shut up!' yelled Danlami.

'Put her down, and then we can talk. I am glad you managed to find your way back. I was worried that you wouldn't.'

The rage on Guppy's face changed to utter disbelief and he began to walk forward. With a jerk, Danlami pulled the makeshift knife towards Kambiri, and Yejide's hand tightened on mine.

'Stay back!' he shouted, the knife hovering over the baby's head. Guppy skidded to a halt, held up his hands and backed away.

Joseph's body tensed, but whether from fear or anger, I couldn't tell. Then he gently rolled his shoulders before speaking. 'No one will hurt you here. But you must put down the child. We can talk.'

'I have not come here to talk! I have not lived like an animal for five days, eating the scraps from your filthy kitchens, just to talk!'

'I can help you.'

'I do not want your help! You have taken everything from me! There is nowhere for me to go. The Oba has turned everyone against me. You must pay for what you have done.'

'What do you want?'

'I've had plenty of time to think about that. At first I thought I would take the *oyinbo*, or maybe the whore he sleeps with, or perhaps the cripple. But you sent them away. Then I knew it was you – it had to be you who dies. I want everyone to watch, to see the great Joseph on his knees at my feet. You have a simple choice: your life or the child's.'

Murmurs clattered through the silent air, but nobody moved, and I wiped the sweat from my face.

'You will kneel in the dirt in front of me,' continued Danlami, 'and then I will release the child.'

'This is madness. You cannot escape from here, whether you kill me or not.'

'I don't care any more. There is no way out for me now. You have seen to that. And I will watch you die before I go.'

'No. You want to kill me in front of these people. But this is your chance to prove to them that this is not who you are.'

'Then it will be the child who dies!'

'No. We worked together once – don't you remember?'

'That was a long time ago. You were a fool then and you are a fool now.'

Joseph took another step forward. Danlami was moving back, towards the gates. 'Stay here,' he said.

'Never. I gave children homes, families. What do you give them? A flea pit! And you dare to lecture me!'

'Please.' For the first time, there was emotion in Joseph's voice, a hint of pleading. 'They will not hurt you here. I have spoken to the Oba. He will not attempt to enter Ilakaye. My work here is respected. He has given me this chance, but if you refuse. . .'

I remembered Mrs Bath saying that someone had made a request, something to do with Danlami, and I suddenly understood who had made it and what it had been.

'There is a way out,' continued Joseph, cracks forming in what I had always thought was an unbreakable voice, 'a way for this to be resolved through the proper authorities. The right way.'

'Your way, Joseph. . .'

'*Our* way. Don't you remember. . . ?'

I looked at Danlami: his body shook and sweat

streaked his face. He stared at Joseph, who extended his hand, and for an instant there was a flicker of something across his eyes – a memory? A feeling? But it was faint, uncertain, a speck of dust caught for a moment in the sunlight.

'This is not the way you are. You can't do this,' said Joseph. 'You believed in the orphanage in Port Rose. You believed we could make things better. You have just lost your way.'

'And you want to help me now?'

'Of course. You will have to answer for what you have done. But not to the Oba. And then Ilakaye will be open to you – if you want it to be.'

Danlami seemed to sink further into the ground, as if his legs could no longer support him, and I thought I saw a tear at the corner of his eye.

Then his strength seemed to return. He straightened his shoulders, his eyes cleared, as if seeing where he was for the first time. A smile formed at his mouth and he tilted his head to the side, his gaze moving to Kambiri. He lowered her to the ground and backed away, his heels striking the gates and sending a deep metallic ring across the courtyard.

Mairead and Guppy hurried forward. Mairead scooped Kambiri up and, with Guppy at her side, she carried her towards the orphanage.

I felt Yejide's hand slip from mine and I knew she was going after the others. But I couldn't take my eyes off Danlami. He still wore that half-smile on his face, and he stared at the makeshift knife. He opened his fist and watched it fall to the ground, shattering at his feet. For a moment nobody moved, and I stood listening to the rhythmic drip of water from an overturned cup.

Danlami looked at Joseph and made to speak, but no words came.

Joseph took a step forward. 'That's right,' he said, exhaling the words. 'That's right. Now we can talk, now we can—'

But before Joseph could finish Danlami turned, pushed open the gates and strode out into the middle of the road, where he stopped completely still, his head bowed.

Joseph stood frozen, his arm still outstretched, then it dropped to his side, 'No. . .' It was a little more than a whisper. Then he lurched forward a step. 'No!'

And in the same instant I realised what Danlami was doing, and I found myself stumbling forward on trembling legs. 'Come back, get back inside. For God's sake get—'

The roar of an engine filled the air, followed by

shouts from the road. But Danlami did not move.

Joseph was running now, calling something I couldn't hear, and I found myself following.

Joseph had almost made it to the gates, just a few feet from Danlami's motionless form, when a truck skidded towards them. Danlami offered no resistance as they pulled him into the back like a rag doll. The man in the red shirt stood upright in the flatbed, one hand gripping the cabin, the other a tyre.

Joseph ran on, followed by Abacha and Mairead, but the truck sped away, spitting dust at Joseph's cries: 'Michael! Michael. . .'

◫ ◉ ◻

They dumped Danlami's body outside the church. He was naked, but it was impossible to tell whether his clothes had been removed or burnt. The remains of the tyre had fused with his shoulders leaving trails of rubber along his scorched body. His face was unrecognisable.

Joseph went out and laid a sheet over him while Abacha got a stretcher, and they carried the body inside. People lined the road but they didn't linger; quickly they turned away, some clearing the tables left from the party, others heading off to work in the workshops or kitchens.

Guppy and I dug a grave at the back of the compound and we buried him. Mairead said a few words while Joseph and the three of us looked on. Nobody else was there. I looked down at the mound of earth and I felt the void, deep inside, that could never be refilled. I heard Mrs Bath's voice in my mind. *Remember tonight*. But it was already distant, a place and time lost in the smoke from Danlami's smouldering body. I had walked – no, I had run through to a place I could not return from. Danlami lay dead, and, for good or bad, it was because of what we had done.

'I knew him for so many years,' sighed Joseph. 'In the beginning he did believe. We were friends once, brothers. Oh, not real brothers – not brothers the way you and Charlie are, Guppy.' It was as if he was talking for his own benefit, not ours. 'Then greed took over. It was easy for him to blame everyone else for our country's problems. He would not listen to me. Now I suppose he will have to answer to whichever god will question him. I don't. . .'

He stopped, the power of speech ripped from him, and clasped his hand to his mouth. I drew Yejide gently away, indicating for Guppy to follow, and we left Joseph sitting on the ground, the dusk creeping in around him, crying by the grave of his friend.

◧◉◨

Gunter leant against the bar in the living room, the discussion he was having with my parents melting into a thick silence as I walked through the door. For a moment nobody said anything, and then my mother rushed over and enveloped me in a hug.

'I've been worried, about you,' she said.

'I'm fine.'

'Gunter told us what happened to that man today. Dreadful. Ilakaye doesn't sound like a very safe place for you any more.'

I had been afraid of this. But before I could protest, Gunter's laugh stopped me.

'There's nothing to worry about. After all, the man's dead. Besides, the police were already on to him, thanks mainly to Charlie here. Fortunately a gang of thugs saved them the trouble of arresting him.' He caught me with a look that suggested contradicting him would not be wise. I glanced over at my father, who nodded, conspiracy in his eyes.

'If gangs of thugs are wandering that area

necklacing people, I don't want Charlie anywhere near it,' said my mother.

'There's crime all over the city. All over any city,' said my father. 'You can't keep him locked up.'

Gunter obviously thought this was the funniest thing he had ever heard.

'And I've been told there will be police checks on both ends of the street from now on,' continued my father.

'Oh that makes me feel *so* much better,' retorted my mother.

'Mum, it's fine,' I said. 'What else am I going to do? I haven't put this much time and effort in, just to jack it all in like that.' She blinked at the click of my fingers, and I realised my voice had been louder than it should.

'I'm sorry. I'm just tired. . . I think I'd better go and have a shower.'

'It's OK,' she said, a little taken aback. And I went through to my bedroom.

I sat on the bed for a while listening to the clicking of a gecko and the voices from the bar, but I couldn't hear what they said. I didn't really care. Gunter was masking the truth from my mother, perhaps from everyone, and I was sure he would be able to turn her around, especially as he seemed to have my father on his side.

The wedge of light spilling through from the corridor widened, and my sister peered around the door.

'Will you help me with my reading, Char— oh, you stink!'

'I think I need a shower first.'

She nodded in agreement and sat down cross-legged at my feet. 'Are you in trouble again? I heard Mummy talking. I hope you haven't been expelled from Ilakaye.'

I couldn't help but smile. 'No, I haven't been expelled from Ilakaye. There was a nasty man there, but he's gone now. Mummy's worried there might be other men like him.'

'What happened to him?' She placed an elbow on her knee, settling down for a good story.

In the background I could hear my mother joining in one of Gunter's laughs. It seemed Gunter had spun the right tale.

'The policeman came and took him away.'

'Wow. Will he go to prison? Did you see the policemen? Did they have guns like they do at the checkpoints? They scare me a bit, but not too much.'

'I didn't see them, Katie. I was busy.'

'Oh well, perhaps you'll see them next time.'

'Perhaps.'

'Oh, what's that?' she said, pointing at the bed next to me. My handkerchief had fallen out of my pocket – the one I had found at the rubbish tip the day the boy had vanished. 'The flowers are very pretty.'

'You can have it if you like. But you'll need to give it a wash.'

'Where did you get it?'

'I found it.'

'What if the person comes back and wants it?'

I closed my eyes and sighed. 'I don't think he will.'

'I'll keep it safe, just in case.'

'That would be nice. Now go on, I'll come and help you with your reading in a minute. She got up and headed for the door, her eyes never leaving the handkerchief clutched in her hands.

I leant against the wall of the shower and lifted my face into the stream of water, hoping it could wash away the images that flickered in the dark behind my tight-shut eyes: the glass knife, Kambiri, Joseph crying on the ground. Then suddenly he was there, scorched and smoking, and with a gasp I thrust my head forward, my eyes wide open. I turned off the taps, breathing heavily, watching the water spiral down the hole in the tiles. I could hear Katie's voice calling me from her room, and it drove back some of the shock.

'I'm coming.' I dried myself quickly, pulled on a clean pair of shorts and T-shirt and hurried over to Katie's room.

'I thought we were supposed to be reading,' I said, looking at toys scattered at my sister's feet.

'Oh, I've done my reading,' said Katie dismissively. 'Here, you can have Mr Bundle.' She handed me a small, stuffed toy that looked a little bit like a mouse standing on its hind legs.

'What does Mr Bundle do?'

'He comes over to play. First, we play hide-and-seek, then it starts to rain and we go and dance in the monsoon drain. Would you like that?'

I looked at her sun-browned face, her hair falling in tangles around her ears. 'Yes, I would.'

Dinner was a quiet affair. I stayed with Katie until Gunter left, not wanting a cross-examination on his stories. Gunter's tale had won my mother over – on the surface, at least. But there was something in the way she looked at me that said she wasn't convinced. Hardly surprising; she knew Gunter as well as anyone and I wondered if she had spoken to Mairead, but I knew we would never discuss the whole truth. The story lay buried too deep, weighted down with half-truths and secrets. Perhaps it was better that way.

My mother went to bed early and I tried to watch a video, but even by Norman's standards the quality was appalling and I gave up after half an hour. My father sat at the bar as I walked past, whisky bottle and tumbler poised ready for his evening vigil on the diving board.

'Goodnight,' I said.

'Hang on, Charlie. Would you like a drink?' He reached down and pulled out another tumbler. 'I was going to sit outside. Like to join me?'

'OK,' I said, trying to hide my surprise.

'Good. Here you go.' He handed me my whisky and we walked outside together.

The Dobermanns rushed up and my father bent down, stroking each one in turn before walking around to the pool, the dogs following at his heels like shadows. He took his usual place astride the diving board and the dogs slunk off into the dark by the generator shed. I sat down and let my legs slide into the pool. The underwater lights broke through the turquoise haze and I felt the lukewarm water tighten gently around my skin. My father looked up suddenly and a bat swooped down, kissing the water as it drank, before arching back into the cloudless sky.

I took a sip of whisky and felt the heat slide down my throat. My father sat in silence smoking a cigarette. Finished, he flicked the butt away and reached into his pocket for another.

'It was awful, what they did to him.' It wasn't until the words were out that I realised how much I had wanted to say them. 'I never expected anything like that.'

My father sat there, watching, listening.

'There were times I wanted him dead, especially when the baby died. But now. . . Perhaps there was some hope for him, some form of redemption. Perhaps he saw what he had become at the end. I don't. . .'

'You didn't kill him, Charlie.'

'I feel like I did.'

'You were the witness, not the executioner. The Oba works through the people outside the government. That's why Joseph wants nothing to do with them. For someone who kills and trades in children there was only going to be one sentence. And it was the Oba who decided.'

'Gunter should have told me.'

'Would that have made it any easier? Things like that can't be imagined, they have to be experienced. The minute you asked Mrs Bath for help, it was already out of your hands.'

'It's hard.'

My father nodded and his hand rested on my shoulder for a moment. 'It should be. But you have done a good thing. Did he deserve to die? That was never for you to decide.'

I nodded and took a sip of whisky, washing his words down and feeling them seep through me. The humidity closed in, wrapping itself around me like cotton wool, and I made peace with myself as I sat silently with my father, two men and their thoughts in the African night.

CHAPTER 23

We made quite a crowd at the airport: myself, Joseph, Abacha, Joshua, Mairead, Guppy with Kambiri in his arms and several of the nurses. Simon had driven down the day before and stayed to see her off.

We hadn't had much time together. The work at Ilakaye remained as frantic as ever, and I had to go home each night to a lonely bed. We hadn't really talked about Danlami. There was no need. We knew we would carry the memories for ever, and we found comfort in our own ways: Yejide with the needs of the sick, Guppy and I with the hammering of nails and the shovelling of earth.

'You take care now. And don't you forget us, you hear?' Mairead choked back her tears as they embraced, the noise of the airport drowning Yejide's reply. One by one, they all said their goodbyes. Guppy held Kambiri up so Yejide could kiss her and then they turned and moved away, allowing us a final moment together.

'Take care, Charlie.'

'You too.' I felt the warmth of a tear running down my cheek. Yejide smoothed it away with her finger.

'I'm going to miss you.'

'Where will you go? When you've finished, where will you be?'

'Here, Charlie. Of course I'll be here. This is my home. Where else would I go?' She leaned in against me and our cheeks touched. 'Where will you be?'

My hand came to rest on the back of her neck. 'I don't know,' I whispered.

She kissed me and then pulled away. 'I do hope you choose here.'

Then she turned, and I watched her as she walked away, choking back tears, until she was gone, swallowed by the crowd.

◼◉◻

I hammered the last of the nails through the roofing sheet into the timber frame of the orphanage roof. Then I sat back and pushed the straw hat off my forehead, wiping the sweat away with the bandana wrapped around my wrist.

'Done,' I called down.

'Excellent,' replied Guppy. 'I will be up in a minute.' I watched as he carried Kambiri back towards the orphanage, vanishing out of sight under the newly completed roof. An ambulance moved slowly out of the gates, carrying AIDS victims to the hospital. It came so often, we hardly noticed it any more.

Guppy emerged a few seconds later, accompanied by cries from Kambiri, and climbed the ladder to join me. When he wasn't working he was playing with her, and when he was working she cried for him.

He crawled across the roof and sat down next to me. 'We are almost there.'

I nodded, and he scrutinised me for a moment. 'Are you all right? She has been gone for a week, but you haven't said anything. I'm worried about you.'

'I'm fine.' It was a half-truth. I had buried my feelings in my work and slowly it had got easier, but I still looked for her everywhere.

'If you ever want to talk. . .'

'I know.' I put my hand on his shoulder. 'Thank you.'

'Well,' he coughed, 'just the painting to do, and then it's finished.'

And it was. My girlfriend was gone; the school year

was at an end; the orphanage was completed and my parents had booked our flights back to England for the long holiday.

I looked out over Ilakaye and wondered what it was we had done. Danlami was gone, it was true, but despite the walls of concrete blocks that I sat on, I found it hard to discern anything solid in our contribution to Joseph's work. I remembered our night at the Eko Club and the words of the Expert as he dipped his finger into the glass of water: *You see that hole? That's how much difference your efforts are going to make.*

'What are you going to do, Guppy?'

'I need to speak to Abacha about obtaining the paint for the walls.'

'No. What are you going to do after we've painted the walls?'

'Oh. Well, we must go and collect our grades from school. How did you do, by the way?'

'Not as well as you, but OK. After that?'

'I will ask Hagit to the dance.'

After all this time, after everything that had happened, he still clung to the date he wanted with the best-looking girl in school.

'I have to admire your dedication, Guppy, but I think you know what I'm talking about.

Did you speak to your father?'

He stared out across Ilakaye, and wiped his forehead with his handkerchief. 'Not yet. But I'm going to tonight. I've made my decision.'

'Go on. . .'

'I will go to Harvard, I can't waste such an opportunity, but I won't stay in the States. After I've finished my schooling, I'll come back here.'

I smiled. 'I thought you would say that.'

'Do you think it's stupid?'

'Not at all. A Harvard-trained lawyer is going to be a lot of use to Joseph and his work.'

'I thought so too. You see, when we were in Ibe, things made sense to me. I wanted to stay. I knew I would go back. I think I've known for a long time, I just haven't really realised until now. ' He smiled, his eyes lighting up. 'I can see everything much clearer. It's such a relief. I'm happy. I hope my father will understand.'

'I'm sure he will.'

'Maybe. And what about you? What are you going to do?'

I had no answer for him and I envied his clarity. I needed to go to university, but the thought of returning to any kind of formal education after everything we had done seemed absurd. Yet it was more than that. I was English, I lived in Ilaju and spoke with an accent that placed me somewhere in the middle of the Atlantic. My best friend was Indian and my girlfriend was a Sengharian. I had no idea where I belonged.

'*There* you are.'

I looked down and saw Joseph staring up at us. 'I have a job for you. We need some tarpaulins at the market. Rains are coming.'

I looked out over the horizon and saw the gathering clouds.

'But you'll have to be quick. The light is fading and the storm will be here soon.'

By the time we had loaded the truck, the sun was struggling to stay above the horizon, and the wind whipped at our faces.

The newly set up police check stood deserted as we passed, the barrier raised, and I assumed they were changing shift, or had given up and sought shelter from the impending rain, and we shot past, racing the clouds. I screeched to a halt outside the market and we heaved the tarpaulin out of the back. With Guppy leading the way, we ran through the alleyways, sharing the load over our shoulders, and made it to the Ilakaye shop just as the first drops of rain exploded on the ground.

'Well done,' shouted Abacha over the noise of the storm. 'I was worried you would not make it in time.' The wind threatened to drag the tarpaulin into the sky as we struggled, half-blinded by the rain, to cover the stall.

'I must stay,' shouted Abacha. 'You get back.' We nodded and hurried away.

I slammed the truck door shut and swore. I was soaked. The water streamed off my clothes, forming a puddle under my feet.

'Quite a storm,' remarked Guppy, trying to wipe the water from his eyes with a saturated handkerchief. 'This section of the road will be a mud bath in minutes. I don't want to get bogged down here.'

I nodded, gunned the engine and felt the wheels spin before catching, and we lurched forward.

The wipers allowed me to see flashes of the road and I managed to avoid the worst potholes, but I felt the tyres slip more than once. The lights of the compound came into view and I allowed myself a smile. 'Nearly there, Guppy.'

I almost didn't see the barrier. I slammed on

the brakes and we slid to a halt inches from the steel bar. I heard a rap on the window and I wound it down. A policeman thrust his head through, water pouring from his face.

'*Oyinbo*, wha' you have for me?' his breath stank of palm wine and his pupils were pinpricks in his reddened eyes.

'We have nothing. *Mo tọrọ àforíjì.*'

His face flashed with anger. 'Out! Out!'

'You've got to be kidd—'

He wrenched open the door, cutting me short, grabbed my T-shirt and pulled me from the cab. I leant back against the truck and saw Guppy running from the other side to join me.

The policeman stood before us, his rifle over his shoulder, and repeated his slurred question.

'We have nothing,' I shouted.

The man screamed with rage and almost lost his footing in the mud. I leaned in closer to the truck. He was dangerously drunk. I glanced up the road. The lights of Ilakaye shone through the night, just out of reach.

'You have money!' he yelled.

'We have nothing!'

'Liar!' and he swung his rifle from his shoulder

and pointed it at my chest. My breathing stopped, and I forced myself to inhale. This couldn't be happening. I held up my hands in submission and opened my mouth to try to reason with him, but a shout from up the road stopped me. I turned and saw a second policeman, an officer running towards us through curtains of rain.

The man lowered his gun and turned to face his colleague. They stood and yelled at each other, the words lost in the screams of the storm. The officer gestured for the gun but the policeman refused, pointing at us and shouting. I glanced at Guppy, my legs beginning to weaken.

With a single swift move, the officer lunged for the rifle. There was a flash and a clap of thunder and I instinctively shut my eyes. When I opened them, the policeman was running away up the road, his rifle lying in the mud. The officer watched him go, and then turned to us and froze. It took me a moment to realise he was staring at the ground.

I turned, and saw Guppy lying in the mud, a crimson stain spreading across his shirt.

For a second I couldn't move, I just stood there and stared. The officer began shouting into a radio, but he gave up and threw it in the mud. 'Help him!'

he cried, and pushed me towards Guppy, before sprinting up the road towards Ilakaye.

Shaking, I dropped to my knees. His eyes were wide with shock. He opened his mouth to speak, but no sound came.

Help him.

I ripped off my shirt and pressed it against his chest, but his eyes filled with pain and I eased the pressure. 'Oh no. . . No. . . Guppy. . .'

Help him.

I could hear the officer's shouts in the distance. I tried to use the shirt as a pillow, but it just sank into the mud. Guppy blinked against the rain and his hand caught mine. I held it tight, trying to think of some words to say.

There were other voices now, growing closer.

Help him.

'I don't know how!' And my answer, hurled at the sky, tore through my soul.

I knelt in the mud beside my friend, my brother. And I watched as the life slid from his eyes, his hand slipped from mine, and his last breath was carried away on the monsoon wind.

CHAPTER 24

The mole stretched a hundred metres into the sea, a jagged line of rocks that kept the bay safe from the currents of the ocean.

I walked slowly, jumping occasionally over the larger gaps. I arrived at the end and sat with the waves breaking at my feet. I turned at the sound of an outboard motor and saw the white spray thrown up by a bumboat as it skimmed around the other mole on the opposite side of the bay. It seemed to stop for a second before launching forward, its occupants grabbing their hats as it hurtled towards the beach.

The only way to reach Clipper Bay was by boat, its white sand a haven for expats. Some, like my father, had access to the chalets that lined the hillside, flashes of colour in the tropical forest. It was a sanctuary from the city, and it was where my parents had brought me.

I remember Joseph's hand under my arm, pulling me out of the mud; Mairead crouching beside Guppy's body; the doctor running through the rain, and a walk back to Ilakaye; a cold wait and my mother's face filled with tears. There was the numbness, the shock, and the phone call my father took at home confirming Guppy's death.

Two days later, Samson had driven my parents and me to Ilakaye. Mairead had organised a memorial service. Guppy, it appeared, had been a Christian – something I should have known. Words were said, but I don't remember what they were. We left immediately afterwards. I didn't speak to anyone. I left my father talking to Joseph while I waited in the car. On the way home, my father had told me that Guppy's parents had taken his body back to India.

Yejide had called, and we talked for a while. She said she wished she were there for me. But she wasn't. I told her about our trip to London and we arranged to meet, but I had hung up the phone without emotion.

The salt spray clung to my face and I took a deep breath, holding the air deep in my lungs until I could bear it no longer. I exhaled in a gasp, the gasp turned to a sob, and I began to cry. All the fear and pain that had built up over the last week flowed from my eyes and dripped into the sea.

I cried for the boy with the accent and the limp, my dearest friend. I had abandoned him in Ibe, choosing to spend my time with a girl who had now left me, and he had died in the mud on the side of a nameless road. I pictured him there, his eyes filled with pain, and the thought turned my sorrow to anger. I picked up a stone and hurled it into the sea with a scream of fury, followed by anything else I could find around me: shells, driftwood, an empty can. I kicked and punched at the rocks until my voice cracked, my hands bled and, fighting for breath, I slumped down, my cheek pressed into the cold wet rock, and stared at an apathetic ocean. My eyes closed and I longed for sleep.

I saw my school and Max and Wael, Ilakaye and Joseph, Samson in the front seat of the car, Danlami preaching in his church, Yejide smiling at me in the Akari spring.

And I saw Guppy. He sat, perched on a chair in Joseph's office, cotton wool shoved up his nose from our fight with the man from the secure compound.

'Nits nalnight. Nits not boken.'

A smile warmed my face.

I heard Joseph's voice: '*I understand if you do not want to stay…*'

And there was Guppy's shocked expression: '*But we have not finished…*'

We had not finished. My eyes shot open, I pulled myself up from the rocks, wiped my face on my T-shirt, and bounded down the mole towards the beach.

⊟◎◻

Joseph stood just beyond the gates as I walked through, his hands in his pockets, as if he had been waiting for me.

'Good morning, Charlie.'

I nodded, unsure of what to say. I hadn't behaved well at Guppy's memorial.

'I'm sorry. About not—' But Joseph interrupted me with a wave of his hand.

'There is nothing to be sorry about. We all deal with these things in our own way.' He stood and looked at me, a gentle smile on his face. A gust of wind pulled at his greying hair and he scratched at the scar under his eye as he waited for me to speak.

'I've come to finish the orphanage.'

He nodded, 'Would you like a cup of tea first?'

'I think I'd better get started.'

'Excellent. The paint is ready for you.'

Kambiri's face lit up at my approach, and I lifted her from the nurse's arms. Immediately she began looking over my shoulder, squirming, searching the empty courtyard.

'He's not coming,' I whispered. 'I'm sorry.' I kissed her forehead and handed her back.

⊞◉◻

It took me three days to paint Guppy's orphanage. Abacha offered to help but I refused. I took two short breaks a day for something to eat and a game of peek-a-boo with Kambiri.

I put the paintbrush down for the last time and walked into the centre of the courtyard for a better look. The white walls glowed a gentle orange in the late afternoon sun and I allowed myself a smile. The compound was quiet except for the rustling of the trees and the laughter of a little girl. I looked down at my hands, I should get some ointment for the blisters, I thought. But I didn't want to speak to anyone.

I walked around to the back of the dormitories and opened the door to Yejide's room. The bare mattress creaked under my weight and I ran my foot through the dust collecting on the floor. Reaching into my back pocket, I pulled out the photograph that Samson had taken of the three of us in Ibe and stared at the faces of my friends. Guppy sat, squashed between Yejide and me, a slurred smile on his face.

'It's finished, Guppy.' I said. 'I wish you could you see it.'

'Oh, excuse me, Charlie. . .' Mairead stood in the doorway. 'This has become a good place for me to hide when one of my Muslim patients is praying. Do you mind?'

I gestured for her to join me on the bed and she sat down with a sigh.

'May I see?' she asked, and I handed her the photo. She stretched out her arm and squinted down her face at the image. 'Oh, isn't that gorgeous! A lovely memento.' She handed it back and I slipped it into my pocket.

'Why are you hiding from your patient?'

'No women allowed during prayer time.'

'Shouldn't you be trying to convert him?'

She laughed. 'If my patients leave here better Muslims, atheists, pagans – whatever, then I've done my job. And if the Lord calls to them, they'll be better equipped to hear Him. Although I must admit, having to skulk in here is feckin' annoying.'

I laughed.

She drummed her fingers on her knees. 'The orphanage looks grand.'

'Thank you.'

'He would be very proud.'

I felt the tears welling up, and she slipped her hand around my shoulder. 'He was a lovely young man.'

'He was my best friend. But. . .'

She waited.

'. . .I didn't tell him properly. When we were at school I laughed at him . . . Then I spent all my time with Yejide in Ibe. I tried to tell him, I offered to go with him one day to Simon's compound. I should have . . . I don't know. . .'

'We always want more time. That's everybody's wish, to go back and say things, to do things. But you mustn't feel guilty, Charlie. You were a good friend to him and he knew it. Don't smudge his memory with unnecessary guilt.'

I nodded, savouring the reassurance. 'He was one of the finest people I have ever known.'

'And you'll always remember him that way.' She squeezed me against her for a moment. 'I'd better go and see if my patient has finished. See you around, Charlie.'

'I'm not sure you will.'

'Why's that?'

'We're flying back to the UK on Monday, I think, for good. My father's been offered a job in London.'

'Good for him. Take care, Charlie.' I watched her go. I had expected more of a goodbye.

I sat for a while longer in Yejide's room, remembering the day we had set up the camera here, making our plans against Danlami. But now it was just a memory, with nothing left but the wind and the dust. I took a last look around and left, closing the door gently behind me.

Adebayo stopped me on the way back to the orphanage. He held a wooden board in his hands and I reached out and took it. It was the painting of the boys in the bush, the first one I had ever seen him working on. But the faces were changed, and there, smiling for ever under a tree in the savannah, sat Guppy and I.

I stared at it in wonder. It was beautiful; but before I could say thank you, he shuffled past me and vanished into the kitchens.

'Charlie!' Joseph and Abacha stood by the orphanage, waving me over.

'Abacha has made something that I think will make a nice final addition to the orphanage,' said Joseph. Abacha held up the small plaque and I rubbed my fingers over the words engraved in the wood.

'I think he would like it,' said Abacha. 'You go gree?'

'Oh, yes. I go gree. He would like it very much. Thank you.'

'I will go put it up.' And he carried it over to the orphanage.

'I hear you are leaving us,' said Joseph.

I nodded. 'It seems that way.' I saw a strange look in his eyes, one I couldn't place.

'Don't worry. You will find your place in the world. Just don't ignore it when it calls.' And he patted my cheek before pulling me into a hug. 'Thank you for everything, Charlie. God bless you.'

▣◉▣

The wall beside the steps leading into the school was uncomfortable and I had been sitting there for half an hour. The noise from the courtyard upstairs began to fade, meaning that everyone was moving into the hall for the prize ceremony.

I hadn't wanted to come for myself, but I wanted to collect Guppy's certificate for his parents. They weren't contactable by phone, but my father had an address. His father would like it. I hoisted my bag onto my shoulder – I didn't know why I had brought it – and felt my hand slipping over the brass handrail as I made my way up.

A few stragglers remained, but they slowly moved away, burying their Walkmans in pockets and bags. I stood under the American flag and looked at the empty alcove where we had met every morning. Where Max and Wael had taunted Guppy and they had listened to my stories of the Ibarajo Road. Where Guppy told me he could come for the weekend, and it had all begun. But there would be no more stories, not here.

I turned and crossed the classroom-ringed space to the hall. The principal's voice drifted out; it had begun. I pushed open the door and took a seat at the back, unnoticed. Scanning the rows of heads, it didn't take me long to find Max's bleached spikes. He was sitting next to a girl, and he leant over and bit her ear. She turned, smiling, playfully pushing him away. It was Hagit.

'. . .Here, at the Ilaju International School, we are proud of our academic achievements, proud that we educate the leaders of tomorrow, global citizens.'

The principal waited for the scattered applause to die down, before continuing. 'And now for the Honour Roll.' He tugged slightly at his tie and switched on his grin. 'Although every student deserves to be very proud of their accomplishments this semester, the Honour Roll recognises those with a grade point average of 3-6 or higher.'

He began to rattle off the list of names, and students trooped on to the stage in single file to collect their certificates.

Mine was the last one called, and every head in the hall turned as one. I stood up and walked towards the stage, my footsteps echoing in the now-silent hall, slowly joined by a breeze of whispers.

I reached the stage and the principal held up his hand for silence, but all over the hall heads still touched in frantic gossip.

'Charlie is also here to collect the certificate for one of our finest students.' He peered at the writing on the certificate and stumbled over the pronunciation of Guppy's name, drawing chuckles from the audience. I felt a sudden burst of anger.

The principal handed me the certificate and continued: 'He was a credit to this school in all he did. His dedicated charity work was an outstanding example of the ideals that our school nurtures in its students, and if he were still with us, I think I know what he would say about being on the Honour Roll. He would be as proud as we are of him. Whaddya say, Charlie?'

I stared at him, saw his smile begin to crack, and the hall fell silent once more.

'I say, you don't know what you're talking about. I say, you don't even know his name.' And I walked off the stage towards the exit.

The principal recovered quickly, ushering on Mrs Fay to talk about her charity cookie bake-a-thon; but I never heard how much she had raised. I walked straight out of the hall, dropped my bag into a bin and, clutching Guppy's certificate, headed for the gates.

'Wait for your driver,' said the guard.

'Open the gates.'

'Wait for your—'

I pushed past him, pressed the button and the gates slid back. With a nod to the guard, I walked out and headed down the road.

Samson was waiting at a small bar ten minutes' walk away.

'How did it go?' he asked, calling for beer with a flick of his hand.

'Just as I expected. But I got the certificate. I hope it reaches his parents.'

The barman clunked the bottles down on the table and we each grabbed one. I raised my bottle to him. 'Thank you, Samson. I won't forget you.'

'I never go forget you, Charlie.'

And our bottles caught the sun as we drank.

■◎▫

My sister sat beside me in the First Class cabin, playing with the seat controls. My mother leaned over from one of the seats in front.

'Everything OK?' she asked.

'We're fine, thanks,' I said, and gave her a reassuring smile.

My father had taken the job. We were leaving Africa.

The plane lurched in some turbulence and Katie gasped.

'Just an air pocket,' I said.

She looked at me. 'I don't want to go to London. I want to stay at home.'

'You'll be fine.'

She nodded with a sigh, pulling the handkerchief with the red flowers from her pocket. She held it in her hand, rubbing her fingers across the fabric. I still wondered about the boy and where he was but, deep down, I knew he was lost for ever.

I turned and stared out at the sky. Ilaju shrunk away behind me, the roads merging with the towns, the towns merging with the city, the city lost in the enormity of the land. But somewhere, buried deep amidst it all, behind a pair of anonymous gates on a dusty road stood a white-walled orphanage with a plaque above the door.

I dipped my finger into my glass of water, watching the ripples as I withdrew it. The words of the Expert came back to me again: *You see that hole? That's how much difference your efforts are going to make.* I shrugged off the memory and plunged my finger back into the water. But this time I held it there.

And then I knew, I knew for certain. I felt it creep through my body as assuredly as if I had buried my foot in the earth. I knew I would go back, that I belonged with the people of Ilakaye. I knew that I would take the carvings to market, with the truck bouncing over the potholes; that I would play with

Kambiri on the steps, listening to her laughter and the sounds of the workshop; that Yejide would walk back through the gates, her degree in her hand, and we would be together.

And I knew I would stand in the shade of the orphanage, as I do every day, read the words engraved on the plaque, and remember my friend.

For Gunaratna Vellasamy
who built this orphanage.
He was our brother.

HARRY ALLEN was born in the UK,
but spent most of his teenage years in Nigeria.
He was educated at International schools in Lagos
and London, and at Leeds University.
After graduating with a degree in Theatre Arts,
Harry worked as an actor, director, teacher and
writer and has had several plays for young people
produced in collaboration with companies in Europe
and Australia. He lives in Singapore with his wife
and two children.